Praise for th

MW00423030

## Guardian Angel

Becky Harmon is becoming one of my favorite authors and this book just ensures that. What I loved about this book is that you could tell it was well researched by how she described the countryside and the issues, especially regarding women and slavery. I just didn't want this book to end...
-Michelle P., *NetGalley*

*Guardian Angel* is one of those books that I crave. Two strong women with very different backgrounds and a bit of thrilling suspense. The author is adept at building chemistry between the two leads while weaving in a thread of danger while living abroad. Honestly, I wish this book was longer.
-Cathie W., NetGalley

There's a lot to like about this story. Harmon does a superb job of describing the setting, a US embassy in the middle of a charged Mauritania society. I loved the disparity between cultures and really enjoyed reading about a country that wouldn't normally fall on my personal radar. Having this story be between an ambassador and her security agent perfectly fell in the beloved "protector" trope, but it was also fresh enough to be new based on the setting. Truly, the international setting and the action/adventure in this story is really what sold it for me.
-Bethany's Reviews, *NetGalley*

## Listen to Your Heart

*Listen to Your Heart* is filled with the off-again, never really on-again, allure of the two main characters' romance. Jemini is convinced she must return to her fulfilling career and unrewarding personal life because she feels Riverview holds nothing for her but unpleasant memories of rejection by her beloved grandmother. Stephanie's job as deputy sheriff makes for an interesting subplot as she pursues a peeping tom. Harmon's story has enough mischief and intrigue to keep readers interested. This tale of romance—with a little mystery thrown in for good measure—is an attention-grabbing read that will entertain readers to the end.

*-Lambda Literary Review*

## *Tangled Mark*

This debut novel is an action-packed tale of security agents Nikki Mitchell and Mel Carter, who both work for the same private agency but on opposing sides. Both agents are strong women; they did not get the jobs they have by not being so. And yet what Harmon reveals as we learn more about them is that they each carry vulnerabilities when it comes to matters of the heart. A good debut, and I'm intrigued to see what Harmon will write next.

*-Rainbow Book Reviews*

I took pleasure in reading this book and it was exciting to see such sexiness written into an action book. If you are an action reader and looking for a book with engagement and some passionate loving, I'd recommend this book.

*-The Lesbian Review*

# Out of Focus

Becky Harmon

## Other Bella Books by Becky Harmon

*Tangled Mark*
*New Additions*
*Illegal Contact*
*Listen to Your Heart*
*Brace for Impact*
*Guardian Angel*

## About the Author

Becky Harmon and her wife live near Mickey Mouse and believe he is the best neighbor anyone could ask for. Though they hesitate to call Florida home, they do like the weather (most of the time). They share their life with a dog that rolls in anything stinky, chews on her own nails, and spends ten minutes moving the blankets and pillows on the bed before she can sleep at night. But they love her.

Becky spends her days surrounded by books and her evenings reading and writing them. She enjoys traveling and spending time with nature. *Out of Focus* is her seventh published work. All are available from Bella Books.

You can reach Becky at beckyharmon2015@yahoo.com

# Out of Focus

## Becky Harmon

BELLA
B O O K S

2023

## Acknowledgments

Many thanks to Linda and Jessica Hill. Both of you, and all the behind-the-scenes staff at Bella, are amazing. I am proud to have the Bella Books logo on all my books and to share that honor with so many fantastic authors.

Once again, Medora MacDougall, you have polished my manuscript and made it shine.

Thank you, Bella Books, for ignoring my ideas for this cover. Heather did a fantastic job creating a beautiful one that reflects the story.

To my fellow author, Jessie Chandler, thank you for always being in my corner. You are a wonderful cheerleader. (And yep, everyone that knows you has seen those legs!)

To Carol, thank you for your love of lesbian fiction. You will have to sleep at some point.

As with everything I write, this book is filled with fiction and no animals, not even the snakes, were harmed in the writing of this story.

To the readers, thank you for picking up this book. I hope you enjoy sharing a little piece of my world.

Lastly, to Deborah, thank you for choosing me. Life is better together.

# Dedication

For Deborah. Always.

# CHAPTER ONE

"You can't be here."

Bailey Everett turned in surprise as a deep voice broke into her tranquil hike. In the hour she had been walking, she had not seen or heard anyone or even a vehicle in the distance. Her breath caught as a figure emerged from the cluster of trees beside the trail. She saw nothing but the pistol strapped to their waist. The few feet between them seemed like inches as she tried to process the level of the threat in front of her. Her fear quickly gave way to irritation at being disturbed as she spied the Florida Fish and Wildlife patch on the sleeve of the tan shirt.

Bailey didn't know anyone that enjoyed being surprised, especially in the wild where a sudden visitor, animal, or even human could mean danger. Her eyes traveled across the stitched law enforcement badge on the protective vest and up to the face of the interloper—and she was surprised once more. A woman with the stance of authority now stood blocking the path. She bit back a response that would match the officer's rudeness.

"I have permi—"

"Now," the officer demanded, interrupting Bailey's explanation. "You need to leave this area. Now." Her dark eyes seemed to challenge Bailey to object again.

The FWC, or Florida Fish and Wildlife Conservation Commission, was the guardian of the forest and exactly the state agency Bailey would expect to find in a wildlife management area on the coast of Florida. She would never enter a restricted area without permission or challenge a law enforcement officer's authority, but this officer obviously didn't know who she was. Reining in her anger at being startled was easy compared to ignoring the officer's rudeness.

Bailey knew she had followed the proper procedures to be in this area and she only needed to explain without being interrupted. She stood her ground and stared back at the woman, realizing for the first time that she was not only a woman, but an extremely attractive woman—and in uniform. The fine lines at the corner of her eyes seemed to be lined up for a dance and Bailey wondered what would happen to them if the woman ever smiled.

Realizing there was no chance of that happening now or that she would be given the opportunity to speak, she unzipped her bag to produce her camera. Taking photographs was her reason for being here and normally all the authorization she needed. She did have written authorization to be in this location and in any other state park in Wakulla County as well, but showing the camera was quicker than digging in her bag for paperwork.

"No pictures," the officer said, spreading her arms as if to block Bailey's view of something.

"Captain Westmore said—"

"That's great." The woman's voice faltered and Bailey thought she saw a flash of realization at the mention of the FWC commander. If she had remembered that Bailey had authorization to be here, it was clear it didn't matter as soon as she spoke again. "You need to return to your vehicle."

Bailey resented the way the officer had suddenly appeared, destroying her peaceful walk, interrupting her work, but most of all she resented her for scaring her. She had spent several days researching and mapping her path on the two hundred acres of forest that reached to the shoreline of the Gulf of Mexico. She had even gotten approval to have Chewie, her four-year-old goldendoodle, with her. Chewie's scent never seemed to hinder Bailey's ability to photograph wildlife, but more importantly, Bailey needed her company. Today she had hoped to find her first teaser shots for the website to promote her next photography book—*Florida: Wildlife of the Northern Panhandle and Forgotten Coast.*

"I was told it would be okay," Bailey said, making one final push.

"Normally it is, but not today. You need to leave immediately."

The woman's tone had softened, but she still sounded like a broken record—jarring and repetitive. Her eyes flickered across the area behind Bailey. It wasn't the first time Bailey had noticed the woman's gaze moving rapidly. It was like she expected someone or something to appear from any direction. Her creepy behavior was starting to weird Bailey out. Plus, she was not interested in wasting time arguing. She was on a deadline, and if she could not get her pictures here, then there were plenty of other locations.

"Fine," Bailey said, raising her palms in surrender. "I'll return to my car."

She patted her leg as she turned, and Chewie followed on her heels. She knew she had not done anything to justify the woman's rude behavior. The stitched name tag on the woman's chest identified her last name as Smith. Bailey made a mental note. If the opportunity arose to gain more information about Officer Smith, she would be interested to know if this was her usual attitude or if Bailey's presence had brought out the less than the best in the officer. In the meantime, she would try not to take it personally.

Sadly, Officer Smith's poor disposition had not detracted from her attractiveness. Her light brown hair was pulled back into a ponytail, showing a shaved section around the base of her head—a style Bailey wished she was bold enough to attempt. It was feminine and sexy, and that was the last thing Bailey wanted to admit. The flutter she felt in her stomach annoyed her too. She wanted to blame it on the sudden interruption of her tranquil stroll and not on the alluring good looks of the wildlife officer.

"Where's your vehicle?"

Bailey jumped as the woman spoke directly behind her.

*Really?* She was following her.

Bailey gritted her teeth and spun to face her. "I'm parked at the west entrance."

"That's too far. We'll go to my truck."

Bailey felt her touch before she looked down and saw it. The pressure was gentle on her elbow, a contradiction to the woman's gruffness.

"Do you have a leash for that dog?" the officer demanded as she began to guide Bailey in the opposite direction.

Bailey kept her mouth shut, quickly snapping the leash around her waist to Chewie's collar. She knew Chewie would not stray from her side with a stranger so close, but there was no need to say that. Her words wouldn't be heard even if she got them out.

She shook her arm free from the officer's tightening grasp. She would go with her, but she would not be escorted like a criminal. In a different circumstance, she might have found this woman's bold mannerisms intriguing, but today they did nothing but piss her off. If asked, Bailey would describe the officer as rude and pushy. And those were not traits Bailey found attractive.

*And why is the west entrance too far?* She had started out at a leisurely pace, enjoying the chittering and chattering of squirrels and birds hidden in the trees. If she had to guess, she could not have walked much more than a mile.

*And too far from what?* She considered asking, but the woman was walking quickly, forcing Bailey to make a few hurried steps to keep up with her.

"You have to stay with me," Officer Smith said, taking Bailey's elbow again.

*Seriously?* Bailey bit her tongue to keep from lashing back at her. She worked hard to keep a good relationship with the federal and state park service personnel. She did not need their cooperation, but it certainly made her job easier. Bailey had not been pushed around so much since she had moved out of her parents' house twenty years ago. She shook her elbow free again and put a step between them.

A frown creased Officer Smith's face and she stopped walking. "I was serious. You have to stay right beside me."

"I'm close enough," Bailey growled, unable to hold back her irritation.

"I can't watch you. I have to feel your location so I can protect you."

*Protect me? What the hell is going on?*

Bailey looked around. She did not see anything ready to attack them. Now that she looked, though, she could see the hair on Chewie's back was stiff and her nose was in the air. She looked up at the officer. Her back was rigid too, and her eyes moved rapidly from side to side. Bailey suddenly had the feeling she wasn't being included in this nonverbal conversation.

The officer released a deep breath and put an arm out, pushing Bailey behind her. "It's too late. Walk slowly and keep a tight hold on your dog's leash."

Possible risks tumbled through Bailey's mind in an image avalanche. Pictures of every scary man or monster she had read about or seen on a movie screen.

"What in the hell is out there?" Bailey asked in a squeak she wasn't sure she recognized.

"We aren't sure."

*An unknown monster!* Her mind flashed to *Keepers of the Cave*, the one and only novel she hadn't been able to read by her favorite author.

Bailey gasped and tried to cover it with a throat-clearing cough. She ignored the silencing look Officer Smith shot her and tried to swallow her fear. In a gulping grunt, she pushed out the words she was not sure she wanted an answer to. "Human or animal?"

Officer Smith shot her a surprised look before returning her focus to the forest around them. Her voice was softer when she finally spoke. "It's an animal. Maybe a panther, but I won't know for sure until I see it."

Bailey stayed close beside her as they began walking again. The hint of a smile playing across the officer's lips annoyed Bailey and pushed away her fear again. She could see how her question could be funny if they were not in the middle of a forest being stalked by—something. She hated to admit it, but she felt safer with Officer Smith beside her.

After a few more steps, Bailey allowed herself to be pulled to a stop. Officer Smith grasped the radio microphone clipped to her shoulder and calmly gave instructions into it.

"Joey, I need you to pick up a hiker about a half mile south of Gopher's Fork."

"Roger," came the immediate response, a man's voice echoing through the silent forest.

Bailey did not resist as the woman continually moved in circles, keeping Bailey shielded from the darkest parts of the forest. The silence was heavy. The birds and squirrels she had enjoyed listening to earlier had abandoned her and the quiet sent shivers down her spine. She found no comfort in cowering behind the officer's wide shoulders and it was impossible to see over them. She turned, putting them back-to-back as they continued their bizarre dance.

Bailey studied the shadows on each side of the trail for any threat that might be coming at them. The forest floor was thick with underbrush and palm leaves. Fallen trees and limbs added frightening shapes to the darkest areas, making them appear even more menacing. Large oak and pine trees stretched high above them, blocking out the sun like giant beach umbrellas. She could feel Chewie pressed tight against her leg, and she longed for the comfort of running her fingers through the soft curls on her neck.

Chewie only stood about two feet tall and weighed less than twenty pounds, but her impact on Bailey's life was immeasurable.

Chewie reminded her to eat and to go for walks. She provided a much-needed balance to Bailey's otherwise obsessive picture-taking lifestyle.

She wished she could wipe her sweaty palms on her pants, but she wasn't going to let go of Chewie's leash or her camera strap. She would have put the camera back in her bag, but she had not realized until this moment that she was still holding it. It would be too much movement to reach the pack on her back. Besides, having it nearby was a good idea in case something appeared.

Putting the camera lens between her and any threat was instinctual and probably what made her a great photographer. If she were not in the process of being removed from the area, she would find a seat at the base of a tree and wait. Getting a picture of a panther in the wild would elevate her career to another level. However, as much as she wanted the opportunity, she would not take any chances with Chewie's safety.

Within a few minutes, she heard the hum of an engine and sucked in a relieved breath. A gray Ford F-150 with FWC stenciled on the front fender rumbled to a stop on the trail in front of them. Would they make Chewie ride in the back of the truck? She didn't know. She only knew she was going to be sitting wherever her dog was.

Officer Smith pulled the passenger side door open and held it for Bailey.

"My dog, too?" Bailey asked, looking back and forth between the officers.

Officer Smith nodded. "That's probably the safest."

Bailey gave a tug on the leash and motioned for Chewie to jump in. Sliding in beside her, she looked back at Officer Smith. The relief on her face was evident. Realizing how worried the officer had been, she instantly regretted her irritation and wished it had not taken her so long to understand the threat and to cooperate.

"Thanks," she said through the open window; she received only a nod from Officer Smith.

"I'll be right back, TJ," the man called as he eased the truck forward. He radioed their location and destination to the dispatcher before increasing the truck's speed to a slow crawl.

"We're leaving her alone?" Bailey asked as she watched the woman's silhouette fade in the side mirror.

"Her choice," he said with a shrug. "And she can handle it. I'm Joey, by the way."

His fiery red hair was cut short, and he had a thin patch of stubble across the top of his lip. Even with the attempt of a mustache, she was sure he was not much older than twenty. His face still showed the eagerness of youth and the adventure of a challenging job.

"Thanks for the ride, Joey. I'm Bailey and this is Chewie."

He patted Chewie's head and gave Bailey and the camera on her lap a quick glance. "So, you're the photographer we've been hearing about?"

At least some of the field officers were aware of her presence. "I am."

"That's cool. Wish we could let you get some photos of the panther."

"Yes, maybe in a different situation that would be great. Today might have been a little closer than I'm comfortable with."

Joey smiled. "I understand. Once we catch it, though, maybe TJ can call you."

"Yes, I would like that." She could feel the instant heat on her face. She did want TJ Smith to call her. "I...I'd like to get a photo." Yeah, a photo. That's what she was thinking.

# CHAPTER TWO

TJ Smith turned and walked in the opposite direction from where Joey's truck had disappeared. She was thankful the woman and her dog would be safe and was only moderately annoyed that Joey's truck had probably cost her a chance of seeing the panther.

She followed the trail back to the last place she had seen a track. She studied the imprint in the sand. Four toes and no claw marks. Probably not a dog or even a coyote as some of her coworkers had hypothesized. Although the Florida panther had five toes on its front feet, the fifth one never showed in a print. She could see three distinct lobes on the center paw pad, but it was too large to be a bobcat.

She had felt a rush of panic when she first sensed its presence earlier. A panther would be attracted to the little dog, but its instinct should have been to avoid the humans. She had felt more than seen it circling them. She was a bit surprised by that behavior, but for now she would chalk it up to hungry predator. She rolled her shoulders and sucked in a breath, relieved at getting the woman and the dog out of the area before something bad happened.

In the last few days, she had tried not to put a name to the animal they were tracking. The locals were gossiping about the possibility of a panther, but she preferred not to echo that hypothesis until the animal was seen or at least caught on camera. Whatever anyone from her department said would be taken as the truth and hearing from the FWC that there was a panther in the area would make people panic. Not to mention attract poachers wanting to shoot it and stuff it like a carnival prize.

The Florida panther was native to Florida—hence its name—and historically had roamed the entire southwest United States, but they were rarely, if ever, seen in the northern part of the Panhandle of Florida these days. With so much construction in the state, most were found in the southwest, around the Everglades and the areas of the wildlife trail. It was almost like there was an invisible barrier splitting the state in half that kept them from moving north. In any case, since there were fewer than one hundred and eighty left in the wild, it was TJ's desire as well as her job to help protect them.

Working for the Florida Fish and Wildlife Service was TJ's first and only job. It had taken most of the last sixteen years for her to become proficient in handling the wide variety of creatures found in the state, some more easily than others. She would happily go head-to-head with a panther or even an alligator rather than a snake. Not that she had not battled her share of snakes growing up in this county, but she'd managed to keep her dislike of them from her coworkers. Men liked to be pranksters and finding even a nonvenomous snake in her truck would likely kill her. Luckily, there were plenty of officers from all over the United States who voluntarily moved to south Florida specifically in order to be involved with the largest snakes found in the Everglades.

As she walked along, she did not squat or bend to study the prints in case the animal was still nearby. Avoiding the appearance of being prey also made her keep her arms close to her body and as still as possible. She slowly turned in all directions, staring into the dark patches between the trees, and felt confident that she was now alone. All sightings in the last few days had been within a five-mile radius of this area, though, and she had to imagine that the animal had not gone far.

She settled into her comfort zone, letting her mind wander but remaining vigilant. She released a small involuntary sigh. Under different circumstances she might have taken a few minutes to ask the woman's name or at least be friendly. Her gaydar was certainly not proficient, but she thought she might have felt a vibe.

She had learned years ago not to judge women by their clothing. Her friends always joked about lesbians wearing flannel and comfortable clothing, but this garb was not a means of lesbian identification in the South. Both were a common selection for all women—no matter their sexual preference—due to them working outside, liking patterns that easily covered spills and splashes, or stealing articles of clothing from a husband or boyfriend's closet.

The woman had not been wearing flannel, but she was wearing comfortable clothing: multi-pocketed pants that had hugged her hips and a matching vest over a white, long-sleeved shirt. Even so, it was not her appearance that made TJ's gaydar ping; it was the way she moved and presented herself. Her restrained rebellion at being asked to leave the area was sexy and, lesbian or not, TJ had felt drawn to her. She wished they had met under different circumstances.

Her dating options in this county were minimal. Oh, there were a few lesbians, but she had either dated them or removed them from her list before she turned twenty. She never spent much time thinking about being alone and now was certainly not the time to do so.

She needed to get eyes on a tawny-colored Florida panther. Normally a night dweller, this panther had been seen several times during the day and within a nearby residential area. It was either looking for food or for a new territory to claim, but that didn't matter for now. She had a process to follow—one that didn't involve analyzing why it was here, but started with the surveillance cameras that she and Joey would soon be hanging.

As if on cue, Joey's truck came into sight and pulled to a stop beside her. She dropped the rear tailgate and began sorting through their equipment.

Making daylight appearances and coming near humans weren't normal behaviors, so she had to be concerned with the risk of rabies. There had not been any attacks on domestic animals or people, and her goal was to prevent that. If it turned out the panther was a female, there was always a chance there were babies nearby. As far as documented data was concerned, though, a female had never bred this far north. In fact, only the males seemed to wander away from the southern part of the state and even those did not come this far west.

She handed five four-inch cameras to Joey and wrapped their cables around her own arm. If possible, she preferred to use solar-powered equipment with a battery for backup. Avoiding returning to the area often to replace dead or defective batteries would increase their chance of catching the animal on video. It would take several cloudy days in a row to diminish the output of her solar panels and that did not happen very often in Florida, even in October.

Cautiously, she walked the slightly beaten-down trail. Even though she was confident she and Joey were alone for the moment, she still listened intently to the sounds around them. It seemed unlikely that the panther would attempt to attack. There had never been a panther attack on a human in Florida. Past experiences had taught her that animals most often acted with instinct unless they were provoked or trying to protect their young.

She stepped into a small clearing and dropped the cables and panels she carried. Stuffing one of the cameras from Joey in her pocket, she picked up one end of the cable and began climbing a nearby tree. The large oak had huge thick limbs starting barely five feet off the ground. Like a step ladder, she used the arms of the tree as rungs and climbed about fifteen feet before straddling the branch. She slid a few tacks into the bark and attached the camera, focusing it on the clearing below. She snapped the cable into place on the camera and switched it on. Climbing down a few limbs, she dropped to the ground beside Joey.

"Nice work," Joey exclaimed.

"Next one is yours."

She moved around to the sunny side of the tree and stuck the sharp end of the solar panel stake into the ground at the base of the tree. She quickly cut the cable to the length needed and spliced it. Attaching a plastic connector, she snapped it into place on the solar panel.

"Let's go," she said, starting off at a brisk pace.

They followed the path another few hundred feet. She waited while Joey climbed the tree, then, when he had the next camera attached, cut the cable and attached the solar panel before handing it up to him.

"Attach this to the limb above you," she instructed. "There's not enough light down here to power it."

After securing three more cameras, they began the trek back to the truck.

"So, did you notice how pretty she was?" Joey asked.

"What?"

"The photographer chick. She was pretty, right?"

"What photographer?"

"The woman you called me to pick up earlier. She's the photographer that Sanders mentioned in the staff meeting on Monday."

She vaguely remembered something about a photographer being given access to restricted areas. She had only partially listened since neither of the two areas involved were in her normal work zones. She had not even noticed if the name had been male or female, but apparently Joey had.

"Oh, right. The photographer."

Joey gave a resigned sigh. TJ gave a mental shrug. It was common knowledge that she was a lesbian, but she never engaged with the guys when they talked about women. And she certainly never talked about her thoughts or private life. She had grown up in this area and in her opinion people already knew way too much about her. Besides, she had not been the nicest, and the photographer would probably never speak to her again if their paths ever crossed.

# CHAPTER THREE

Bailey pulled the door on her Jeep closed and hooked Chewie's seat belt before fastening her own and contemplating Plan B. She knew without studying her maps that there were plenty of locations in this area where she could get wildlife pictures. State parks were not her only options. More than sixty percent of Wakulla County was designated as national park and owned by the federal government. She did not have a federal contact in Florida yet, but she was certain it would not be a problem. Most areas were open to the public, and she had seen a US Forestry office on the road that ran behind the local grocery store.

Positive advertising did not come easy for any type of law enforcement, so there were very few government officials that would pass up the opportunity to be highlighted in a photo book. Captain Westmore, for example, had been eager for her to focus on Wakulla County. That thought reminded her that she had agreed to swing by his office for a face-to-face meeting, as well as of his awkward invitation to have dinner with his family. She hated being social and making polite conversation with people she barely knew.

She headed in the direction of St. Marks. After Joey had dropped her off, she had programmed her GPS with the location of several areas she could explore, and she tapped the button now for the St. Marks Lighthouse. Following Highway 98, she crossed the Wakulla Springs River and took the cutoff for the small riverside town of St. Marks. She followed the brown park signs onto a narrow two-lane road. Both sides of the road were heavily wooded with large swampy areas reaching right up to the edges of the pavement.

She was hoping to capture a few pictures of anything that was native to Florida to submit to Mona, her publicist. Mona had been hounding her daily for something she could use to begin promoting Bailey's tenth book. The nature lovers were already blogging about it and sending out a photo would increase excitement—and in the end make them both more money.

She slowed as she passed the gatehouse but could see that there was no one inside. A large sign pointed her to a pull-off area where a metal box on a post held envelopes. This park, as she imagined many in the area would be, worked on the honor code. Visitors were expected to fill out an envelope with their vehicle information and then deposit their park access fee into the slot in the metal box. She separated the identification number tag from the envelope and tossed it on the dash before slipping the envelope with the correct amount of cash into the slot.

She made a mental note of the hours of operation for the visitor's center in case she wanted to browse there later and then continued south toward the Apalachee Bay. Eventually the darkness of tree cover opened to reveal sunshine and blue skies. Pools of water and marshes stretched until the trees behind them looked like matchsticks. Bailey checked behind her for traffic and then slowed to scan both sides of the road. Marsh grass lined the pool edges and she strained to see any sign of an alligator.

The first vehicle she had seen since entering the park appeared in the bend of the road ahead. They crept toward each other like turtles on a log. The sun reflected off the windshield as the other car approached, and they were almost side by side before she could see it was a battered pickup truck.

"Of course," she mumbled, looking at Chewie. "Wanna bet his political party?"

She and Chewie had arrived in Florida almost two months earlier. As they meandered around getting familiar with the area, she had seen a wide variety of vehicle bumper stickers. While her favorite was zombies chasing a stick-figure family, the majority were political, and she discovered quickly that here she was in the minority party. Trucks seemed to be the worst, though. The larger the truck the bigger the chance she would not see eye to eye with the driver.

A hand emerged from the open pickup window and waved Bailey to a reluctant stop. There was still no other traffic in either direction, so Bailey only opened her window a few inches. She was happy to see that she was wrong on at least one of her assumptions. The driver was female. The tuft of gray hair emerging from under the wide-brimmed hat almost covered the vibrant blue eyes that stared out at her.

"A gator just crossed the road in front of me. If you hurry, you might see him before he slides into the water."

"Thanks," Bailey called as she stepped on the gas. She would take time later to think about why her assumption that the pickup driver would be male was so wrong.

She applied the brakes as she came around the turn, scanning the grass-covered bank. Spotting a green-armored body lying inches from the pool of water, she slammed her Jeep to a stop. Without a thought, she grabbed her camera and threw open her door. Her eyes caught movement in front of her and she saw there was another gator crossing the road.

"Shit," she muttered under her breath as she quickly pulled her door shut. She looked at Chewie standing on the seat beside her. Her eyes were focused on the alligator in front of them and a low growl was emerging from her throat. Bailey watched as the fur on her neck and back rose.

"It's okay, girl. That's an alligator, but you're safe inside."

Chewie gave her a quick glance, clearly hesitant to pull her eyes away from the object in front of them.

Bailey lowered her window completely and slid her upper body out until she could sit on the door frame. It was not the angle she would have preferred, but leaving the Jeep was not really an option. She watched the gator slowly lift its scale-covered body and continue to walk across the road. Right arm and left rear leg. Left arm and right rear leg. It was a surprisingly fast waddle, and she quickly switched to video on her camera. She could pull still images from the footage later.

When the gator reached the edge of the water, it gave one final push, sliding past the first gator she had stopped to see. As its tail disappeared, Bailey checked for traffic and climbed out. Having been surprised once, she quickly checked the area for any other reptiles before moving away from her vehicle. Staying on the edge of the road, she walked away from and then parallel with the alligator. Listening for the sound of oncoming traffic, she held the camera low and snapped a few pictures.

The big beast was about six feet long and did not appear to be bothered by her. Even though it never looked in her direction, she knew she was being watched. After a few minutes she got nervous and returned to the Jeep. Chewie gave her a little whimper when Bailey climbed in, but at least the hair on her neck was no longer standing at attention.

She followed the narrow two-lane road as it meandered toward the lighthouse at the tip of the point. She would have to keep Chewie on a leash in this public area; that was one of the reasons she had not chosen to come here first. Having the goldendoodle along had not interfered with her work yet, but, if necessary, Bailey could always leave her at the condominium she had rented.

Bailey had never intended to get a dog. Or any animal for that matter. About three years ago, though, she had returned to her small studio apartment in New York to compile her photography book on the wildlife in Oregon and ended up spending a day listening to her neighbor's new puppy whine and cry. She met the owners as they left the apartment the next morning and offered to dogsit. They were eager to allow her to do so, and it became a daily routine.

Chewie's curly, red-tinted hair did not shed, and she had fit perfectly into Bailey's apartment and life. During the day, she and the dog discussed the proper layout and wording to use with each photo, and even though Chewie mostly listened, she still felt that the pup's input was invaluable. They walked, napped, and enjoyed an occasional treat at the nearby ice cream shop. Of course, Chewie's treat was made for a dog and hers was a less-calorie-filled sherbet rather than ice cream, but it was still fun. She could barely tolerate the emptiness that filled her apartment after Chewie's owners came to retrieve her each evening.

She had always claimed a pet would not fit into her life, but Chewie had shown her that it was possible. She visited the local animal shelter, but none of the animals seemed to fit her like Chewie did. She finally broke down and asked her neighbors if they would consider giving her up. They sadly admitted that they had acted spontaneously when they got the pup and agreed that she needed a new home.

Now, Chewie was a big part of her book tours and photograph gathering. She was patient and seldom barked or even whined. She would lie quietly beside Bailey while they waited for animals to be photographed and at Bailey's feet while she signed copies of her books. Chewie was her constant companion, and Bailey could not imagine a time when they had not been together.

The only other vehicle in the parking lot when she got there was a sand-colored Ford truck that her Jeep towered over. The multiple dents along its fender encouraged her to leave several parking spots between them. She left the Jeep running but secured the doors with her extra key. She knew that locking the doors on a soft-top Jeep was a bit ridiculous, but undertaking to provide a little extra security to prevent Chewie from being stolen seemed okay. The Jeep was replaceable.

She walked around the base of the lighthouse and climbed the lookout tower. From that height she could see the Gulf waters on the other side of the narrow strip of trees. The water shimmered with the reflection of the afternoon sun. To her left were grassy paths that wound around multiple pools of brackish water. On the right was a single path with Gulf water on one side and a huge brackish pool on the other.

She left the tower and walked along the single path. She took a picture of the sign instructing visitors not to feed the alligators. Mona might want to use it on the book cover or at least on the website. As she walked there was an occasional break in the trees where she could look out at the Gulf waters. There was only a gentle rocking of the water as it met the shore, and it looked calm if not a little stagnant. At one of the breaks in the trees, she climbed over a few tire-sized rocks and made her way to the shoreline.

"Watch your step, little lady. I saw a baby diamondback rattlesnake over there a few minutes ago."

The man's voice surprised Bailey, but it was his words that made her jump.

He chuckled. "I shooed it into the brush, so you should be okay. But watch where you step."

Stepping away from the rocks and onto the beach covered with small pebbles, she felt a little better. Snakes always made her jumpy and on edge. Especially if she knew they were in the area but could not see them. She was a little bit proud that she had not squealed when he told her, though. From this vantage point, she would be able to see something coming at her.

She was finally able to look at the man who had spoken. He stood in front of an open lawn chair that held an aluminum beer can in one pocket and multiple pieces of clothing across the back. His head was covered with a wide-brimmed hat exactly like the one she had seen on the woman she passed on the road earlier. His body was as straight and narrow as the fishing pole he held in his hands. His faded blue jeans were cinched at the waist with a thick belt and their legs disappeared into knee-high rubber boots.

He reeled the line in slowly before pulling back and casting again. His gaze was on the water in front of him, but she saw his eyes flicker toward her occasionally. The snake warning seemed to be all the words he had in him, and she wondered if she should retreat. He didn't seem bothered that she was here and she didn't want to be rude.

"Are you catching much?" she asked.

"Hmpf."

She was not sure if that was a yes or a no, but she did not see a bucket or anything that would hold a catch of fish.

"Thanks for the warning on the snake. I'm not a fan."

"Most people aren't."

So much for conversation. Now seemed like a good time to turn and run. She was not looking forward to climbing back over the rocks, but there were trees reaching out into the water on her right and she was not going to walk any closer to the man.

"Well, good luck."

She turned to leave but turned back when he cleared his throat and began to talk.

"No need to run off before you take your pictures."

"Oh, right," she said, remembering the camera she held. "I'm actually a wildlife photographer."

"Sorry you missed the little diamondback then. Want me to scare him up again?" he said, chuckling.

"Uh, no, please."

"You're not from this area, are you?"

"No, I'm from up north."

He made a little growl in his throat. "A Yankee?"

"Well, I do live in New York, but I'm definitely not a Yankee's fan. I grew up outside Boston, so the Red Sox are my team."

"Then we can agree. I like any team that's beating those Yankees. So, what are you doing in this area?"

"Taking pictures of Florida wildlife for a book."

"Hmpf. Doesn't sound like you like our wildlife too much."

She shook her head. She was certainly not going to try to convince him that she liked snakes, and she thought he might only be messing with her anyway.

"I'm gone for ten minutes and you've already made a friend. Ain't that sweet?"

Bailey jumped at the woman's voice behind her. She wanted to warn her about the snake, but the woman was already over the rocks and shuffling down the beach. Bailey immediately recognized her wide-brimmed hat.

"This here is that photographer Rick was talking about this morning," the man said, turning and making a little motion toward Bailey. "Didn't catch her name, though. Was waiting for you to grill her when you got back."

The woman laughed and slapped him on the back as she sank into the lawn chair. "Rick will be sorry he missed you," she said, giving Bailey a nod. "Rick's an old buddy of Tim's and he overheard those forestry cops talking about some big-time photographer coming here. Rick's pretty famous 'round here. Seems like he's in the newspaper every other week, winning some fishing tournament or competition. He likes to call himself photogenic." She laughed again, reminding Bailey of the grandmother she hadn't seen since she was ten.

Grandma Everett didn't need anyone to laugh at her jokes and she could talk for hours without input from anyone else. As a kid, Bailey enjoyed her company more than that of anyone else in her family. When she was with her, Bailey didn't have to make conversation. She could sit and listen without feeling judged or criticized.

"Now," the woman continued, nodding at Bailey again. "If I remember correctly you're named after some mountain. Everest, maybe."

Bailey smiled. "Close. Everett. I'm Bailey Everett."

"I'm Marge, but you can call me Tubs, and that handsome man is my husband, Tim. I bet he was talking your ear off. Normally he naps when I run to the bathroom. He thinks I don't know, but my seat is always warm when I get back."

"I don't sleep!" He laughed and stepped out of her reach before adding, "You don't leave that seat long enough for it to get cold."

She swatted at him again, catching only air. "You're lucky I'm here to supervise or we wouldn't have anything for dinner."

He gave Bailey a sheepish grin. "I let the smaller ones go. It just doesn't seem right to eat anything that's shorter than my foot."

"Is that what you use to make your decision? I think we should start using my foot instead." Tubs shifted her bulk in her seat so she could see Bailey. "Don't mind us. We aren't happy if we aren't bickering. So you're from New York, huh?"

"I have an apartment there." Bailey looked out at the water. New York was not her home. She could not truly say where home was. When she left Worchester, a suburb of Boston, she had not looked back. Her parents had been extremely happy to be rid of their lesbian daughter.

"You must do pretty well with those picture books to live in New York and still have money to travel all over."

Bailey was not sure that was a question, so she remained silent. She did do well, though, well enough to afford an apartment in New York City and constant travel and to receive more photography awards than the shelf in her home office had space for. She and Chewie didn't want for anything. Well, Chewie might like to have her own yard one day, but she never complained.

It had taken her five years to save enough money for the high-quality camera that had started her career. She still held on to that one, but the one she used today was beyond anything even comparable to that older model.

"That's your Jeep up there, right?" Tubs asked, bringing Bailey back to the conversation.

"Yes."

"I parked beside you. I have another chair in the back, if you want to grab it."

Bailey considered that question. Sitting here on the shoreline with Tubs and Tim seemed like an enjoyable way to spend the afternoon. Before she could respond, Tim cut in.

"Won't be out here much longer, Tubs," he said, motioning toward the western skyline.

Bailey looked up at the same moment that a flash of lightning stretched across the darkening sky. *Chewie!*

"I need to run. My dog doesn't like these Southern thunderstorms."

"We're here every day. Come back and visit us," Tubs called.

"It was nice meeting you both," Bailey said, giving them a wave as she climbed the rocks with only a passing thought of the snake. Chewie would be starting to pant nervously; she needed to get her back to the condo as quickly as possible. Chewie preferred to be under the bed or in the closet when she was scared.

Driving as fast as possible on the curving road back to Shell Point, she thought about her conversation with Tubs and Tim. She had been happy to leave Massachusetts twenty years ago. She had known at a young age that she would leave the small town as soon as she was able. Coming out to her parents had made that dream a reality as soon as she graduated from high school.

She was surprised she had made it to graduation. There had been threats to send her to California to live with her mother's sister. She had encouraged her father to make the arrangements even though she had never met her Aunt Phyllis. Anything seemed better than living with parents who did not want her. Her two younger brothers were her parents' pride and joy. They did not need a daughter too and certainly not a lesbian one, as her father had told her more than once.

Even before she left home, she had felt that being an animal photographer would be the perfect profession. No conversations. No uncomfortable silences. She had embraced the solitary career, especially once she learned to develop her own film. She was happy spending time away from people with only critters to watch and enjoy. With her Canon EOS 5D camera, the Mark I at first but later a Mark IV, as her only companion, she could view the world around her as if she was watching television.

As a kid, she only had an old pair of binoculars. She had found them in a box her father brought home from an estate sale. One of the lenses was hazy and partially blocked with years of dust, but she didn't care. They worked well enough she could watch animals; they became her escape from a house she didn't belong in.

The animals around her house weren't scary. They were cute and entertaining to watch. She would imagine their lives and the conversations they were having with each other. Squirrels and chipmunks were her favorites, especially when they were gathering nuts for the winter. She understood the cycle of life but preferred to avoid the death and dying side of nature.

After purchasing her first camera, it had taken her almost three years to compile enough top-quality photographs for a complete book and to convince a publisher to take a chance on her. Hiring a publicist to tend to the business side freed her time to take photos. Her wildlife books were now quite popular, and she had the money to make a temporary move to a new state every year or so. She would capture as much of the native wildlife there on film and then return to her New York apartment to compile her work and write the descriptions.

Her preparation for each temporary move was extensive. Weeks of Internet searching and reviewing wildlife books that were already published. Compiling a tentative list of animals she'd like to include—that was essential—though she would not lock herself into anything specific. Once she arrived in an area, she would spend a few weeks getting a feel for her surroundings.

Most states, like Florida, would require more than one book to document their wildlife. The animals and reptiles found in the southern part of Florida were nothing like what was found in the northern part. She had decided to start with the northern Panhandle because so many books had already been done on the Florida Everglades and the area surrounding it. And to be honest she was not looking forward to getting close enough to take pictures of anything that slithered. Thankfully, she focused on indigenous creatures and not eight-foot-long pythons. Reptiles weren't all bad. Frogs, especially the little green tree frogs, were awesome, as were turtles and even lizards. Snakes? Not so much. In fact, not at all.

# CHAPTER FOUR

TJ slammed her truck door and yanked the casting material from the bed. She would blame Joey's ramblings about the photographer yesterday for making her forget she needed to make a plaster cast of the tracks. If her videos did not produce anything in a week or so, she would need proof that she wasn't chasing an imaginary beast. She was thankful that there hadn't yet been any destruction of property or loss of domestic animals, but the lack thereof had made her superiors doubtful about the threat.

Captain Westmore was inclined to listen to his officers, which meant he was a small bit better than the previous supervisors assigned to Wakulla County. In the past, egotistical men filled with authority from their title rather than from experience had always known what was best. At least Captain Westmore tended to follow and back up his officers' ideas rather than his own.

Supervising six officers in Wakulla County was apparently a position that few ranking Fish and Wildlife officers wanted. Mostly it was used as a stepping-stone to somewhere bigger and more prestigious. Funding was divided between all the sixty-seven counties in Florida. It took an extremely vocal negotiator to make sure that Wakulla maintained its share of the funds.

Captain Dan Westmore was good with the public; she would be able to judge just how good he was at pulling his own weight, however, when he returned from the state meeting this winter. If he lasted that long. She had been hearing rumors about his departure for several weeks now. He had only been there for about three months and they were just starting to get him trained. His wife and two sons had settled in quite nicely. Sarah Westmore even had an article in the weekly paper. Something about tourism and the local attractions.

TJ didn't read the county paper and certainly not the fluff pieces. She would take reading a lesbian fiction book any day over reading the news, though she tried to keep up with world news, especially with the state of today's political affairs. Weekly staff meetings made sure she knew anything about local news that might pertain to her job. Her boss did seem to like being a part of the local news. Which explained why he had allowed a photographer into their forests.

When TJ arrived at the Fish and Wildlife detachment, she went straight to her office. The small brown building barely had space for the officers assigned, a receptionist desk in front, and Captain Westmore's office in the rear. TJ's office, or rather her nook, contained a small desk and chair. Visitors were greeted in the lobby, and paperwork, if it couldn't be completed online, was filed behind the receptionist's desk.

She settled into her desk chair with her work laptop beside her. Hitting a few buttons, she tapped into the live stream and began to watch her own panther television. Sadly, there was no panther to be seen. She watched for a few minutes, willing the tawny animal to appear, but still nothing. She pressed the intercom button on her desk phone and punched in the three-digit code for the office down the hall.

"Randy, I'm back."

"I heard you come in. I'm headed out." His gruff voice called to her from her open doorway.

She switched the phone off and looked up at him. Randy Sanders's six-foot-three frame filled the doorway. He would be retiring in the next year or so, and she would miss him. He was quiet with a sarcastic sense of humor, and she had enjoyed learning from him when she first came on the job. He was the field supervisor directly under Captain Westmore, but he did as much if not more field work than the other officers assigned here.

"Lunch?" she asked.

"Yep. Did you grab something when you were out, or do you need me to bring something back for you?"

"I'm good. Thanks."

He gave her a limp salute and stepped out of her sight.

"Thanks for reviewing the video from last night," she called.

His muffled response drifted down the hall, but she couldn't identify his words. Probably something sarcastic. No one enjoyed watching an empty screen.

She liked everyone in her office. She was lucky in that, she guessed, but that didn't mean she wasn't working with five testosterone-filled men. Joey was the newest addition, and he had only been in the office for about nine months. Randy and Neil had the longest tenure. Kurt and Chandler were the office jokesters and always the ones begging her to join them after work for a beer.

She switched the video monitor to detect movement and pulled her personal laptop in front of her. They had been watching the stream for over twenty-four hours now with nothing but squirrels, raccoons, and armadillos to see.

She scrolled through her email until she found one from Randy listing the details from the last staff meeting. The name of the photographer and the date she would begin work was listed in the last paragraph. She opened a search window on her laptop and typed in the name Bailey Everett. There were hundreds of links displayed, but she started with Everett's official website. The photos were amazing. She quickly added all nine books available to her cart and then realized how crazy that was. She removed all but one, Utah. It was a place she had never visited. Yielding to a last-minute impulse, she paid the extra money for overnight delivery.

* * *

Bailey slowed as she approached the white St. Marks Lighthouse. Its black top shimmered in the midmorning sun. It had been several days since she had driven along the six miles of scenic roadway. She had made the hard decision to leave Chewie at home today. The dog had watched her leave with big sad eyes, but it was easier for her to work at this location without her friend, especially after the diamondback sighting. It wasn't safe for Chewie to be out of the car.

She had gotten an early start this morning, stopping for gas at a Crawfordville gas station that turned out to be a local breakfast hangout. She had noticed the food sign on one of her previous trips through town, but gizzards and livers weren't her thing, even if they were the best in town as the sign claimed. She couldn't find the words to describe how that made her stomach feel.

Tubs and Tim had been at a back booth when she entered the store and made a ruckus until she joined them. After introducing her to everyone in the store, they prodded her with questions from personal to professional. When they found out she was traveling without Chewie today they coaxed and begged until she agreed to come sit with them for a while.

She walked around the lighthouse and read the information placards she hadn't noticed on her previous visit. This was the second-oldest lighthouse in Florida and the oldest one on the Florida Gulf coast. It was built in 1842 and had been recently renovated. The keeper's house was available for tours two days a month. Not today, though. So she walked the grassy path that ran between the Gulf shoreline and the pools of brackish water.

A few boats in a variety of sizes speckled the Gulf water and she watched one leaving the river at the end of the point. It was white with a thick, vibrant red stripe along its length. It accelerated as it hit the open water like it had been holding back and then she saw the signs marking the river as a No Wake zone. She passed the path where Tim and Tubs would be fishing and walked closer to read the posted sign. A blue-and-black sign with a huge gray animal with a mermaid's tail that said "Manatee No Wake Zone."

She usually only skimmed over aquatic animals when doing her research; her camera wasn't made for underwater shooting, and she had never been interested in pursuing that aspect of nature photography anyway. The manatee pictured on the sign reminded her of a gray Shmoo from the old *Li'l Abner* comic strip. The Shmoo was a nonaggressive fictional creature that lived only to delight people. She resisted the urge to stop and research manatees on her phone, instead returning to the path that led to the shoreline. She carefully stepped over the rocks, watching for anything that slithered.

She heard Tim's chuckle before she cleared the narrow strip of brush and trees.

"I chased all them creepy crawlin' critters away 'cause I knew you were comin'," he called to her.

"Hey, Bailey, so glad you could join us," Tubs said.

Bailey was glad too because beside Tubs was an empty lawn chair that had apparently been brought for her. She casually picked up the chair and repositioned it to put more distance between the chairs. It wasn't that she didn't like Tubs; she didn't like anyone in her personal space.

"What can you tell me about manatees?" she asked as she sat down, shifting sideways in her chair so she could see Tubs.

"They're a big sea cow," Tubs answered.

"Big? No. Those suckers are huge," Tim exclaimed. "If they were meat eaters, people wouldn't go in the water again."

"What are you talking about, Tim? We swim in the river with the gators." Tubs waved her arm at him like what he said didn't matter. "Manatees eat plants and they're gentle as can be."

"I'm not really familiar with them. Are they in the Gulf as well as the rivers?"

Tubs nodded. "Yep. They mostly come up the rivers in search of warmer water in the winter months. Shallow water is warmed easier by the sun. Plus a lot of the rivers are spring fed and they remain the same temperature year-round."

Bailey shifted in her chair to reach her cell phone in her pocket and then immediately straightened again. She couldn't wait to do research on these animals, but she would. Tim and Tubs had invited her to sit with them, not to watch her face glued to her phone. She had always admired the beauty of the animals she photographed, but she loved the eager feeling that came along every so often when she discovered something new. She anxiously awaited the first convenient moment to politely make her escape.

That moment came when Tubs announced she was making her bathroom run.

"It's almost noon, I should get back and let Chewie out," Bailey explained.

Tim gave his usual hmpf, but Tubs linked arms with her as they walked toward the rocks leading out to the parking lot.

"I always keep an extra chair in the back of the truck, so come back anytime," Tubs encouraged her.

"I will," Bailey called as she slid behind the wheel.

Back in her condo, she sat down at the small kitchen table which she had claimed as her workspace. The chair at the end looked across the narrow living room and out the window to the docks and water inlet below. She opened her laptop and began to research manatees in depth. The more she looked at the huge water cows the more she began to fall in love with them. They were famous for their gentleness; the truth was they were five hundred pounds of plain old cuteness.

# CHAPTER FIVE

TJ pushed the lever to drop the bucket to the ground and then pressed the foot pedal to push the tractor forward. When the bucket was filled with dirt from the pile beside her house, she pushed the lever to lift it. Torrential rain had destroyed her driveway, but dosing it with an occasional bucket of dirt helped avoid deep puddles when the downpours came. October wasn't normally a rainy time but with climate change things weren't normal.

The compact John Deere tractor had been her first investment when she moved in with her grandmother. It was a necessity. She used it for mowing the pasture, carrying dirt, and anything else that needed scooping or moving. Like the mulch that the landscaper had dumped in one big pile at the edge of the yard.

The John Deere was also good for pulling stumps out of the ground. She was reminded of this as her right front tire sunk into a hole as she crossed the pasture. She turned the tractor around and dumped the bucket of dirt in the hole. When her grandmother had had the area around the house cleared years ago, the man she hired sawed the trees as close to the ground as possible and then covered them with dirt.

Now, years later, as the tree stumps rotted, little mini sinkholes were developing all over the pasture. It was annoying and one of the reasons she crossed the pasture often with the tractor. She would rather find the sinkhole with the tractor than have a cow or horse break a leg. Of course, she didn't currently own any cows or horses, but she often leased the pasture to nearby neighbors. That way she got the joy of seeing the animals every day but didn't have to tend to them.

It wasn't that she didn't like farm animals. She did. She had considered many times purchasing or rescuing a horse or even a donkey. The pasture was about ten fenced acres and could comfortably hold two or three animals. It was perfect for cows, horses, donkeys, or goats, but she preferred to spend her time outside riding her dirt bike. Her bike didn't demand daily attention. If a few days passed and she didn't ride, she never felt guilty like she would if she couldn't make time for an animal.

She returned to the dirt pile and scooped another load. She dumped it on the low spot in the driveway and then drove back and forth over it until it was packed down. The afternoon sun was beating down on her, and she was soaked with sweat and covered in dust. She parked the tractor back inside the shed and looked longingly at her dust-covered motorcycle.

This was the first day in weeks that she had time to even think about taking a ride. Straddling the 250 Honda, she kicked the starter. It took a few strong kicks before the engine caught and held. She revved the engine, pushing gas through the lines.

She had spent many hours during work and after skimming video footage. Randy and Joey had helped, but she was glad she was the one to make the initial identification. Everyone in the office was surprised a panther had wandered into their area, and she was pretty sure they were a little jealous too. An official announcement was made to the public along with the reminder to keep close tabs on pets and livestock. Now that the presence of the panther had been confirmed, the fun was about to begin.

She had compiled as much data about it as possible, where it traveled during the day and where it hid at night. Now state and local agencies would come together to capture the beautiful creature. Until then, though… She pulled through the shed and grabbed her helmet from the shelf. She needed the escape from the thoughts continually running through her mind.

Everyone in each agency was in agreement. The panther would be captured and relocated. She had trapped and relocated more animals than she could count but never something like this. A panther was like the Loch Ness Monster to her. She had never seen one in the wild and she could barely wait.

She rode all the trails that traced the edge of her property to make sure nothing was out of place. There were a few new paths leading back to the swampy area behind her house, but they were all low to the ground, indicating they were made by animals and not humans. Once she was certain that everything looked okay and no trespassers were camping or building fires, she increased her speed and ran the main trails again.

She had created the trails to avoid riding on the main road with her bike. At first, they were only small paths, but over time and with the use of the tractor she had been able to widen them. Now she could drive her truck on them if she wanted. Keeping the limbs cleared away and the grass and weeds mowed gave her somewhere private she could jog if she felt like it, and it was great fun to run them on the motorcycle or four-wheeler. Especially after a hard rain.

After an hour or so of riding she parked the bike back in the shed and drove the tractor over the trails to cover any ruts she might have made. As she walked back to the house, she admired the greenery around her. This summer had been wet, and despite the heat, the grass in the yard and pasture was still growing strong. Stopping for a moment, she admired her little one-story brick farmhouse and its wraparound porch and swing.

The house had been built by her father's great-grandparents and passed down to each generation. It was the only place she had ever called home. After her mother left when TJ was five years old, TJ and her father had moved into it with Grams. The petty crimes her father couldn't seem to stay away from had kept him in jail most of TJ's teenage years, though, and in the end were the cause of his death.

Grams was the only parent she could remember. Their relationship was one of comfort now, unlike during her younger wild years. Now they each did their own thing but often returned to dine together in the evenings. Grams loved to cook and TJ was willing to clean up afterward so the relationship worked. Grams wasn't here at the moment, though. TJ wasn't sure when Grams would return from visiting her friend in Ohio, but she was looking forward to her next home-cooked meal.

She slid her boots off on the porch and carried them inside to the closet. Leaving any shoes on the porch made a welcome home for unwanted critters. Her pace slowed as it always did when she passed through the living room. The big wide windows on either side of the front door brought in plenty of natural light. Two framed pictures sat on the mantel above the fireplace. She smiled at the one of her and her grandmother. It was hard to tell from the picture where they were, but she clearly remembered taking the selfie on the porch swing outside.

The other picture was of her and Breezie. The golden retriever sat with her head held high and her mouth slightly open in a pant that looked like a smile. Breezie, with her long reddish-golden fur, regal frame, and eyes that seemed to see everything, had been the love of her life. When she had finished her probationary years with FWC, she had returned to work in her hometown. Grams had insisted she move back into her childhood home and Breezie had been welcomed as well. She was pretty sure Grams missed Breezie as much as she did, but they didn't talk about that dreadful evening they had found her struggling to take a breath.

She walked through her bedroom and into her private bath. There was a matching L-shaped shower in Grams's bathroom on the other side of the house—one of the improvements they had agreed on. No moldy shower curtains or cramped hard-to-clean stalls for them.

Stepping into the shower, she turned the water nozzle toward the wall before turning it on. The water could take five or ten minutes to warm so she made her way to the kitchen for a snack.

She loved this house and it was the perfect size. When she was growing up, her small bedroom had been nestled between her father's room and Grams. She couldn't remember ever having to fight for use of the single bathroom back then, but when she moved back in as an adult, she needed more personal space. So they knocked out a few walls and made two master bedrooms with a bath.

The kitchen was as spacious as the living room, but Grams's decorating had managed to keep the cozy feel amid the new appliances. Grabbing a few slices of pepperoni and a slice of cheddar cheese, she looked around the room and inhaled deeply. As always, Grams's favorite room smelled of cinnamon and apples. It had been weeks since an apple pie had been baked but the room somehow held on to the good smells. Happily, it also released the bad. Grams could steam cauliflower or make a crock full of sauerkraut, and when they were eaten the scent would go with them. It was like the house had the ability to clean itself.

She surveyed the room with satisfaction. Years of dirt and grime had been removed when the 60s' floral wallpaper was steamed off, taking not only old smells but also bad memories. One moment she could smell her grandfather's cigarette smoke and hear her father yelling about why his latest scam had failed and the next she could hear birds chirping and smell Grams's apple pie. Grams hadn't been shy about reminding her of the history she was removing with her remodeling, but she was confident in the end that Grams liked the changes too.

She dropped her clothes into the bedroom hamper as she stepped into the spray from the shower. Dust clung to her hair and body and she watched it disappear down the drain. It was one of the things she would never get used to in Florida. Dust was in the air. It didn't matter how many times you cleaned the furniture or wiped off the windows, before you knew it they were covered again.

She hated to admit it, but Randy had been right. Taking a day off to mentally regroup before they would make the final push to capture the panther had been refreshing. Now as she made dinner and prepared for bed, she could barely think of anything else. Like a ballplayer might run through an upcoming game, she could see the tranquilized panther falling out of the tree into her net. She hoped it would go as smoothly as she imagined.

* * *

Bailey rested her camera on her knee. The Canon EOS 5D she was using today only weighed 800 grams, about the same as an eight-week-old kitten. It was not heavy at all when cradled against her chest, but holding it to look through the viewfinder made her arms shaky and affected the quality of her photos after a while. She had a tripod, but setting it up while trying to be stealthy was extremely difficult.

She used the touchscreen to flip through her last grouping of photos. The sky was starting to darken as the sun set and she knew the deer would be moving soon. One of the many advantages of her older camera, the Mark I, was its easy and silent switch for low light photos. She knew it was fast becoming a dinosaur in the photography industry, but it was still her favorite. Its photo capacity and protection against inclement weather were as important to her as its ease of use. She carried a Nikon Z9, the Mercedes-Benz of the industry, in her bag as well, but her hand seemed to gravitate to the molded handgrip of the Canon.

She listened to the coastal white-tailed deer snort and watched them stomp their hooves as the wind occasionally carried her scent in their direction. They weren't concerned enough to flip their trademark white flag tails up so her slow progression into their area was working. This was day eight in her search to locate where they spent their evening hours, a time that would lend a different quality to her photos.

There were five adults, four does and a six-point buck, along with two fawns. Through hours of research she knew white-tailed deer were found throughout most of the continental United States. Florida was home to three subspecies; white-tail and coastal white-tail were both smaller than their northern counterparts, and the Florida Key deer were half the size of the other Florida natives.

She quietly stood, keeping as low to the ground as she could. The deer slowly moved down the trail near where she had parked her Jeep earlier in the day. Thanks to a local farmer, she had easily found the two fawns, with a smattering of white spots on their backs, hidden in the tall grass of his pasture. The first couple of days she had maneuvered close enough to take pictures of them and then followed at a short distance when the doe retrieved them for the night. Following the adults wasn't easy and had to do more with being patient and not moving until they were used to her smell.

She followed them across the small two-lane highway that led to a rural farm area outside Crawfordville. Based on the number of steps registered on her Fitbit, she estimated they traveled over a mile down a narrow path to a barely noticeable clearing. The deer circled several times before the fawns moved in for their nighttime feeding. She settled onto a clear spot away from downed limbs and trees. The low brush was enough to hide her and made it easier for her to see creepy crawlers if they approached.

Much to Chewie's disappointment, she had been left at home for this trip and the previous attempts to get close. Bailey wanted the deer to get used to smelling her so she could get close after they had settled in for the night. These were the money shots. The impromptu photo of the alligator she had posted on the blog a few weeks ago had satisfied her followers. It was the picture they expected when she told them Florida would be her next book. For her, though, the pictures that took days to set up were what made her work special—to others and to herself—speaking as they did to her craftsmanship as well as her talent.

Being an acclaimed photographer—yes, she could call herself that now—was a joy she had never imagined. She had made it to this day, past the many rejections of her photographs, all thanks to Mr. Anderson. Unbeknownst to her, he had submitted her photos to magazines all over the world. The first photo accepted by *National Geographic* had won their photo contest as well and brought her agent, Mona, into her life.

Mr. Anderson had done so much for her. When she was discouraged, he would remind her that capturing a story in a single shot took determination, dedication and most of all patience. He was more than a father figure or a mentor. He taught her about life. Now, looking into the eyes of the doe as the fawn nursed, she felt their struggle and their love for each other. Life was never simple, but if you could find the joy in that moment, then it could feel simple, and easy, and yes, joyful.

She silently moved back several paces every few minutes until she was far enough away to move freely without stirring up the deer. A rumble of thunder made her break into a sprint. Chewie would be in a panic if she didn't get to her quickly. The last time she didn't make it home before the storm hit Bailey had found her quivering in the bathtub.

She threw the Jeep into gear and flew west on Highway 98. Five miles down the road she veered right at the fork and followed the signs to Shell Point Beach. The small town was filled with golf carts and with boats, thanks to the many-armed inlets that allowed Gulf of Mexico water to flow through the town. She passed the inlet access on the left and then the brief stretch of white sandy beach on the right before turning into a two-story building that held six condominiums. Her temporary home was in the middle, sandwiched between that of an elderly gentleman who used to be a fisherman, and a couple from Michigan.

Karl Maxwell was overly friendly and clearly always in search of someone to chat with. He was over six feet tall, as he liked to tell anyone that would listen. The tufts of gray hair above each ear reminded her of the frayed ends of Chewie's rope toy. Karl had spent his entire life on the waters of the Gulf of Mexico. His stories were entertaining and often long. This was firsthand knowledge for Bailey, as he always seemed to catch her when she was walking Chewie. Often, he had offered to keep Chewie when she was out. Maybe one day she would take him up on it, especially given the random thunderstorms that seemed to pop up at a moment's notice.

Mike and Janet, on the other side, were happily enjoying their newly started retirement and not looking for others to share their time. She admired the way they seemed to want to spend every second with each other and no one else. Seeing them always reminded her how alone she was. Not that she minded being alone, she reminded herself.

She had tried to date a few times over the years but had never felt close to any of the women. It was always a role she felt like she was pretending to enjoy. Having a companion was what people expected, and she was always good at doing what people expected. Except for this. She would make all kinds of excuses, but usually the one that worked best was her constant moving from state to state. Maybe she was only making excuses, but Mona was the only one that seemed to care if she had someone by her side at events. Sadly, Mona preferred that everyone who escorted her be a male like she had. He didn't have to be a permanent part of Bailey's life, she said, but he did need to clean up nicely.

Being alone had become her way of life; she didn't like anyone to get too close, physically or emotionally. Her private space, whether it was her apartment in New York or something she was renting, was off-limits to anyone.

Mona might play dumb, but she knew that if Bailey ever allowed someone to share her life it wouldn't be a man. Unfortunately, that didn't stop her from using her male friends to escort Bailey at events. It was on those evenings that Bailey couldn't get home fast enough. She liked knowing her things would be exactly where she left them, including the television remote. She couldn't imagine a time when Chewie wouldn't be her favorite companion.

Even though the sky was already blue again, after she parked in her numbered spot Bailey hurried to the building's white staircase. She wouldn't complain that the storm had passed to the north once again. The weather in north Florida was hot and sunny unless it wasn't and then it was a torrential downpour and thunder. It seemed like the weather could change in a second, and she had heard many locals saying if you didn't like the weather to just wait for a moment.

Chewie met her at the door with a whimper and Bailey bent to scratch her head before clipping on her leash. The beach had been deserted when she passed it, so she and Chewie walked in that direction. When they arrived, she removed Chewie's leash and let her run through the sand. She sat on the picnic table and rested her feet on the bench.

Chewie alternated between splashing in the water and chasing the little white birds that ran along the shoreline. They were sanderlings, Bailey knew, because she had looked them up online after she took photos of them. They were mostly white in color and ran in little quick steps, racing to stay in front of the waves.

Mr. Maxwell sank heavily onto the bench at her feet.

"I thought Chewie was in the apartment alone."

His tone was a bit accusatory, but she detected a hint of sadness too.

"I'm sorry, Mr. Maxwell. I promise to let you know the next time I leave her. Most of the time I take her with me, but sometimes it's not convenient. Did it thunder much here?"

"Only once or twice and they weren't too loud."

"Good."

With his chastising out of the way, his tone immediately changed.

"What were you photographing today?"

"I've been following a family of deer. I was able to get close for a few photos today." She realized how excited she was to download the photos and start looking at them. "I guess I should head back in and get to work."

Chewie made one more detour to chase a few birds off the ground before following her to the sidewalk. She clipped the leash to her collar, and they walked with Mr. Maxwell back to the condominium.

"Let me know when you're going to be away," he said as they parted in the hallway.

His door was closed before she could answer, so she didn't. Pushing into her condo, she released Chewie and scooped some kibble into her dish. She didn't feel hungry yet, so she settled in front of the computer with a cup of tea.

The first ten photos or so were disappointing, but she could see the colors brighten and the shadows disappear as she had settled into her zone. The angle of the shots shifted as the deer, watching her closely, moved into rest beside the babies. Several remained standing and she assumed they were keeping watch. As she moved through the clips, she felt the familiar excitement of realizing how good it felt to capture a special moment.

Her favorite shot was a baby stretching up to touch noses with an adult standing beside it. She dropped that one into the final folder and selected a shot that showed the spots on the babies as the best one to email to Mona for another teaser release. Then she began the slow process of writing up where the pictures were taken, a task made easier by the GPS on her camera. It was well past midnight when she finished identifying each one and remembered she hadn't eaten dinner.

# CHAPTER SIX

After a week of late nights, early mornings, and one all-nighter, TJ was relieved it was finally time to attempt the capture. She had been able to anticipate the panther's path the last two days, so Randy had summoned an FWC crew from the Florida Panther National Wildlife Refuge in southwest Florida to assist them. Their daily work involved sedating and tagging panthers for monitoring and research purposes. Even though she had wanted to make the capture with only their local staff, she understood his decision to call in experienced help. If they missed today, the probability was low that the panther would stick around, not after he had been pursued by dogs.

She slid behind the wheel of her truck and reached for the open bottle of water in the center console. Finishing it off, she tossed the empty bottle in the growing mound of plastic containers on the passenger side floorboard. Tomorrow, she would drop them off at the recycle bin. She tried to always think conservation and normally only used her refillable glass water bottle. Over the last week following the panther, she never knew how far she would go or when she would be able to return to her truck. For an FWC officer, getting heat stroke or falling behind due to dehydration was more than a little embarrassing.

She pulled into the gravel lot at the west entrance to Shell Point Wildlife Management Area and parked beside several other state vehicles. She could hear the baying of beagles through the closed windows of her truck. Their eagerness made her pulse race. She hadn't been this excited since—well, she couldn't remember ever. Maybe when she had first started working for the FWC. She took a deep breath and jumped out to join the other uniformed individuals.

"Are we ready for this?" she asked as she joined the group.

"Oh yeah!" Joey responded quickly. She was glad to see he was as excited and eager as she was, but her ego hoped she hid it better.

"As ready as we'll ever be," said Dr. Harroway, a wildlife biologist employed by the FWC. His geographical input had allowed TJ to anticipate and track the path of the panther.

FWC Officer Charlie Bregg opened the rear of his truck and clipped leashes to two brown and white beagles. TJ was surprised when they leapt from the truck and began to pull Charlie toward the forest. Charlie's two assistants followed close behind.

In the previous week, TJ had had numerous Zoom calls with Charlie and Dr. Harroway. Charlie had explained that he would release the dogs in the area TJ had identified as the one the panther was operating in, and that when they found the scent the dogs would sit until he attached their leashes and gave the command to go. As often was the result when dealing with animals, their lengthy discussions and planning were superfluous now as the dogs announced they were already on the trail.

"Here we go," he called over his shoulder as he followed the dogs off the path and into the forest.

TJ sprinted to catch up to them, dodging limbs and jumping fallen trees. Snakes be damned, she wanted to stay on Charlie's heels. She knew the path the panther had followed the last few days, and it looked like they were in for a couple-mile run. A few times the dogs stopped and began to circle; Charlie gave them room to move and locate the scent again. While the dogs followed the smells, she and the other officers watched the ground for signs of scat or scrapings.

Following tracks would be the easiest way to track it, but finding a print around the pine needles and other forest debris wasn't likely. Locating the panther's scat would at least confirm they were on the right path. Panther scat was tubular shaped with tapering at both ends and normally contained hair and bone fragments from their kills. She also watched for piles of debris or pine needles, leaves, or soil. These scrapings were a means of communication with other panthers and were made by pushing backward with their hind feet.

About thirty minutes into the forest, the beagles stopped and sat at the base of a tree.

"What now?" TJ asked as she stopped beside Charlie. They had passed the area where she would have started the search a few minutes back. Circling back wouldn't take long if the dogs needed help finding the scent again.

"My work is finished," Charlie said, pointing up into the tree.

TJ looked up to see the whitish-gray belly of a tawny-colored panther about fifteen feet above her. Its dark eyes pierced into her, and she felt a shiver of fear. Not the panther's but her own. The set of its strong jaw and its black mascara-lined eyes sent a chill through her body. On more than one occasion she had happened upon a bear, but she had always been able to back out of those situations without a confrontation. This was the fiercest beast she had ever stared eye to eye with.

The panther shook its head and swiped its huge paw along the branch it rested on. The scrape of nails along the wood reminded TJ of the sound her pruning saw made when she cut down small trees. The panther opened its mouth and let out a sound somewhere between a meow and a growl. A long and mournful distress call. The sound echoed through the trees and TJ thought she felt the ground beneath her boots vibrate.

She stood mesmerized until Joey bumped her shoulder.

"Are you going to shoot it?" he asked.

"Uh, yeah," she stammered. "It's just so beautiful."

She had watched hours of video footage of panthers being sedated and tagged, but this was her moment. One she would never forget. The image of this creature would be forever imprinted in her mind, but at this moment everyone was waiting for her to act.

She took the tranquilizer gun from Charlie's assistant and loaded the dart as Charlie's crew quickly deployed an inflatable air cushion and a net below the branch the panther rested on. When they were done, she lined up her shot and hit the panther in its right hip, which was exposed.

"Nice shot," Charlie said, walking the dogs away from the tree.

"Yeah," Dr. Harroway agreed. "Let's step away and give the tranquilizer time to work."

TJ watched the panther's head begin to wobble as it gave a hissing growl, far less menacing than the first one. As its body sank deeper into the wedge between the trunk and the branch, TJ could see it was going to need help getting out of the tree.

She grinned at Joey.

"Go get the ropes. It's time to climb."

Joey took off at a sprint to the FWC truck that was waiting on the trail to transport the panther.

"Are you sure you want to do this?" Charlie asked, stepping beside her and giving her shoulder a friendly bump with his. "We do this all the time. One of my team can scramble up there."

"I know and that's why you should share this opportunity with us. I wouldn't pass this up for anything."

"Yeah, but what about him?" Charlie stuck his thumb in the direction Joey had disappeared.

"He'll do whatever is expected of him. Besides, deep down he wouldn't want to miss this opportunity either."

Charlie laughed. "Let me tell you about my first panther capture."

When Joey returned a few minutes later and dropped the ropes at her feet, she was still laughing. And also praying that her first experience would not end with a weak bladder like Charlie's had. In her opinion men had few advantages over women, but relieving their bladder without removing any clothing was certainly one of them.

She tied a rope around her waist and began to climb. Adrenaline raced through her, increasing her intake of breath to almost a gasp. She forced her breathing to match her slow climb, taking a few extra seconds to force each breath to completely fill her lungs before letting it out again. She would never live it down if she passed out and fell out of the tree.

As her breathing slowed, she let the thrill of the moment envelop her. She would memorize each step to replay and savor later. She was also sure at least one person on the ground was filming on their phone. She certainly hoped so.

"Are you sure he's asleep?" Joey called as he followed her up the tree.

She flashed him a grin that said they would soon find out. She had trust in the veterinarian that told her which dart to use and trust in the animal above her that told her he would be letting them know if he wasn't asleep. She slowly approached the large cat, reaching out a tentative hand to stroke his fur. It was thicker than it looked and coarse. The thick strands reminded her of the bristles on her kitchen broom.

"Now what?" Joey asked as they stared at each other over the tawny cat.

"Go a little higher so you can lift him by the scruff of his neck. I'll lift his butt. Once we get him away from the tree, we'll drop him."

"Really?" Joey asked with a little panic in his voice.

She nodded at the net and the men waiting below. "They'll catch him."

"Okay." Joey grasped the cat by the fur on his neck and pulled him up.

TJ pushed up on the cat's hindquarters until he was out of the wedge. Together they balanced him in the air until the men below gave the okay to drop him.

"One, two, three, release," she instructed Joey.

# CHAPTER SEVEN

Bailey poured a second cup of coffee as she sat in front of the print newspaper folded on her kitchen table. Her first cup was always enjoyed with the online *New York Times* even if a print copy was available. This morning she decided she deserved a second cup as a reward for attempting to tackle the local paper. She flipped the paper open, careful to avoid touching the black print.

She scanned the political articles, quickly moving on to more interesting topics. The annual craft bazaar would be held at the 4-H pavilion this weekend and all vendor tables had been rented. She made a mental note to avoid that area on Saturday. She already knew beach traffic was heavy along the main strip through town on Sundays.

The next article advised everyone not to miss the "exercise in the park" event. The local clinic doctor had volunteered to join walkers for a question-and-answer stroll every evening at six. Several nurses would be present to take blood pressure before, after, and during the event. Everyone was welcome and participants should come by the office to register in advance. *Breathtaking*, she thought.

A small headline in the bottom right corner caught her eye. Florida Fish and Wildlife Conservation Commission were pleased to announce they had captured a Florida panther in the Shell Point area. Credit was given to two officers, TJ Smith and Joey Kimball. She ran her finger across the grainy black-and-white picture. TJ was at least two inches taller than Joey, but his shoulders were wider, giving him a bulky appearance. A large, clearly anesthetized cat was stretched the length of the table in front of them.

Bailey had been thinking a lot about her meeting with TJ Smith and how she might have handled the situation differently. The brusque way Officer Smith had handled their introduction had slowly been forgotten. Now she only remembered the look of relief on her face as Bailey climbed into the FWC truck.

She hadn't ventured back to the Shell Point Wildlife Management Area since the day she had been escorted out. Seeing the size of the animal now, she was glad that she hadn't. She remembered Joey's words about letting her take a few pictures. The article said the cat would be taken to the panther reserve in Immokalee after a thorough examination.

She grabbed her phone off the table in front of her. A panther reserve would be an interesting place to visit, but a quick search showed it was more than seven hours away. Captain Westmore would most likely be willing to let her snap a few shots before they moved the panther, though, if she was able to reach him in time.

Bailey had not taken the time to meet with him face-to-face since first arriving in the area. The hanging dinner invitation had kept her silent, but now it seemed worth the risk. Her cell phone rang before she could search for the FWC office number. The name displayed on the screen made Bailey close her eyes and take a deep breath before answering.

"What?" she asked without bothering with a greeting.

"Is that any way to talk with the person responsible for promoting you and your books?" Mona Caffrey said sarcastically.

"You're a pain in my ass, so yes, that's the best way to talk to you. What do you want?"

"I wanted to check in with you and make sure you were ready to hit the road."

Bailey groaned. Going on tour after each book was a requirement and always did great things for her sales, but it was probably the thing she hated most about her work, the lines of people waiting impatiently for her to sign their copies. Mona always said they weren't impatient because if they were, they would just leave. Maybe she was right. Bailey didn't really look at them. She greeted, made small talk, and signed. Mona moved them along, making sure the line was in constant motion.

"As ready as I ever am."

"That's the spirit. Your flight leaves on Friday and your first signing will be Sunday afternoon. I'll pick you up at the airport. Make sure to bring at least one cocktail dress. We have an invitation to the premiere for the latest Marvel movie."

"Wow." Maybe this trip wouldn't be so bad after all. She had been planning to see that movie as soon as it came out. "How did you swing that?"

"I know how to work magic." Mona laughed. "I'll see you Friday evening."

Mona broke the connection without saying bye and Bailey knew she had already been forgotten. Starting the tour in California had been Mona's idea and now she wondered what her plan might be. She wasn't Mona's only client so she wouldn't assume anything. She didn't like it when Mona used her name to get them special treatment, but this was one she wouldn't complain about. Movie premieres did not have to be social gatherings; Bailey would slip in, see the movie, and slip back out.

She dialed Captain Westmore's office. His secretary said he had just stepped out, but she would have him return her call when he came back.

She set down the phone and swallowed the remaining coffee in her cup. It was cold, and the strong taste lingered in her mouth. She felt unsettled and a bit anxious. Photography was the one thing that she had patience for, especially in the early days when she developed her own pictures. Other than a few of the deer photos, she wasn't overly thrilled with any of the photos she had taken so far.

A few visits to the lighthouse had produced more gator pictures and lots of water turtles and blue herons, but none of them were her best work. The truth was her desire to wander about had decreased since the panther scare. But why? It wasn't the first time she had been asked to leave an area, especially for safety reasons. Could she blame TJ Smith for her distraction?

Her phone rang and she glanced at the paper's picture of TJ and Joey as she swiped to accept a call from a local number.

"Hello."

"Ms. Everett?"

"Yes."

"It's Captain Westmore returning your call."

"Thank you, Captain. I'm sorry my first call is to ask for a favor. I saw in the paper your department has captured a Florida panther and I was wondering if it would be possible to get a few pictures of it."

"Sure. You want to put them in your book?"

"I'm not sure yet. I might do a section on the process you took to capture it."

"We'll probably only have it here for a few more hours at the most. We're waiting on the transport team now."

"I could come in now if that's okay."

"I don't see why not. It's at the veterinary clinic on Highway 98 by the traffic light. I'll let them know you are coming and send an officer to meet you."

"Thanks. I really appreciate it."

She quickly ran around the condo, throwing on a pair of blue cargo pants and a white T-shirt under a multipocketed vest. Grabbing her keys, she was out the door in less than ten minutes with Chewie on her heels.

The drive to the veterinary clinic would take only take a few minutes according to her GPS, so she stopped at the convenience store on the corner of Shell Point Road and Highway 98 and grabbed a bottle of ginger ale to settle her jittery stomach—and a couple of mini peanut butter cups from the tub beside the cash register.

She parked in the lot at the clinic and opened the windows for Chewie. Happily, the morning was cool without much humidity. The humidity in Florida was worse than the temperature. It could be sixty degrees, but if there was any humidity you were sweating before you left the house.

She checked Chewie's water dish on the floor of the SUV and then locked the doors. An FWC truck was pulling into the lot and her stomach did a different kind of flutter when she saw Officer Smith at the wheel. Bailey looked forward to interacting with her again. Maybe this time things would go better.

"Good morning," she called as Officer Smith climbed from the truck.

"Morning."

"Thanks for meeting me. I'm hoping to get some good pictures. Can't get a better subject." She knew she was talking way too fast.

"He was asleep when I left yesterday so I don't know what you'll get. I imagine you'll find him more than a little cranky about his current situation."

*Yikes. Of course.* What was she thinking? This wouldn't be like a zoo. Taking pictures while he strolled around was not likely. This panther was going to be very agitated. Thankfully she didn't have a chance to ramble anymore as she followed Officer Smith to the glass door and inside the brick building.

It was nicer than the vet she took Chewie to in New York City. It was a large building with several rows of bench seating and a public bathroom. To the left was a large open window leading to the three receptionists' desks. On the right wall was a huge painting of an Army soldier on his knees embracing a black Labrador. The dog was also wearing combat gear. The soldier's head was bent, and Bailey imagined he was getting advice from the dog. Thick splotches of paint gave the picture texture. Bailey could barely pull her eyes away.

"Go on back. Dr. Riggins is waiting for you," one of the receptionists called.

TJ acknowledged her with a wave but didn't stop to chat. Bailey followed her through a door in the rear of the waiting room. The area they stepped into was open with a few elevated metal tables. A tall gray-haired man with a matching mustache stood reviewing a folder he held in his hand. Tossing the folder on the counter, he looked up as they walked in.

"Hey, Dr. Riggins. How's it going?" TJ asked.

"It's going great here. The big guy is a little impatient, but I just heard from the transport officers so he's about to go back to sleep again."

Bailey stepped forward and held up her camera. "Hello, Dr. Riggins. I'm Bailey Everett. Is it okay if I get a few shots of your tenant?"

"Sure. I'll put him in the outside area. You'll have better light there."

"That would be great if it won't be a problem."

Dr. Riggins walked over to a door opposite from the one they had entered. He flipped a switch on the wall, and they heard a grinding sound.

"You'll want to give him a few minutes to check out his surroundings. He won't be as cranky that way."

Bailey pulled her notebook and a pen from her camera bag. "What can you tell me about him?" she asked.

"He weighs a hundred and fifteen pounds and stands twenty-five inches. He'd be over six feet tall if he stood on his hind legs. He's alert and in perfect health."

"How old do you think he is?"

"Panther cubs hang with their mothers until they're at least a year and a half to two years old, but he seemed to be traveling alone." He looked at TJ for agreement and she nodded. "So, I'd say he's older than two, but his teeth say he's not more than three."

Bailey jotted down all the important details and listened while Dr. Riggins continued to talk about how wonderful the panther was. His eyes sparkled with enthusiasm, showing his love of animals.

"What other animals do you treat?"

"Well, other than the usual cats, dogs, and horses, I have plenty of clients with snakes, turtles, and birds. We have a local mammal rescue right down the road and a sea turtle rescue in Panacea."

"What kind of emergencies do the rescues bring in?" Bailey asked.

"Sea turtles often have fishing hooks caught in their mouth, but the worst thing I've seen in a while was with two pelicans." His voice grew soft as he squeezed his eyes shut before glancing at TJ. She grimaced but gave him a nod so he continued.

"What happened?" Bailey interjected. She wanted to hear but could tell it would be something heartbreaking.

"A fisherman was annoyed that the pelicans wouldn't leave him alone when he came in with his catch. It's not unusual for them to get pushy or combative for food."

"That's true," TJ snapped. "Especially when you feed them for a while and then decide you don't want to do it anymore."

"People can be stupid, that's for sure," Dr. Riggins added before continuing, "His solution was to slice their necks."

"That's appalling. I can't imagine them being killed like that." Bailey's stomach churned at the thought.

"Oh no," TJ said disgustedly. "Killing them would have been humane. He cut them and left them to wander defenseless."

Bailey took a step back and swallowed hard. Cold coffee acid was rising in her throat. She covered her mouth with her hand.

Dr. Riggins crossed the room in a flash and gave her a quick, hard, side hug. "I saw them last weekend and both are recovering well, thanks to our local mammal rescue. Pelicans aren't mammals, of course, but they won't turn away any animal."

"Thanks to you too, Doc," TJ added, before looking at Bailey. "They each needed over a hundred stitches."

"You caught this guy, right?" Bailey's eyes drilled into TJ.

"Oh yeah," TJ said, nodding.

"Okay, let's see how the boy is doing," Dr. Riggins suggested, drawing both women's attention.

Bailey followed him to a wooden panel in the wall which he opened to reveal two sliding windows. The panther was lying at the base of tree inside an area enclosed with chain-link fence. A strip of privacy fencing stretched into the tree line on both sides.

"You can take your pictures from here or you can step outside." Dr. Riggins grinned. "I don't have to tell you to remain outside the chain-link fence, right?"

Bailey chuckled. "Not even once."

"Then I'll leave you to it and get back to work." Dr. Riggins left them alone.

"What a neat guy. I bet he's a great vet," Bailey said as she pulled several camera lenses from the pockets of her vest.

"Yes, he is. And he's always willing to help when we have an injured animal. I don't think I've ever had him tell me no. Day or night." TJ walked over to join her at the window.

"I wish I could bring Chewie here."

"Nothing's stopping you."

"Except the fact that I don't live here."

TJ shrugged. "Do you want to take your photos inside or out?"

"I'm going to see what I can get from here. After the other day in the woods, I'm not real eager to get close to him again."

"Yeah, about that. I'm sorry if I scared you out there." TJ's head dipped, and Bailey was surprised to see an embarrassed flush cover her neck.

This time Bailey shrugged. "It wasn't you. It was not knowing what was out there or where it was. And then for a minute, it seemed like it was closing in on us."

TJ nodded. "I think he was. Circling us at least."

"To eat us?" she asked, surprised at the waver in her voice.

"Not us, probably, but maybe your dog."

Bailey felt her eyes grow wide. "Chewie?"

"Well, yeah. What did you expect taking a walking snack into the forest?"

"I guess I thought with me there that wild animals wouldn't consider her food."

"Maybe, but not if the animal is hungry enough."

Bailey lifted her camera and began snapping pictures of the panther. She hadn't really thought about the dangers of taking

Chewie into the woods. She had thought that the biggest risk was scaring away her potential photos.

She remembered how freaked out she was in Arizona when she was working on her first book. She had never been an outdoor kind of kid and her time in New York City had been protected by the scores of people. In Arizona, she had plopped herself down in the desert outside of Phoenix without a care in the world, her mind lost and wandering through dreams of becoming famous. Then a Gila monster approached the rain puddle near her and she felt like Elliot when he met E.T. in the 80s movie.

She was beginning to realize how selfish she was being by taking Chewie with her. Her personal desire to have Chewie with her had blinded her to the reality of what she was doing. Chewie wouldn't like being left behind, but that wasn't a reason to risk her safety. Bailey would miss her company, but how would she continue her career if she lost Chewie? Especially not in the way TJ was implying.

"I didn't mean to upset you," TJ said.

Bailey shrugged. "I guess I just didn't think it through very well. I'm feeling kind of stupid."

"It's not stupid. People walk their dogs in the woods all the time. This was a unique situation. Besides everything worked out fine."

"So I'm good as long as you're nearby to save me. My hero." Bailey couldn't stop the grin from sliding across her face before she quickly turned back to photographing the panther. She concentrated for a few minutes on getting the proper light and angle as the panther paced along the fence line, clearly looking for a path to escape. This wasn't the story she wanted to tell, but being so close to this majestic animal was a bit breathtaking and she was more than a little glad she had taken this opportunity. She zoomed in on his face and blurred the chain-link fence behind him. For a moment she saw him in the wild instead of in a world of massive industrial and housing developments where he wasn't wanted.

Taking pictures and hiding behind the lens of her camera wasn't what Mr. Anderson had taught her. She remembered how he had lovingly showed her how to study her subject and absorb the environment. To imagine what they were feeling in that moment and try to see it in the viewfinder.

Animal caregivers had offered in the past the chance to get close to subjects, but she had always declined. When she was behind the lens of her camera she felt protected from the world, and now she felt protected by the very silent officer standing beside her.

TJ's face was hard to read; she couldn't tell if she had offended or embarrassed her. Most officers would have beamed with pride to be called a hero, but clearly TJ wasn't the cocky game warden that she was used to dealing with. She had learned to smile at those a lot and say flattering things so she could have a chance at getting the best possible photos.

"By the way, thanks for that," Bailey said. "The saving, I mean. I can't really let myself think about what might have happened if Chewie and I were left out there alone with that animal."

"No problem," TJ mumbled.

"Great. Then I can count on you always coming to my rescue?"

TJ studied her feet and Bailey mentally kicked herself. Why was she being so flirty? She never said things like that and certainly not to someone she barely knew. Yes, TJ was attractive, but Bailey had clearly made her uncomfortable.

Bailey snapped a few more pictures and then turned to TJ, placing her hand on TJ's arm. She meant it as an apologetic gesture, but the second she felt the warmth of TJ's arm her thoughts ran amuck. When was the last time she had touched someone and felt something? Anything? She couldn't remember. She raised her eyes to meet TJ's and was surprised when she didn't look away. There was a question there that Bailey wished she could read. TJ stepped back, crossing her arms over her chest.

"I'm sorry if I made you uncomfortable," Bailey said, turning back again to the panther. She had all the pictures she wanted. It had been a good opportunity, but the panther's story wasn't the one she wanted to tell; the photo of an animal in captivity really wasn't a good fit for the book. With TJ so close, though, she didn't want to call it quits or leave the room. She liked being around this woman. She liked her quiet demeanor and felt surprisingly at ease with her. So at ease she was saying things she never said. She didn't want to leave until the air between them had been cleared, but she was afraid if she said anything else that she would make it worse.

"It's fine," TJ said, walking toward the door that led into the rest of the clinic. "I'm going to find Dr. Riggins. You're about finished, right?"

She looked up, but TJ was gone. She hadn't even waited for Bailey's response. Maybe she was flirting with a straight woman. TJ certainly seemed eager to get away from her. She had been sure she was catching vibes, but now she was second-guessing herself. It made her sad. She wasn't sure she had ever felt such an instant attraction with anyone before. She had to say, though, that if that was the case this would be the first time she had made the moves on a straight woman. She wasn't sure if she should try to apologize again or not. She knew she wouldn't have a chance when TJ returned with Dr. Riggins.

"Did you get all your pictures?" Dr. Riggins asked as he entered the room with TJ.

She nodded, glancing at TJ. She would have liked to turn the camera on the dark, brooding officer. She imagined TJ strolling through the forest and thought that inside this building, kind of like the panther, TJ was in captivity. That thought made her smile, and she directed it back at Dr. Riggins. "A magnificent specimen."

"That he is. That he is."

He pushed open one side of the window and pointed a small dart gun at the panther. A pop sounded and the panther glared over his shoulder at them.

"It'll take about ten minutes or so for him to fall asleep and then we'll carry him back inside."

Dr. Riggins disappeared into the other room and Bailey was alone with TJ again. She leaned casually against the counter and reviewed the images on the screen in the back of the camera. She wished she knew the words to make the air between them comfortable again.

# CHAPTER EIGHT

TJ watched Bailey flipping through the photos she had taken. It was hard not to be enamored with her. It wasn't only her good looks, though they were hard to miss. TJ liked her easygoing manner, enjoyed watching the joy on Bailey's face as she took pictures. Bailey was good at what she did. TJ knew this from the list of awards she had seen on Bailey's bio on her website and the photos shown there.

She had perused *Utah Wildlife: Home to the Most Breathtaking Natural Landscape* so many times in the last week she almost had it memorized. The photos and the descriptions that accompanied them had transported her to Zion National Park in southwest Utah. She also knew from Bailey's website that one of the photos from this book was a finalist for the Wildlife Photographer of the Year Award. Should she win, Bailey would only be the sixth woman ever to receive this award.

Bailey's confidence showed in the way she held the camera, like it was a part of her. An extension of her arm. Her fingers held the camera firmly while her thumbs gently swiped back and forth between the pictures. It was a loving caress and it stirred something in TJ that she hadn't felt in a long time.

She was confident that she had misunderstood Bailey's flirting earlier. Joey and some of the guys in the office had been determined to find out if Bailey had a boyfriend. She had heard them talking about their Internet search yesterday. It had annoyed her the way her coworkers hypothesized about why there was a different man with her in every photograph they found. TJ knew gay and even straight women sometimes used men to avoid questions about their private life. She wished she had the courage to ask Bailey if she was a lesbian. Not that it was any of her business, of course.

*Geez!* Why was she even thinking about this? Even if Bailey was interested in her, this was a road TJ did not want to travel. Bailey would take her photos and then leave. It wasn't like they could have any type of a relationship. They could date for the few weeks or so that Bailey was in the area and then TJ would be left alone again. *I'll be back.* Her mother's voice echoed in her head the way it had the day she drove away for good. *I'll be back*, her father would say each time he was carted off to jail. He actually returned, though. Until the day he didn't.

TJ grimaced thinking about how Grams would pop her on the back of the head if she could hear her thoughts. Grams's favorite saying was "Goodbye and good riddance." Anything missed in the past was already gone, she said, and anyone who left wasn't worth thinking about. Grams knew how to let things go, and she had tried to pass that practice along to TJ. It didn't stick to her like it did to Grams, but she had heard it enough to learn to enjoy the moment in front of her.

She stepped over beside Bailey. "Did you get any good shots?"

"I think so. Sometimes it's hard to tell until I put them up on a larger screen."

"Understandable. Could you take a shot with me—"

Before TJ could finish her sentence, Bailey turned the camera on her.

"No, I meant with the panther," TJ said, putting her hands in front of her face.

"Oh, okay," Bailey said, but TJ could hear the rapid clicking as Bailey continued to hold the button on the camera down. She couldn't help but laugh. Bailey sounded so agreeable and yet she continued to do the total opposite of what TJ was asking.

"Stop already!" TJ laughingly choked out as she started to dart around the room.

"Okay," Bailey said again, and TJ stopped moving. She spread her fingers so she could see Bailey through them, and the camera clicked a few more times.

TJ spun her back to Bailey and started backing toward her. She was not sure how this was going to end, but she knew she would be a blurry blob if she could get close enough to Bailey.

"Okay. Okay," Bailey said, putting her hand on TJ's shoulder. "I'll stop."

TJ turned and Bailey's fingers lingered a moment too long on TJ's neck before they dropped to her side. Her surprise at the heat in Bailey's touch was mirrored in the brown eyes that looked back at her. *Kiss her. Kiss her now*, TJ's thoughts screamed.

Voices from outside the room seemed to bring Bailey around first. She bumped TJ with her shoulder.

"I don't think I got a single good shot. Maybe you didn't notice, but your hands were in the way."

"Good," TJ said as the door to the room opened and Dr. Riggins with two technicians stepped in. They opened the door leading to the enclosure the panther was in.

"Shouldn't we check to see if he's asleep before opening the door?" Bailey asked.

Dr. Riggins laughed. "Oh, he's asleep. That dosage will keep him napping soundly for the next four to six hours. Enough time for the officers to get him back in the forest."

As if on cue, two men in FWC shirts and jeans stepped into the room. TJ had met them both before and had little fondness for either of them. The last time she had seen them was a few years ago at a training class and their attempts at humor had come across more as sarcasm and disrespect for the female instructor.

"Where's the little cutie pie?" Jeremy bellowed. At over six feet tall and with a thick black beard, he demanded all attention be focused on him. There were so many things about him that TJ disliked, but the beard was at the top. His appearance would never pass inspection at her office, but apparently Jeremy's supervisor didn't care. TJ didn't know if it was his appearance or his words that made Bailey laugh, but she tried to hide her irritation as both men zeroed in on Bailey.

"We seem to know everyone but you," Jeremy said, stepping toward Bailey.

"I'm Bailey Everett. Just here to take pictures," Bailey said, holding up her camera.

"Fantastic. Let's get this photo shoot underway," the other officer said as he struck a pose with his crotch pushed forward. TJ knew him as Knuckles. She didn't know or care why he was called that, but she was pretty sure that was not his real name.

Dr. Riggins laughed. "Enough playing around. Let's bring in the main attraction." Two staff members followed him outside and came back carrying the panther in a sling between them.

"He's sleeping soundly," Dr. Riggins said as they laid the beast on the nearest surgical table. He pulled back the blankets so everyone could get a good look.

"Wow, he's even more impressive close up," Bailey gushed, lifting her camera to snap a few more pictures.

"We sure hate to ruin your fun, Ms. Everett, but we need to get on the road before he wakes up from his nap," Jeremy said.

"Are you coming with us?" Knuckles added.

TJ looked at Bailey. Surely, she wouldn't go with them. To her disappointment, Bailey looked excited at the offer.

"I could see him being released?" Bailey asked and TJ held back a groan.

"Yep, that's where we're headed," Jeremy answered. "You're coming then?"

"Well, I'd like to, but my dog is with me. I'd need to take her home first."

"You definitely can't take a dog with us, but we're working on a tight window as it is."

Bailey looked at TJ. "Could you take her?"

"Me? I don't...what would...for how long?" TJ stuttered. She had been so distracted with her annoyance at Jeremy and Knuckles that Bailey's words caught her by surprise.

"Oh, that's okay. Sorry I asked."

TJ felt the disappointment in Bailey's words, but before she could recover, Dr. Riggins cut in.

"We can keep her here, Ms. Everett. She can hang in my office while I'm seeing patients or one of the techs could run her to your place."

"Really?" Bailey said with surprise. "That would be awesome."

TJ could see the relief on Bailey's face, and she felt like such an ass. Why hadn't she just said yes? She liked dogs and that would have been a good reason to meet up with Bailey later. She could have been the one receiving Bailey's smile now and she missed having a dog around. It had barely been three months since she lost Breezie, her golden retriever and best friend. She still looked for her in the mornings when she got up. There was something about Bailey's dog that reminded her of Breezie. Maybe it was only the color, but it felt like something more.

One of the techs stepped forward. "She's in your car, right? I'll come out with you and get her. Don't worry. We'll take good care of her."

As TJ watched them disappear out the door, she kicked herself for not jumping at the chance to watch the dog.

\* \* \*

Bailey followed the Fish and Wildlife truck down another dusty road. She was thankful to be following them through this labyrinth of trails. She was also thankful for her Jeep. The men had wanted her to ride with them, but she had refused, reminding them of the distance they would have to travel to return her to Wakulla County. They had been on the road for over four hours now, and she knew the big cat would be waking up soon.

They pulled to a stop in front of a yellow galvanized steel gate. A huge sign marked this area as off-limits to unauthorized personnel. They traveled another ten minutes before pulling to a stop in the middle of the road. She jumped out and joined the men as they opened the rear of their enclosed truck. The panther pierced them with a glare as the sunlight covered him. His yellow eyes filled with fear and curiosity.

"We'll carry him to a clearing about two hundred yards from here. Normally they come out ready to run, but we have to be prepared for him to turn on us."

They each grabbed a side of the enclosed carrier and pulled it from the truck. She followed as they slowly walked to the clearing. The panther was silent, but she could tell he was moving around as the men juggled his weight. They set the carrier down in a small clearing and attached a wire to the lock on the door.

"Stay behind us and don't talk," the bearded man said, and she realized that they hadn't taken the time to introduce themselves. Unlike TJ and her associates, these men didn't have name tags on their uniforms. She noticed how quickly their moods had turned serious as they unrolled the trip line that would release the door of the carrier.

They stood at the edge of the clearing behind the carrier and out of the panther's line of sight. She heard the creak as the door slowly began to open. It seemed like hours until the tawny head of the panther emerged. She held her camera about waist high, tilted enough for her to see the rear viewing screen. Remembering the words of caution, she tightened her muscles and moved as slowly as possible to keep her angle on the moving cat.

The panther moved forward with hesitancy, its black-tipped ears flicking as it checked out its environment. Bailey was almost so captivated by the beauty of the large cat that she forgot to take pictures. As the back half of the panther emerged, she could see its trademark unique patch of back fur, standing up like an adolescent boy's cowlick.

The panther turned one last time, giving her the perfect photograph of his black-trimmed nose and yellow-hued eyes before he bounded into the tree line. She followed the example of the guys and continued to hold her position and her tongue, sorting through the many questions that were forming in her head.

"Okay, he should be gone now," the bearded man said.

"Can I get your names to use in my book?"

"I'm Jeremy," the bearded man said. "And this is Ralph."

"Hey! I'm not Ra—well, I am Ralph, but everyone calls me Knuckles," the shorter man answered with a laugh.

"Should I ask?" she said, smiling at him.

"I worked on a chicken farm up north before moving to Florida." He held up his hand. "Big knuckles from holding multiple chickens at a time."

She tried not to grimace as understanding of what he wasn't saying sunk in. Chickens that were being slaughtered.

He shrugged. "Not pleasant, I know, but I do prefer Knuckles to Ralph."

She pushed aside her disgust at the US meat industry and gave him a small smile.

"Do you guys have time for a few questions?" she asked as they made the trek back to their vehicles.

"Sure," Jeremy said.

"Where are we and why did you set him free here?"

"We're northeast of Tampa. From here he can travel safely within the corridor."

"The corridor?" she asked.

"The Florida Wildlife Corridor is a natural stretch of land and water that runs continuously from here to the Everglades. We think he was traveling alone, but if Smith missed something and he tries to go north again, he should be safe."

It was a small statement, but she caught the jab at TJ.

"He was tagged, right?" she asked.

"He was and for the next couple weeks we'll keep an eye on him."

"Why do you think he traveled so far north?"

Jeremy shrugged. "He's young, so he's trying to find his own space. He'll mark a territory of about two hundred to two-fifty square miles. It's possible he was pushed north by other cats.

We're hoping he wasn't in Wakulla County long enough to set up residence."

"And if he was?"

"Then you might get to see him again."

She didn't get the idea that made either man happy.

"Thanks for all the information. I should probably get back on the road."

"Do you need to follow us?"

"Hold on. Let me check." She slid into her Jeep and punched her address at Shell Point into the GPS. After a few seconds, the display directed her to make a U-turn.

"I think I'm good."

"Okay. Let me know if you have any additional questions or if you need more information," Jeremy said, passing her his business card.

"The Crawfordville office has been great, but I'll keep your card in case."

"You might want to watch how much time you spend with some of the folks up there."

She caught the look that passed between them and felt a little chill. Were they talking about TJ? She was suddenly very uncomfortable and wanted to get away from them and this isolated area.

"Well, okay, thanks."

"My cell phone number is on there too," Jeremy called.

She nodded and pulled her door shut. She couldn't get out of there fast enough. She followed the dirt roads back to a narrow-paved road then turned west on Route 44. Finally, when she reached Highway 98, she began to relax. Back in the land of fast-food restaurants and gas stations, she took advantage of both.

The vet clinic would be closing soon, and she still had several hours to drive. She dialed Mr. Maxwell's number and explained where she was.

"How can I help?" he asked.

"Would it be okay if I had someone drop Chewie off with you? I'll be home about seven."

"Of course. Anytime."

"I'll give them your number so they can call before they bring her, okay?"

"That sounds fine."

She disconnected the call and dialed the veterinary office. They said Chewie was doing fine and would be delivered to Mr. Maxwell when they closed. She settled in for her drive. It had been an amazing day. Seeing the panther up close was something she might never see again, but what kept bouncing into her memory was the time she had spent that morning with TJ. The woman was such a mystery and a challenge. One that she might be willing to accept.

# CHAPTER NINE

She didn't think FWC officers were assigned to specific areas so going back to the Shell Point Wildlife Management area wouldn't mean she would see Officer Smith. Or any FWC officers at all. With all the state land around, TJ could be assigned anywhere now. Especially since the panther had been caught. Despite all of that, returning the next day to the area where she had met TJ gave Bailey a rush of excitement.

Shell Point Wildlife Management area was huge, and it was a good day for an outing with Chewie. She could continue where she left off before she was so rudely interrupted. That thought made her chuckle. She had thought TJ was so rude when they first met. Not that she knew her much better now, but she had seen a different side of her at the vet clinic the other day. There were no vehicles in the management area's parking lot when Bailey arrived, so she packed her water and snacks quickly and moved onto the trail.

They had been walking a few hours when Chewie started acting weird. She would stop, tilt her head, and stare into the trees. Bailey couldn't do anything to get her to keep moving.

She looked around nervously, trying to see what Chewie was seeing. She knew the panther was gone, but the words Jeremy and Knuckles had told her about the possibility of it returning had her on edge. Chewie began to move slowly forward on the trail without lifting her nose from the ground. Leaves and scattered limbs covered the path in front of them, and Chewie took the time to sniff each one.

A rustle in the brush beside her caused her to jump. She froze when a strange growling noise came from farther down the trail and she moved a little closer to Chewie. They should turn around, but as the noise grew louder it sounded almost human. She moved forward tentatively and when she eased around the bend in the road, she saw a person squatting at the side of the road. She called a soft greeting and recognized Officer Smith when she glanced in her direction.

"What are you doing here?" TJ asked.

*Great.* Was she interrupting another animal chase? Was she going to be escorted out of the area again?

"I'm walking my dog and taking photos. Is there a reason I shouldn't?"

TJ stood and swiped the back of her hand across her mouth. "Sure. I mean no. You can be here, Ms.…uh…sorry," she said, clearing her throat.

"Everett, but you can call me Bailey. I guess we didn't really introduce ourselves either of the times we met."

Bailey studied her pale face, noticing a faint sheen of sweat across TJ's brow.

"Oh yeah. I'm sorry about that. I—"

Bailey froze in surprise when TJ moved quickly toward a nearby bush. Without moving closer, she leaned back and forth trying to see what had made the officer move into action, her camera at the ready in case it was something she could photograph. Officer Smith dropped to her knees and Bailey recognized the horrible retching sound she had heard earlier.

Bailey took a few steps toward her. "Are you okay?"

TJ stood and wiped her mouth again with the sleeve of her shirt. "I'm sorry. I need to get moving."

"Where? Home? You're obviously sick."

"I'm working right now. I'll go home after I finish what I need to do today."

"That's crazy," Bailey said with amazement. Why would someone continue to work in this condition? She looked around. "Where's your truck? We'll walk you to it."

"I can't—"

TJ bolted into the trees. Bailey turned away from her, unsure whether to offer her assistance or leave her in peace. Somehow, she felt like the woman would rather be alone than to have her leaning over her. Although strangely enough, she thought about holding her hair and rubbing her back.

TJ returned to the path. "It was good to see you again. Enjoy your day."

She began walking in the opposite direction and Bailey followed her.

"Wait. Where are you going?"

"I have another trap to check before heading back to the office to finish my paperwork for today."

"But you're sick."

TJ shrugged.

"Fine. If you won't leave now, then we'll go with you."

"I can't stop you."

Bailey trotted to keep up with her and Chewie followed at her heels. She wasn't sure why she felt any generosity toward this woman. She hadn't been exactly welcoming to Chewie and only a small bit better to her. She always seemed to find people intriguing when they were good at their jobs, though, especially a profession that she found interesting. TJ carried herself with a poise that she found very attractive. Even today, when she was sick, TJ still moved with a sense of mission, intent on carrying out whatever responsibility she had in the moment.

After the second time TJ moved off the path to be sick, Bailey couldn't take it any longer. It was one thing to be dedicated to your job and quite another to be just plain stupid. She looked at TJ's pale face and noticed there was now no sheen of sweat on her face. She wiped the sweat off the back of her own neck and looked at TJ.

"You aren't sweating. I think you're dehydrated. What is it that must be done today?"

TJ was silent for a few minutes and Bailey wasn't sure she was going to answer. She was prepared to counter whatever argument TJ gave her anyway.

"I have one more trap to check. Leaving an animal trapped inside would be inhumane." TJ's eyes flicked across to hers. "I'm sure you'll agree with me."

"I do, but isn't there someone you can ask to help you?"

"Everyone has their own job to do. I'm not going to ask someone else to do my job."

She couldn't believe how hardheaded this woman was. The day she had taken the photos of the panther, TJ had been reserved and almost shy. It seemed like she had been a different person. It was hard for her to say which woman she liked more. She tried to hide her smile as she realized she liked the hardheaded TJ more. Then she remembered the bossy TJ from the first day they met.

"I need to rest for a minute," TJ said, leaning against a tree at the side of the path.

Bailey stopped in the path and watched her. She could see how much effort it was taking for the woman to continue walking and she made a decision.

"Where is this trap?" Bailey asked.

"Just ahead. Not too far."

"Fine. Stay right here. Chewie and I will check the trap and be right back."

"I don't—"

Bailey held up her hand. "Just stop. I can't take the macho crazy lady anymore. You're sick. Just wait here."

Bailey didn't wait for a response. She headed up the path at a quick pace, Chewie on her heels. She honestly hadn't been sure if TJ really knew how far it was, but she was relieved to see the wire from the frame not long after leaving her. She strained her eyes to see inside the cage and was almost ready to call it empty when she noticed a small ball of black fur in the far corner.

"Crap. Chewie sit," she commanded, leaving the dog in the middle of the trail as she moved closer.

The door of the trap was closed, but the fur ball moved as she approached.

"Hey, little guy. I'm not going to hurt you."

Ignoring her gentle voice, the raccoon turned his narrow nose in her direction and showed her his teeth. A barely audible hissing noise came from him as he tried to back farther into his corner.

"Great, now what do we do?" Bailey said to Chewie. She hadn't asked TJ what she was supposed to do if something was in the trap. If she released the raccoon and she was not supposed to that could be bad, and besides TJ was in no condition to check this trap again today. If TJ wasn't willing to ask a coworker to help her today, then tomorrow wouldn't be any different. Bailey decided to take the trap and raccoon with her. She slowly walked toward the trap and leaned down, grasping the metal handle on top.

"Hold on, little guy. We're taking a trip."

Once she was headed back toward TJ, she called Chewie to follow her. She didn't have to tell her to keep her distance. Chewie followed several feet behind her with her nose on the ground as if she was leading the way back. Her actions made Bailey laugh, but she stopped quickly as TJ came into view. She sat on the ground with her back and head resting against a tree. Her eyes were closed. At first Bailey wasn't sure if she had fallen asleep, but her eyes flew open as they approached. Bailey watched as TJ struggled to her feet. Spreading her legs wide, she braced herself on the tree.

"What are you doing?" TJ asked.

"I'm sorry. I didn't want you to have to walk any farther and we didn't talk about what to do if something was in the trap."

"I'll need to take him to the office. I don't think I can examine him safely right now."

She could see the remorse in TJ's eyes as she admitted she couldn't do her job.

"*We'll* take him to the office."

"I can't let you do that. My truck is right down the road."

TJ took a step and then stopped. Bending at her waist, she placed her hands on her knees. Bailey watched her ragged breathing. She knew her Jeep was too far away, and it was outside the gate so she couldn't get on this trail anyway.

"Give me your keys."

"I can't—"

Bailey held out her hand. "Just give me your keys."

She could tell that TJ wanted to argue more but she didn't. She held her keys out like they weighed twenty pounds and Bailey barely grabbed them before TJ's hand fell back to her side. She quickly grasped her arm and helped her slide back to the ground.

"Chewie, sit. Stay." She patted her head before dropping her camera bag to the ground beside Chewie and hurrying down the path.

She liked to pretend she was in shape and she did hike a lot, but the Florida heat and humidity was more than she was used to. In only a few minutes, she was breathing heavily and could feel the sweat sliding down the middle of her back. Remembering the look on TJ's face was the only thing that kept her moving. When the gray truck came into view, she ran the last couple of steps and slid in behind the wheel.

It fired up on the first turn and she breathed a sigh of relief. She hated driving other people's vehicles and she was sure there were rules against a civilian driving a government vehicle. As soon as they got outside the park, she would switch them to her Jeep. It would be easier for someone from TJ's office to come get her truck than for Bailey to retrieve her Jeep later.

She pulled to a stop beside Chewie and jumped out. The dog ran to her side and she gave her a few pats for staying as commanded. She helped TJ to her feet and then put an arm around her waist as they walked toward the truck. She could feel the muscles in TJ's back and side twitch each time her hand moved. This was the wrong time to think about how sexy this woman was.

With TJ secure in the truck and the caged raccoon in the back, she motioned Chewie to climb in on her side. TJ glanced her way as Chewie sat beside her, but she didn't say anything. Once again, she could see that TJ didn't like Chewie and she tried not to take it personally. When they got to her Jeep, Chewie could sit in the back seat, but she wasn't putting her in the bed of the truck alone.

She leaned around Chewie and looked at TJ. If possible, TJ's face was even paler than it had been in the muted light of the forest.

"I'm not sure which way to go to get out of here."

"Straight. Left at the first fork."

Bailey pushed the truck into gear and crept slowly forward. TJ's eyes were closed again, and her head rested against the back of the seat. There seemed, if only for the moment, to be a break in the puking and Bailey was relieved. The few times in her life that she had been around other people when they were sick had caused her to throw up too. In fact, just the thought of it made her stomach start to churn.

She took a few deep breaths and glanced over at her two companions. Chewie was still sitting, but her body rested heavily against TJ's side. Chewie gave her a look and then stared out the front windshield. Her eyes suggested that she understood TJ's situation and she wanted Bailey to get them wherever they were going quickly.

* * *

"Can you stand?" a voice very close to her said.

TJ forced her eyes open and tried to focus on the woman standing beside her.

"Can you stand?" the woman asked again.

Why? Why did she need to stand? Couldn't she stay here? She was almost comfortable, and the left side of her body was so warm. Her head felt like a bowling ball and she struggled to hold it upright.

"Officer Smith, we need to take this raccoon to your office."

Oh yeah. Now she remembered. She was in the forest with that beautiful woman with the pretty blond hair. The photographer. The one she was pretending not to like. What was her name?

She slid out of the truck and leaned heavily on the woman as they walked. She tried to make herself stand up straight, but her body wasn't cooperating. This really wasn't cool. She needed no one. Why was her body betraying her? Her stomach rolled and she could feel her esophagus spasm. She was going to be sick again. She stumbled a few steps away from the woman and fell to her knees. Her stomach heaved but very little came up and each convulsion ripped through her body. When it felt like she was finished, she raised up to her knees and crawled a short distance to a patch of grass. She lay down and rested her head against the cool grass.

"No, no, no. You have to stand."

"I'll just lay here for a few minutes," she mumbled. Why wouldn't this woman leave her alone? This was a perfect spot to rest and she only needed a few minutes to feel strong again.

"Up. Come on. Get up. You can sit in my car."

The woman tugged on her arm and even though she tried to bat her away, she persisted. TJ finally gave in and lifted her forty-pound head as she pulled her knees under her. Her legs were wobbly, but she balanced on them with the help of the woman. She was guided to the open car door and collapsed onto the seat.

Okay. This was comfortable too. Not the same as lying down, but it would do for the moment. Doors closed around her and she thought she heard a dog growl before everything went fuzzy again.

* * *

There wasn't anyone at the front desk and Bailey didn't take time to look around. She knocked on the first open door in the hallway and forced herself to stand her ground at the glare the man behind the desk gave her.

"Is...uh...Joey around?" she managed to get out.

"Ms. Everett?"

She looked down the hallway and saw Joey striding toward her.

"Officer Smith is sick," she informed him. "I found her in the forest. The place where I met you."

He nodded. "I'll go get her."

"No, she's with me. In my car. Outside." She struggled to string her words together in a way that would make sense to him. "But she's really sick and I have a raccoon."

He shook his head, looking at the other rangers that had joined them in the hallway.

"You have TJ and a raccoon outside?"

"Yes, and someone will need to pick up her truck."

"I'll take her home and take care of the raccoon." He looked at the others around them again. "Can someone grab her truck?"

"Yeah." A woman Bailey hadn't seen before stepped forward from the group and took the keys Bailey held. "Carl can give me a ride over."

"Let's go get her so I can take her home." Joey put his arm around Bailey's shoulder.

What Joey had been saying finally registered on her. He was going to take TJ home. Of course, he was. What did she think? She had been going to take TJ back to her condo. That was crazy.

"Take her home, right," she agreed. "But she can't be alone. She's really sick."

"She won't be alone," he said, ushering her toward the door.

"Wait, Joey. Katie is out of town," the woman informed them.

"Oh," Joey said, hesitating as he pushed through the door.

*"Oh" is right! Who is Katie?* Now wasn't the time, Bailey thought as different words spilled out of her mouth. "I can take her...I mean, I can take her home with me and keep an eye on her."

Joey nodded. "I guess that's the best idea then. Since Katie's not at home."

She followed Joey out the door and nearly ran into him when he came to a sudden stop in front of her Jeep.

"Is she okay?" he asked, looking through the windshield at TJ's head resting on her chest.

"I think she has the flu, but if she's not better in a day or so I'll take her to the doctor. Can you let her boss know she's going to be out the rest of the week?"

"Yeah, I'll let him know, and I'll cover for her when I can."

She opened the back of her Jeep and stepped aside for Joey to grab the raccoon.

She slid behind the wheel, relieved to have that over with. It had been awkward. She really had not thought through what she was going to say to TJ's coworkers when she arrived at their office.

A knock on her window made her jump and then she saw the woman who had taken TJ's keys standing beside her door. Bailey rolled down the window.

"Do you need any help getting her home?" the woman asked.

"Well, I...uh...think I can handle it."

The woman leaned down and peered in the window at TJ. Chewie growled. Her eyebrows raised at Bailey as she stepped back again. She pulled a card from her pocket and handed it to Bailey.

"Here's my card. My cell phone number is on the back. Call if you need anything. Smith and I work for different agencies, but we're friends. I know where she lives if you need anything from her house."

"Thanks. Thanks for taking care of her truck too."

"No problem."

Bailey put the car in reverse and backed out of the parking space. She made a quick stop at the local drugstore to pick up flu medication, Gatorade, and snacks. She parked as close to the entrance to her condo as she could. Leaving all her purchases in the car, she convinced TJ to stand and walk again. They made it to the elevator and up to the second floor before TJ's body started to heave. She knew there was nothing left in TJ's stomach, but she knocked the lid off the trash can in the hallway and helped TJ lean over it.

A bit of heaving and gagging, which Bailey looked away for, and then they made it the last few steps to her door. She took TJ straight to the bedroom and dropped her onto the bed. She knew it made more sense to put her on the couch, but then she wouldn't be able to move around her apartment without worrying about waking her. She took the lid off her kitchen trash can and put a fresh bag in it before setting it beside the bed.

Chewie rested on her dog bed outside the bedroom, but her eyes watched Bailey as she left the condo. She hurried to the car and grabbed her purchases before sprinting back up the stairs. She put the Gatorade in the refrigerator and pulled a pack of chicken from the freezer. She knew it would be a while before TJ was ready to attempt food, but she'd have the soup ready by then.

She walked into the bedroom and watched TJ for a few seconds. Her breathing seemed okay. She rested the back of her hand against TJ's forehead; it felt warm. She went back to the kitchen and grabbed a dose of medicine and a bottle of Gatorade. Convincing TJ to sit up wasn't easy, but she finally went along with it and Bailey was able to get her to take the medicine and drink a few sips of Gatorade. Then she removed TJ's boots and pulled a throw blanket over her.

# CHAPTER TEN

Bailey spent a fitful night on the couch. In the morning, after a quick bathroom walk for Chewie, she threw the ingredients for the soup into the slow cooker. It would be ready by midday. She was looking forward to it. It was her first time cooking since she came to Florida and she knew without TJ in her house she probably wouldn't have made the effort.

TJ had only stirred once in the night and Bailey had taken advantage of it to shove more medicine and Gatorade in her. She had also pulled TJ's uniform pants and shirt off and put them in the washer. Of course, she had been careful not to look too closely at TJ's boxer-style underwear with the moose heads on them or the outline of her bra through the white T-shirt.

It felt weird having someone else in her space and especially in her bedroom. At first, she had tiptoed around, but now she was sure it would take a sledgehammer to wake TJ up. She tried not to stare at her when she went in to check her breathing, but it was hard. TJ did not dress glamorously or to impress others, but Bailey found her more attractive than the movie stars she had occasionally met on the red carpet in LA. The soft line of TJ's jaw and her high cheekbones made her physically attractive, but it was TJ's own style that set her apart from others.

As if she could feel Bailey's gaze on her, TJ stirred and rolled onto her back. She kicked her legs until one foot and leg found its way out from under the blanket. Her leg wasn't tan like Bailey expected of someone who lived in the land of sun. Its paleness was almost blinding, and Bailey smothered a chuckle. If they were better friends, or even friends at all, she would definitely give her a hard time about it. Her own legs were darker and she had spent most of the summer in New York.

Chewie walked past her and sprang up on the bed beside TJ. "Chewie, no!" she whispered. "Come here now."

Chewie rolled onto her back, resting her head on TJ's shoulder. The look on her face said she had no plans to move. Bailey's eyes grazed TJ's face as she patted her leg, trying to convince Chewie to leave the bed. She was surprised to find TJ's eyes open and staring at her.

"Oh, wow. I'm so sorry Chewie woke you."

TJ glanced at the dog resting comfortably at her shoulder.

"I can make her move if she's bothering you."

TJ shook her head and Bailey took that to mean she didn't need to. She couldn't remember the last time Chewie had jumped on the bed without being encouraged.

Bailey picked up the cup on the nightstand and held it toward TJ. "Drink?"

TJ took the cup and swallowed a few sips.

"Do you think you could eat something?"

TJ vehemently shook her head.

"I didn't mean anything major. Maybe a cracker. Or a piece of dry toast."

She didn't wait for TJ to decline but hurried to the kitchen and grabbed two saltine crackers. TJ didn't look willing but she took the crackers and bit off a small bite. Bailey watched her face, waiting to see any signs that the bite wouldn't stay down. When TJ took another bite, she hurried to the kitchen and refilled her glass with cold Gatorade.

TJ was burrowed under the blanket again when she returned, but she was able to convince her to drink a few more sips. Her eyes drifted shut quickly and Bailey left her to sleep with Chewie nestled into her side. Traitor dog.

* * *

TJ groaned under the heat of the blanket, kicking her legs to push it off. Her head was fuzzy and her body felt like she had been run over by a train. A ray of sunlight shone in her eyes and she struggled to figure out where she was. Her bedroom only had direct sun in the evening. Wait. Was it evening? Why was she still in bed? When did she fall asleep? And who was the warm body pressed against her back? Had she brought someone home with her? She couldn't remember. In fact, she couldn't remember coming home.

She reached a hand behind her and was surprised to feel soft curly fur. *What the hell?* She rolled over and stared into the blue eyes of the photographer's dog. What was its name? Shelly or Smelly? Her brain contemplated other variations as the dog's nose inched forward and touched her arm. The nose was warm and dry. Didn't that mean something was wrong? Wasn't a dog's nose supposed to be wet? She couldn't remember. She shook her head to try to clear the cobwebs. What was this dog doing in her bed?

"Are you sick too, buddy?"

The dog pushed its nose against her arm again. A noise from the other room drew her attention to the door and she noticed the rest of her surroundings. The room was a powder blue with a white chest of drawers situated at the base of the bed. She lifted her head and slowly looked around. A strange sensation overtook her as she realized she didn't know where she was. She pushed her feet over the side and started to sit up. Her stomach rebelled as soon as she was upright. Her head throbbed. She dropped back onto the pillow and stared at the dog.

"Where are we, buddy?"

TJ looked up when a shadow slid across the room. The photographer! She pushed herself to sit up again.

"Don't do that," Bailey said as she stepped closer to the bed and felt TJ's forehead. "You're probably feeling weak. At least you don't feel hot anymore, so that's good. Are you ready to eat?"

Just the mention of eating made TJ's stomach growl loudly.

"My stomach is a little unsettled, but food sounds good," TJ croaked.

"I made chicken noodle soup. Want to try that?"

She nodded. This woman was being so nice, and the food sounded really good. She hated to be rude, but she really wanted to know where in the hell she was. And why?

"Where am I?" TJ asked.

A faint blush appeared on the woman's face.

"Well, you're...uh...you're at my place. It seemed easier than trying to figure out where you live."

TJ nodded, though she wasn't sure why.

"You're that photographer, right?"

The blush on the woman's face deepened. It was kind of cute. What was she thinking? Somehow, she had ended up in this woman's house. Not just in her house but in her bed and she needed to know why.

"Oh, right. I'm Bailey. Bailey Everett. I found you in the forest and you were really sick."

TJ shook her head. Things did feel fuzzy, but she couldn't remember being sick.

"I'm going to need more details than that, but at this moment I'd rather eat."

"Of course," Bailey said, disappearing through the bedroom door.

TJ shifted the pillow behind her and found a half-lying down, half-sitting position that didn't cause her head to throb so badly. The dog shifted its nose to rest against TJ's side and she placed a hand on its head, moving her fingers slowly back and forth, alternating between rubbing both ears. She didn't feel like she could hold her eyes open any longer, so she closed them.

"Do you still want some food?"

TJ opened her eyes and reached for the bowl. She couldn't remember the last time she had eaten. Although she really didn't know what time it was now. The sun was bright, so it must be still in the morning.

She sipped from the spoon. The soup was warm but not hot. She held it in her mouth for a second before swallowing. She felt the liquid pass all the way to her stomach and was very pleased when her stomach didn't object to it. She had noticed the trash can beside the bed and was glad she didn't seem to need it anymore.

"So, give me the highlights, please. I probably need to get back to work before I'm missed, right?"

"Yesterday morning I was taking pictures and our paths crossed. You were, uh, puking along the trail. You couldn't stand very well and had a high fever."

"Wait. Did you say yesterday?"

"Yes. You've been here overnight."

TJ felt her eyes grow large. She had to get to work! She had responsibilities. She couldn't just disappear for twenty-four hours.

Bailey quickly continued, "We took the raccoon in the trap back to your office—"

"You transported the raccoon in a trap?" TJ slapped her forehead.

"Well, yeah. What was I supposed to do with it? Let it go?"

"No, you should have brought it to me so I could check it for any injuries or weird behavior. Then I would have let it go."

"I did bring it to you," Bailey huffed. "But you were sick, so I took it to your coworkers and told your boss that you would be out for a day or so."

"You talked to my boss?"

"Well, not exactly. One of your coworkers took care of that for me. Everyone was very nice and agreed to check your other traps. It should be fine."

She set the half-eaten bowl of soup on the nightstand beside her. It wasn't okay. She had a reputation at work. Now she did feel sick. Had she really puked in public? She had never used any of her sick leave and she had certainly never let someone else lead her around.

Bailey must have been able to read the look on her face. "You were really sick. You didn't have a choice but to go with me. I couldn't leave you alone."

TJ nodded. She should be more appreciative of this woman's help. She had to admit she couldn't even remember being in the woods yesterday morning. She did remember that breakfast hadn't settled well on her stomach. She tried to hold her eyes open but finally gave in when it became too difficult. She also felt herself give in when Bailey shifted the pillows underneath her head. She tried to lift her hand to find the fuzzy head beside her, but her arm wouldn't obey.

"Dog," she mumbled as she drifted off to sleep.

* * *

Bailey called Chewie before pulling the door closed.

"Sorry, girl. I don't think she likes you any more than she likes me."

She shouldn't have been surprised that TJ seemed a little upset about her situation. She knew it was weird that she had brought her here, but what was she supposed to do? Even if she found out where TJ lived, it wasn't like she could have dropped her off. The other officer had offered to take her, but Bailey couldn't really explain how that made her feel. She only knew that she didn't want to turn TJ over to her.

She settled on the couch and pulled her laptop onto her lap. She opened the file with the photos from the vet's office first. She had just one photo of TJ's face. The rest were of TJ's hands moving closer and closer to the lens. She had surprised TJ with the first shot. Her mouth was open, caught in the middle of saying something, and her brow was furrowed.

She stared at the photo, studying every inch of TJ's face. After a few seconds, she glanced up as if she expected TJ to have emerged from the bedroom. Nope, she was still alone except for Chewie resting on her cushion in the corner. Chewie's lids were partially closed but her eyes were focused accusingly on Bailey.

"What?" she said. "I'm not being creepy. I'm working here. Go back to your nap."

Chewie's eyes gave a roll as her lids closed and Bailey sighed. Maybe it was creepy to be studying TJ's picture with her in the next room. Her eyes moved to the next picture—no rings on any finger. Her pulse raced, but then she remembered the woman Joey had mentioned that TJ lived with. How would this woman feel about TJ's current situation and how would TJ explain it? Professionally and courteously, she hoped.

Looking through the work pictures she had taken so far, she was disappointed to see that she didn't really have much of anything. The release of the panther and the deer photos were definitely worthy of inclusion, but she needed a lot more than that. She needed to get to work. It wasn't like she worked on a deadline, but she knew that she needed to release books on a regular schedule or people would forget about her and her sales would drop. When she had worked in Mr. Anderson's shop she had a regular paycheck and an affordable place to live. Now that she depended on income from her books, it applied a bit more pressure.

She put her laptop back on the table and unfolded the map of Wakulla County. Pulling out the calendar, she began making a schedule for the next week. She needed to spend some quality time in the forest.

Once she had a plan in place, she felt a little better. She returned to the files in her laptop and began going through them, more slowly this time. Her trips to the lighthouse had given her about two hundred photographs and she needed to sort out the best ones. As expected, most shots were of Florida softshell turtles, with their flattened pancake-like bodies, long necks and elongated heads, but a few were dragonflies in varied colors. Along with a chance sighting of a flock of Wilson's Phalaropes headed for South America. Phalaropes were riveting to watch and photograph given their distinctive feeding process, which entailed swimming in small, rapid circles in shallow water to create a whirlpool that drew crustaceans and small insects from the bottom of ponds and bays. Female phalaropes were larger and more colorful than the males; they took the lead in courtship and left the males to incubate the eggs. Her readers would be fascinated.

Most of the afternoon had passed before her stomach reminded her she hadn't eaten any of the soup earlier when she had dished up a bowl for TJ. Making her way to the kitchen, she fed Chewie and then brought a large bowl of soup back to the couch. Not feeling very productive, she turned on the television and randomly flipped through the channels. She wanted to check on TJ again, but it felt a little different now that her fever had broken. TJ only needed rest now. Not a nurse.

Besides, by morning she would probably be ready to go home. She realized how disappointed that thought made her. It had been nice having TJ with her. Maybe it wasn't TJ specifically, just having someone nearby. Was she changing and now she wanted someone in her space? Would anyone work? Or did it have to be TJ?

* * *

TJ rolled back to the other side of the bed. She had tossed and turned for what felt like hours. It was dark outside, and she kept hoping the sun would appear. She felt like she had been asleep for days and now she desperately needed to get up and move around. She willed herself to go back to sleep until morning. No matter how bad she wanted to get up, she couldn't.

Her watch was gone from her wrist and she had no idea where her cell phone was. Surprisingly there was no clock on the bedside table, either. She rolled back in the direction she thought was the door. No light showed from that direction, but she was pretty sure the door was closed.

There were two windows in the room, and she could see a very faint light shining through them. She couldn't tell if it was a streetlight or the moon, though. As quietly as she could, she sat up and then stood. Her legs were stiff from lying down for so long. She twisted from side to side and stretched every muscle she could find. Her stomach felt empty and not the least bit upset. She wished she was at home and could fix herself a big turkey and provolone sandwich. She wondered what the photographer would think if she found her rummaging through her cabinets.

What did the photographer think about anything? TJ didn't know. What kind of person took in a stranger when they were sick and cared for them for several days? A really nice one, apparently.

She stretched as high as she could and then bent at the waist. Her body was sore, and she wished she had a better reason than lying in bed alone for two days. Or was it three? Honestly, she didn't know how long she had been here. She flipped on the ceiling light and almost screamed as it pierced her eyes. Flipping it off, she sat on the bed for a few minutes, waiting until the spots in front of her eyes started to disappear.

She couldn't leave the house in only a T-shirt and underwear. She thought she had seen some clothes on top of the dresser, so she felt around, finding a pair of shorts that didn't belong to her. She pulled them on anyway. She would wash them and return them later. Now for transportation. She had no idea where her truck keys might be or even where her truck was.

Maybe she could call someone to come and get her. She crossed to the window to see if she could identify where she was. The light she had noticed earlier was the moon, but there were a few streetlights in the distance. It looked like she was about two or three floors up and there was a body of water leading right up to the back of the building. She must be in Shell Point. It was mostly a retirement community and a lot of the condos were rented out for part of the year. It made sense that Bailey would have found a place here.

Now she knew where she was, but her house was on the other side of town. Unfortunately, the bustling town of Crawfordville didn't have any taxi cabs. She had been meaning to load the Uber app to her phone but hadn't really had a need for it before now. She would willingly take harassment from Joey, though, if she had a phone to call him with.

She found a lamp by the bed, switched it on, and searched for her phone. No luck. She did find her watch, though, and now she knew it was only a few minutes past midnight. It probably wasn't a good idea to call anyone to pick her up at this hour. Even if they would do it, she would be the butt of office jokes for months if not years. No, she needed to tough it out for the night. Her stomach made a huge grumbling sound. Maybe she could find some food.

She switched the lamp off and waited until her eyes adjusted to the dark before pulling open the door. There was a faint glow leading down the hall to what she assumed was the living room. *Bummer.* She had hoped that there was another bedroom and that Bailey would be sound asleep there. She walked slowly down the hall, placing each foot carefully to avoid making any sound. When she reached the end of the hall, she could see a body on the couch. Even from the glow of the television, she couldn't tell if it was Bailey or not. She took a step closer and her foot collided with a dining room chair.

"Ouch!" Her hands flew to cover her mouth, but it was too late.

Bailey sat up on the couch and rubbed her face. A fuzzy dog face appeared beside her on the couch.

Great. She had woken both of them.

"Sneaking out in the dark of night?" Bailey asked, her voice a bit gravelly from sleep.

"No, not really. I was looking for food."

She heard Bailey chuckle. "That's a good sign. Let me find you something."

The glow from the television silhouetted Bailey as she walked around the couch, leading the way into the kitchen. Her hair was disheveled, and TJ touched her own head self-consciously. No way did she looked as cute as Bailey did in the middle of the night.

She followed her into the kitchen, appreciating the soft glowing lights from under the cabinets that Bailey turned on instead of the overhead light. The kitchen wasn't very big, but it had everything necessary. Bailey pulled open the refrigerator door and then lifted her head to look at TJ over it.

"More soup or a sandwich? I have deli turkey."

"Yes," TJ answered.

Bailey chuckled again. It was a pleasant sound. Not a taunting laugh that someone might make when they were making fun of you.

"Soup and sandwich, it is then." After removing the ingredients from the fridge, Bailey began pulling bowls and plates out of a nearby cabinet. While the soup heated, she placed several slices of bread on the plates. With a nod from TJ, she added turkey, mayonnaise, and a slice of what appeared to be provolone. Her stomach growled again. It was the sandwich she had been dreaming of and her mouth watered in anticipation.

Bailey dished steaming soup into two bowls and handed one to TJ. She pulled two bottles of Gatorade from the refrigerator.

TJ picked up everything Bailey didn't carry and followed her into the living room. They sat on the couch facing the television and Bailey pulled the glass-topped coffee table within reach. With their meal spread out in front of them, TJ began pulling off pieces of her sandwich and dipping it in the soup. She held her other hand under the soggy bite to avoid dripping on the floor or the couch.

The television was displaying the end of a Sandra Bullock movie. TJ couldn't remember the name of it but knew Garth Brooks had written the theme song. It was one of her favorite songs by him.

"I can turn the channel to anything that suits you," Bailey offered.

"No, this is fine. I hate watching the end of movies unless I've seen them."

"You've seen this one?" Bailey asked as she followed TJ's process and dipped a piece of her crust in the soup.

"Yeah, lots of times. I like the theme song and it's a sappy romance."

She watched Bailey's face as she dropped the piece of dripping crust into her mouth. Her face contorted as she chewed and swallowed the sodden bread.

"That's terrible," Bailey said after taking a drink.

TJ smiled. "I didn't make you try it."

"You seemed like you were enjoying it, so I was tempted. It was disgustingly soggy, though."

"I like soggy. It's better than dry."

"That's what mayonnaise is for." Bailey reached for the remote as the end credits of the movie played. "I like that song too by the way. Garth Brooks, right?"

"Yep."

"Are you a country music fan?"

"Sort of. My grandmother is and I live with her."

*Lives with her grandmother? Was that Katie?* She wouldn't ask. "I like Lady Antebellum."

"Unfortunately, my grandmother only plays 70s and 80s songs, so I'm not really familiar with newer musicians. Thanks to Sirius XM Radio, though, I can listen to the Prime Country channel."

"I can handle that channel, but I prefer The Beat. It has a modern mix." Bailey pulled her feet up on the couch in front of her. "Let's surf and see what's on now."

TJ shifted to get comfortable, pulling her legs up on the couch too. She kept them close in front of her to avoid touching Bailey. The flickering of the light from the television cast a glow across Bailey's face. The few times they had been together she had noticed Bailey had a habit of brushing her hair back from her face. She would use her fingers to push the hair directly above her ears. Sometimes she would do both hands at the same time and hold the hair in a little ponytail for a minute or two before dropping it.

"How about this channel?" Bailey asked.

She focused her attention back on the television and her mouth dropped open. A woman stood beside a stand holding a purple dildo as she described all of its features.

"Close your mouth," Bailey said, kicking her feet out to nudge TJ.

She glanced at Bailey and then back at the television. "What channel is this?"

"Want to memorize it so you can watch at home later?"

"No, I just can't believe how descriptive they are."

She listened to Bailey laugh as the woman moved on to the next displayed toy.

"Seriously, hit the guide. I want to see the channel. Is that what happens after everyone goes to bed? It's like QVC for adults only."

Bailey pushed the guide button on the remote. "Channel 21. Adult toy auction. There you go."

"I think I watched a movie last week on this channel."

"Was it porn?" Bailey laughed even harder.

"No, it was not. It was about a dog who saved Christmas."

"Are you sure that wasn't the Hallmark channel?"

She shook her head. "I'm sure. I watch the Hallmark channel a lot."

She was pretty sure she had never admitted that to anyone else. Even Grams, who she spent hours with watching movies in the weeks leading up to Christmas. She always tried to make it seem like Grams was picking the channel.

"Me too."

Bailey's words were soft and TJ almost didn't hear them. She glanced at her, but Bailey was flipping channels again and didn't look back at her. She didn't feel the need to continue the conversation, especially once Bailey found a movie still in opening credits on the Hallmark channel.

TJ drifted off to sleep and when she woke up there was light outside. Bailey was asleep too and she tried not to wake her as she untangled their feet and legs. Apparently in their sleep, they had both slid down on the couch and their heads rested on opposite ends.

TJ stood slowly, working out the kinks in her body before moving. The sunlight coming through the window made it easy to look for her belongings. After she placed all their dishes from the previous night in the sink, she walked through the house to gather everything. Her uniform seemed to have disappeared, but her boots were sitting by the door. She shifted the set of keys on the table in hopes that hers were hiding underneath.

"Can I help you find something?" Bailey asked, sitting up.

"My keys."

"Your truck isn't here."

She noticed her phone on the table and grabbed it.

"No problem. I can call someone to come get me." She clicked a button, but the screen didn't light up. *Shit!* So much for getting the hell out of Dodge. She ran her tongue over her teeth as disappointment settled in her. She was stuck here, and she desperately needed a toothbrush.

Bailey stood. "I can drop you wherever you want. Do you mind if I shower first, though?"

"That's fine." She needed a few minutes to decide where she wanted to go. Home was the best idea. Joey could pick her up there and it would avoid any office gossip about her appearance or where she spent the night.

"I washed your uniform and it's hanging in the closet. You're welcome to shower, but I imagine you'd like a complete change of clean clothes first. There's a new toothbrush by the sink in the bathroom if you want to grab it before I shower."

Boy, would she ever. She tried not to sprint into the bathroom. The blue plastic-wrapped toothbrush was right where Bailey said it would be and she ripped it open. Lining the brush with toothpaste from the sink top, she left the bathroom. She didn't want to be rushed. She wanted to savor the minty taste and scrub each tooth individually. Bailey smiled at her as they passed in the hallway.

It was weird to be in someone else's space and to share domestic rituals. She finished brushing her teeth over the kitchen sink and placed the toothbrush with her phone. She had to guess that Bailey didn't want the brush back.

Bailey was quick in the bathroom and came out with her hair still damp. She was dressed in cargo shorts and T-shirt with several buttons at the top and a single pocket over her left breast. She carried a hanger with TJ's uniform over her shoulder.

"Here, I'll take that," TJ said, stepping forward.

Bailey relinquished the clothing and picked up her keys off the table.

"How about stopping for breakfast?" Bailey asked.

She almost said yes without even thinking. Did she dare spend any more time with this woman? She had enjoyed the previous night. Maybe even a little too much. It had been easier to keep her at a distance before the subtle flirting over the panther and before the closeness of last night. She needed to keep her distance, because she could already see she was starting to like her. And that was not a good idea. She didn't know much about Bailey, but she did know that she wasn't a one-location kind of woman.

"It's probably not a good idea. I'd hate to be seen by anyone from work before I make it back in."

"Another time then?"

"Yeah. Sure."

*Crap!* Now she had agreed to see her again. Oh well. Bailey would leave when she had her photos and their paths would never cross again.

# CHAPTER ELEVEN

Bailey stopped in the FWC's parking lot and turned off her Jeep. Did she have a good reason to be here? Not really. Except for the fact that it had been over a week since she had dropped TJ at her house. The memory of that quiet ride still bothered her. Their night on the couch had been fun, filled with joking and laughing, but the next morning had been just plain uncomfortable.

She sighed. What did she think would happen? Like magic, they would connect while TJ was trapped at her house? That sounded creepy even to her. It was a weird situation and undoubtedly even more so for TJ. Bailey had tried to be patient, hoping they would accidentally run into each other around town. But that hadn't happened, and now here she was.

She sighed again and pushed herself out of the car. The concrete sidewalk lined with vibrant, green plants was welcoming, but the clank of the metal hooks bouncing off the flagpole reminded her she was entering a government office. A blast of cold air hit her when she opened the door and she took a moment to look around. Rows of racks with pamphlets lined both sides of the small lobby. Pamphlets for everything nature-related and at least one for the local parks, a few with fishing regulations and locations, and a whole section for all the different hunting seasons.

Unlike the last time she had been here, a woman with shoulder-length light-brown hair occupied the front desk. She looked up as Bailey approached.

"Can I help you?"

"Yes, please. I'm Bailey Everett. I was wondering if Captain Westmore had a moment to talk." She smiled broadly, proud of her ability to quickly come up with a logical reason for being here.

"Oh, sure. You're the photographer, right?"

"I am."

"He was on the phone earlier, but I don't see his extension light on anymore, so let me go check."

She forced herself to lean casually on the counter as the woman walked down the hall. Two doors on the right were closed, but the two on the left were open. The woman disappeared as the hallway made a sharp right turn. Bailey could see name plates to the left of each door but she couldn't read any of them. Was TJ's name on one of the closed ones or the open ones?

Two men came out of the first open door. They both wore cargo-style pants and green forest ranger shirts. She recognized Joey and gave him a wave.

"Ms. Everett. It's nice to see you again."

She shook Joey's hand and then reached out to the taller man. "Hi, I'm Bailey."

"Randy Sanders."

"It's nice to meet you, Randy. And good to see you again, Joey. Is it a slow day? No panthers to chase?"

The men chuckled.

"We just came by the office to close out our notes for the day. It's almost quittin' time."

"Big plans for the evening then?"

*Yikes.* Why did she say that? It sounded like she was fishing for an invitation.

"Just headed over to Dave's for some oysters and beer. That's the bar that sits on the water in Panacea. Have you been there yet?" Joey asked.

"No. I heard about it, though." What was she supposed to say to avoid an invitation? "I pretty much have my dog with me everywhere I go so I don't eat out much."

"Oh, they have outdoor seating and dogs are welcome."

*Crap.* She was digging herself in deeper. She tried not to look relieved when Captain Westmore appeared in the hallway. She recognized him from his picture in the paper.

"Captain Westmore." She stepped toward him and away from the two men. "So nice to meet you."

"Yes, Ms. Everett. I wondered when we would have a chance to visit in person."

She shook his outstretched hand and searched her mind for a reason for her visit.

"Thanks for the opportunity to photograph the panther. Do you have any comments or information you would like to add if I use any of the photos?"

He gave the men a wave as he turned back toward his office. "Come on back and we'll talk."

"Enjoy your evening, officers," Bailey called, relieved to follow Captain Westmore down the hall. She slowed her pace at the first open doorway and gave a casual wave when she saw TJ. She didn't wait to see if TJ waved back since Captain Westmore had already disappeared around the corner. She followed him into the last open door at the end of the hall.

His office was three or four times the size of TJ's. He had a large dark-colored glossy desk in the corner with two chairs in front of it and still had room for a leather sofa to one side. He tossed his glasses on his desk and motioned for her to have a seat on the sofa. He took a seat on the other end, leaving the empty cushion between them.

"I really appreciated the opportunity to get photos of the panther."

"No problem. Once he was caught, I didn't mind showing him off."

She recognized the nervous chuckle and knew he must have had a lot of anxiety waiting to capture the panther. She had seen it in TJ's face too.

"So, you got some good shots?" he asked.

"I did. Something in captivity is not my normal photos, but the capture and release is an interesting story. If I don't find a spot for it in the book, I might submit it to a nature magazine. I'll inform you before anything is published though."

"I appreciate that, and I don't have anything to contribute. I only want to make sure the officers that participated get recognition."

"Of course."

"I hope you're enjoying your time here. I heard the boys giving restaurant suggestions, but I'd stick with Angelo's in Panacea for seafood. Dave's is a bit of a dive."

"I'm certainly enjoying the scenery. I don't dine out much, but I'll keep Angelo's in mind."

"So, you're traveling alone?" he asked.

"I have my dog. It's hard to bring anyone else when all I do is work." Hopefully that implied that she had someone that she could have brought with her.

"True. True. Sarah and I want to have you over to the house for dinner. She's planning some kind of festival, an event thing, but when that's over she'll have some free time. How long do you plan to be around?"

"Another month or so. Maybe longer since I have to leave soon for a book tour."

"That's exciting. How long do those last?"

"Usually a couple weeks. We cram as much as possible into each day, but we only hit the major cities. We'll start in California and end in New York. This book focused on Maine, so we'll probably stay a few days there too."

"Well, that sounds like a lot of fun."

*Really?* Where was the fun? To her it sounded exhausting. All those people in all those towns. Fun would be hanging with friends and watching football. But what friends? She had left her hometown so suddenly she hadn't even attempted to pretend she cared about anyone there. Since she had been on her own, she didn't stay in one place long enough to cultivate any relationships. Who was she kidding? She didn't try to make friends.

"Keep in touch and if anything good comes through the office we'll make sure to let you know."

"Thanks. I really appreciate your support."

"We appreciate the free publicity," he said, standing.

She took that as her cue to leave.

She followed him to the door and shook his hand again before she left. Sounds of laughter came from the lobby and she walked in that direction. TJ's office was empty and she couldn't help hoping TJ was in the lobby too.

Four men stood near the front doors. She caught the tail end of a story about two raccoons in a trash dumpster.

"I told him to either put a lock on it or enjoy the wildlife. What the hell did he think anyway?" one of the men said.

"Yeah, even a cat will climb in a dumpster. It doesn't have to be a stray one either. Trash is breakfast, dinner, and dessert to any animal," another said.

"My dog would climb in one if he could," Joey chimed in as he waved Bailey into the conversation. "Maybe Ms. Everett would like to stake out the dumpster for some photos," he suggested.

"Sounds beautiful," she said, laughing with them. "But I think I'll stick to catching animals in their natural habitat."

"That's as natural as it comes around here," one of the other men said as he turned and offered introductions.

Bailey tried to memorize their names, but she was distracted by seeing TJ standing behind the receptionist's desk. Her back was to Bailey and her head was bent toward the receptionist as if they were deep in conversation. Bailey knew TJ had to have heard her voice, but she was making no effort to acknowledge Bailey's presence.

* * *

TJ could feel Bailey's eyes on her, and she fought the desire to meet them. She had heard Bailey arrive earlier before she disappeared into the captain's office. She could have taken that opportunity to sneak out, but she hadn't. She wanted to. Boy, did she want to. She couldn't be more humiliated by her sick episode than if she had collapsed in front of her. Oh wait, she did. And she puked! Too many times to count apparently. She tried to push all of those thoughts away, but that was why she was standing here at the desk pretending to discuss a memo about tracking deer that had been released two weeks ago.

She heard her coworkers say their goodbyes to Bailey when it became clear they weren't going to convince her to join them for drinks. She looked up when Joey called out to her and gave him a wave. Her eyes met Bailey's.

"Hello. It's good to see you again." She tried to sound casual. How was one supposed to sound when they met up with the woman that held their head while they puked? She certainly didn't know. She took a deep breath and tried to find a friendly smile. "So what animals are you looking for today?" She wasn't sure she wanted to help, but maybe she could point her in the right direction. Then she wouldn't feel guilty for not offering more assistance.

"Pretty much anything."

"Anything?"

"No reptiles," Bailey said with a shudder.

"Did you just cringe?"

"Well, they're not my favorites."

"A nature photographer who doesn't like a big alligator. How can that be?"

"It's not the alligators." Bailey glanced around her and dropped her voice conspiratorially. "It's the snakes."

TJ tried to hold back her laughter, but her whole body began to shake.

"Go ahead and laugh," Bailey said dismissively. "I guess now you'll try your best to find me a snake." She started toward the exit.

*Crap!* She hadn't meant to make her angry. "Wait!" She hurried to catch Bailey as she opened the exterior door. "Wait." She touched Bailey's shoulder. "I didn't mean to laugh."

Bailey turned to her. "Yes, you did. You're exactly like all the other testosterone-filled men I deal with every day."

She couldn't believe the hurt she saw in Bailey's eyes. She glanced around to see who else was listening to their conversation. An officer stood in one of the doorways, but she didn't bother to look and see who it was.

"Come with me." She grasped Bailey's arm and escorted her through the front doors of the building.

Bailey yanked her arm free.

"Are you kicking me out?" Bailey asked, glaring at her. "I photograph snakes for almost every book. Just because I don't like them doesn't mean I don't deal with them."

TJ stepped between two vehicles, using her truck to block them from a direct view of the building.

"First, I'm not kicking you out. I only wanted to have a conversation without the entire office listening."

"Oh."

"Second, I wasn't laughing because you didn't like snakes. I was laughing at the way you checked the hall and lowered your voice before you said it."

"Well, I have to be careful. Sometimes nature people get upset if I don't love every aspect of it and then they won't help me if I need something."

"That's crazy. I work in the field and I don't love every aspect of it."

Bailey's voice dropped again. "Really? I thought all conservation officers were nature lovers."

She chuckled. "I am a nature lover, but I still scream like a five-year-old girl every time a snake surprises me."

Bailey laughed. "I find that hard to imagine."

TJ glanced up in surprise as her boss stepped off the curb to join them.

"I'm glad to see you guys hanging out. TJ, why don't you take her for a run up the Wacissa tomorrow," Captain Westmore suggested.

"I have to clear the traps at Highland Pass tomorrow." Was she arguing against spending the day on the river with a woman that she found completely alluring? What was wrong with her?

"I'll have Joey do the morning check," he stated.

TJ shrugged and glanced at Bailey.

"Sounds like we have a river date tomorrow. Want to meet me here about seven thirty?"

"Sure. That sounds fine."

"And don't bring the dog."

\* \* \*

Bailey rubbed Chewie's head. *And don't bring the dog.* What did that woman have against dogs? Chewie didn't understand being left behind and she wasn't sure she did either. Of course, there were trips that Chewie couldn't go on, but it was the way TJ had said it. As if she was trying to end a negotiation that Bailey hadn't even started.

She walked across the hall and tapped on Mr. Maxwell's door.

The door swung open and his face glowed with excitement to see her. "Ms. Everett!"

"Please call me Bailey, Mr. Maxwell."

"Okay. Bailey, what can I do for you?"

"Can you give Chewie a walk tomorrow about noon? I'm going to be gone for a few hours and I know she'll appreciate an escape."

"Why don't you just leave her over here with me? She can hang out and play in my backyard."

She looked past him into the apartment. "I didn't realize you had a backyard."

"Well, I share it with Tom downstairs, but there's a grassy area in front of the dock. I don't have a boat anymore, before you ask. Wish I did though. I could show you some good areas. Maybe I'll ask Tom if I can borrow his. Then I could take you into Panacea on the water. You could see the fishermen gathering oysters—"

"That sounds great. About tomorrow, though. Can I drop her off about a quarter after seven? Will that be too early for you?"

"Nope. That'll be fine."

She gave him a wave and stepped away. "I really appreciate this."

"It's no problem. Bring her food and any treats she's allowed to have. We'll have a wonderful day."

She gave him a wave and quickly returned to her apartment. He was such a nice guy, but she couldn't take too much of him at one time. She hoped he would forget about borrowing his friend's boat. She wasn't sure how she would get out of something like that if he offered.

Going out with Officer Smith, or rather TJ, was a different story, though. She was really looking forward to it. Tomorrow couldn't come fast enough.

She fed Chewie and raked together a few items for her own dinner. She had never been much of a cook. Living in New York gave her access to any type of food at any hour and cooking had never really had much of a draw. When she began traveling for each book, she had learned to make a few staple items, like spaghetti and chicken noodle soup, but unfortunately her fallback was always cheese and crackers. She was a bit of a snob, though, when it came to the cheese. It couldn't be anything prepackaged. Her selection had been limited at the local grocery store, but she had found a market in Tallahassee that carried homemade local selections.

She cut a wedge from the block of cheese and sliced it into thin strips. The crackers were some kind of healthy whole grain and a bit dry, so she added a spritz of light olive oil to each one. The cheese was made by a local goat farmer and had a wonderful smoky taste. She added a few grapes to her plate and poured a glass of wine. Taking her dinner with her, she joined Chewie in the living room. Chewie had scarfed a few pieces of kibble as soon as they had arrived home and was already napping on her corner bed.

She watched Chewie's steady breathing. In and out. In and out. Her chest rose and fell along with the antenna on the stuffed bumble bee that lay in front of her nose. A flitter of her eyelid and a flick of her ear acknowledged Bailey's movement around the room. But soon she was back to sleep with only an occasional paw twitch as she chased bunnies in her sleep.

Chewie was the best thing in her life. Chewie never judged her for eating only cheese and crackers for dinner. She never asked how much money she had spent shopping. Chewie only asked for attention, and Bailey always felt better afterward, not guilty like people made her feel if she neglected them.

Wait. Was she comparing her dog to past relationships? Yes, she was. And why not? Chewie was her companion in every part of her life. Well, except for that one area. And intimacy wasn't something Bailey liked to spend time thinking about anyway. It was the single reason that she couldn't hold on to a girlfriend.

She was starting to understand that it wasn't that she didn't want someone in her space but more that she didn't want a stranger in her space. She wanted someone to share everything with. Not a couple of limited things. Not a part-time lover who was more of a roommate. She wanted a shared bank account, shared property, and shared time. A consistent hand to hold. She couldn't share a bed and then buzz in and out of someone's life. There had to be more.

No one had ever seemed to understand that about her. Or maybe it was that they didn't care enough to try to understand. Either way it had still led to heartache. And that had led her to living alone with a dog. Truth was she was happier now than she had ever been. Chewie liked to travel with her and hadn't complained even once about her upcoming book tour even though it meant spending a lot of crate time in airplane cargo holds. Happily, she was a great traveler. Bailey couldn't imagine weathering the stresses of a book tour without Chewie by her side.

# CHAPTER TWELVE

TJ hoisted the canoe from the back of her truck and walked it to the water's edge.

"Are you sure I can't help?" Bailey asked again.

"No, it's not that heavy. I do this all the time by myself."

"I can't imagine going out on the river alone."

TJ watched her glance around again. Bailey's face was lined with stress and her voice was a little squeaky.

"Are you scared?" TJ asked.

"Of course not," Bailey answered quickly. "Well, okay, maybe a little."

"Can you swim?"

"No. I mean yes, I can swim, but I'm certainly not going to," Bailey said adamantly.

TJ held back a laugh. "I wasn't going to suggest that you swim. Although you could if you wanted. The water is cool and, in another hour or so, it'll feel really good."

"I could never swim in water with snakes and alligators."

"Okay, relax. I was only asking if you could swim because I could see you were a little nervous. I thought maybe you were scared of the water, but now I understand. You're more worried about what might be in the water."

"And the thin piece of plastic I'm about to climb into."

"It's Kevlar, not plastic, and it has never leaked before." This time she couldn't stop the chuckle. This woman was an eminent professional and she was acting like a scared little kid. She stepped to the side of the canoe and reached out a hand to Bailey.

"Trust me. You'll enjoy this."

Did she know that was true? Yes, she did. Bailey would enjoy a day with nature. And she was going to enjoy sharing it with her.

Bailey tentatively took TJ's hand and stepped into the canoe. She didn't look confident, but the hesitant smile she gave TJ melted her heart. She was going to enjoy this day.

TJ flipped open the storage area between the two seats and pulled out a waterproof bag. She held it open in front of Bailey.

"Camera and phone, please."

Bailey clutched her camera to her chest, making TJ laugh again.

"It'll be safer in the bag. At least until you get used to being on the water."

Bailey stretched the camera out and dropped it into the open bag.

"And your shoes too," TJ suggested.

"My shoes?"

"They're leather, right? You probably don't want them to get wet or lost in the water."

"Suggesting my shoes might get lost in the water doesn't instill confidence in your canoeing abilities."

"I'm an excellent canoer."

"Really? Canoer? I don't think that's a word."

"It could be."

"Are we going to argue all day or go out on the water?"

"Oh, now you're in a hurry to get out on the water," TJ said as she pushed the canoe into the water. She hadn't been thinking when she had Bailey get in before the canoe was completely in the water. She pushed harder, making a ridge through the sand that was quickly washed over by the movement of the river.

Giving one last push, she hopped into the canoe and settled into her seat. She grabbed the oars and began to row. She quickly found her rhythm, knowing she would need to row hard on the way up the river and then rest on the way back.

"Do you want help paddling?" Bailey asked.

"No, I've got it. And it's called rowing."

"Rowing, paddling, it's all the same. Moving the boat, right?"

TJ laughed. "Well, yes, both make the boat move but they're very different. Oars are attached to the boat and paddles are loose. When I'm by myself I use a paddle and I can face forward. When I'm watching to make sure someone doesn't fall out of the boat, I prefer to have a clear view of them rather than the direction we're moving. Plus, I don't have to worry about losing a paddle when the oars are secured to the boat."

"Okay, I get it. Thank you for schooling me. I prefer to face the direction I'm moving. Although, your head is directly in my line of sight," Bailey said, shifting her head to the right and then left to see around TJ.

"I can move if you'd like," TJ teased, rocking them back and forth until Bailey clutched the sides of the boat. "Or I could just jump out. It's a nice day for a swim."

"Stop already!" Bailey scolded. "Do not leave this boat."

"Then quit worrying about logistics and enjoy the view."

Bailey nodded and took her eyes away from TJ, but every time she glanced from side to side her gaze lingered on TJ. It was an appreciative look and TJ liked the goosebumps it caused on her arms. She concentrated on her rowing technique in hopes she looked experienced and, maybe, just a little cool—or rather hot.

She used the distraction of rowing to study Bailey. Today she was wearing a dark green ribbed tank top and tan cargo shorts. Her face was a masterpiece of concentration as she looked from side to side. TJ followed her gaze and caught the glimpse of a blue heron as it waded along the edge of the river, its long beak plucking small fish out of the water.

Bailey's wide eyes caught hers again and TJ smiled. When it came to nature, Bailey had seen so much, but her face was still eager for what she might see next. TJ couldn't wait to share something she loved with someone that would appreciate it as much as she did.

They were almost to the spot where they would turn around. It was a wide area where the river's current shifted in many directions, and she often saw manatees and river otters there. She was confident that both would be something Bailey would like to see.

* * *

Bailey readily took the bottle of water from TJ's hand. She hadn't realized how thirsty she was. From the moment their journey up the river had begun, she was captivated by the thriving nature around her. She had easily forgotten her fears of snakes and alligators slithering around her. The picture of the river she had in her head had been filled with murky waters and deep dark forests stretching as far as she could see. The reality was nothing like she had imagined. The river was shiny and glimmered in the reflection of the sun. The edges were lined with vibrant green leafy vegetation and dotted with an occasional purple or yellow flower.

"You're going to want this," TJ said, interrupting her thoughts.

She looked up to see TJ handing her the camera from inside the storage area. She reached toward it and felt the canoe begin to rock. Quickly grabbing the sides, she tried to balance as she bobbed from side to side. She glared at TJ, who was laughing and didn't seem to be concerned with their movement.

"Here," TJ said, reaching out the camera again. "There are two little faces over there that want to be photographed."

"Where?" she said excitedly, grabbing the camera from TJ.

TJ pointed to the shore where a mass of downed trees lined the riverbank, stretching into the water.

She searched the area, looking for a face in the mass of shadows. Then she saw it. Water-streaked fur and white glistening whiskers. And little black eyes. Four of them. All focused on her. She slowly raised the camera and zoomed in on the two little river otters.

She loved watching river otters' slide, wrestle, and belly flop on slippery slopes. They were present in all of her East Coast books, Pennsylvania, Vermont and her last book, Maine. Along the way she had learned firsthand that otters, along with other Mustelidae or carnivorous mammals like martens, wolverines, and badgers can all secrete a musky scent from their anal glands, but the skunk was the master at aiming and spraying this fluid.

She snapped several pictures and then glanced at TJ.

"Their feet are so cute!" she exclaimed.

They both laughed as the otters' faces disappeared under the water.

"Oops. I guess I scared them. Did you know they have fingers?" Bailey exclaimed, adding, "Of course you did. You're a wildlife pro."

"Webbed fingers. Don't worry about it. They'll come back in a minute. They're very curious." TJ stroked the water a few times with the oars and turned them around. "Besides there is more to come."

"Oh, like what?"

"I almost always see manatees in this area."

"I've read tons about them online, but it would be awesome to see and photograph one."

"No need to do an Internet search. You're traveling with a well-informed nature lover. I can answer all your questions."

"So, tell me something I don't know."

"Manatees are really big."

Bailey laughed. "I think I knew that."

"Okay. How about this? Did you know that female manatees are larger than males?"

"That's better. Tell me more."

"Manatees grow new molars in the back of their mouth that move forward to replace the front ones as they are worn down."

"I thought they were vegetarians. How do their teeth get worn down?" she asked.

"They are primarily herbivores. They like eel grass." TJ pointed to the long strands of grass rising from the bottom of the riverbed. "And thankfully they like water hyacinth and hydrilla as well."

"Why thankfully?"

"Because neither are natural to Florida or even the United States and they're invasive. Left unchecked water hyacinth will completely cover the surface, affecting water flow and blocking sunlight from underwater plants. Then you have a perfect habitat for mosquitos, and that's one thing Florida doesn't need more of."

"I can agree with that. I've been more than one meal while I've been here."

"I have some stuff that'll help with that."

"Really? That's a secret I'll make you share."

"Get your camera ready," TJ said as she rowed them toward the middle of the river.

"What is it?" she said, trying to spin back and forth without rocking the canoe.

"Your favorite."

"It's a manatee? Where?"

TJ swiped her hand back and forth through the surface of the water, creating ripples. Then she held her palm a few inches above the water. It was clear TJ was doing something, though Bailey wasn't sure what. Unlike when she'd been introduced to black bears in Arkansas and again in Texas and Maine, she was more excited than afraid. Maybe it was TJ's presence, but more likely it was the manatee's reputation. Anatomically, they were unable to bite with their teeth because of their position in the mouth, and being aggressive only meant pushing someone away from them or their calves.

She held back her excitement and watched. Within a few seconds, a gray muzzle appeared and pushed TJ's hand away from the water. She almost screamed as the rest of the manatee's body slowly appeared at the surface of the water beside the canoe.

"You touched it!"

"No, it touched me. There's a difference."

She shrugged. "Same difference. What does it feel like? Can I touch it?"

"No, you can't touch them. But when this big one gets past us, you can see if one of the others will want to check you out."

"No? Well, that's the answer I expected, but I didn't expect you to touch it either."

"I didn't touch it. It touched me."

She frowned at TJ. "I feel like you are making a point that I'm missing."

"It's against the law to touch a manatee with two hands, but I won't arrest you if the manatee chooses to touch you."

Bailey laughed. "You won't arrest me?"

TJ shook her head. The smile on her face may have been the first one Bailey had seen her make that was natural. Even out of uniform, TJ had always seemed to be acting her role. Today she seemed relaxed. Bailey liked this side of her. She was open and friendly, unlike the day Bailey had dropped her off at her house.

"Hey, I wanted to ask you about the trap from the day you were sick and then you mentioned traps again at your office yesterday. Why are you trapping?" Bailey asked.

"Anytime someone reports an animal acting weird we try to confirm it's not rabies. If we get a timely report, we'll set traps immediately to catch the animal."

"Doesn't an animal have to be dead to check for rabies?"

"That's true, but if we can examine one that's acting disoriented or partially paralyzed, often we find out that it's an injury we can treat or that will heal on its own. Folks around here think every time they see a raccoon in the daylight it has rabies."

"Isn't that true?" Bailey asked.

"Yes, if you see it in your backyard in town, but not if you are walking in the forest. You're in its neighborhood."

Bailey laughed. "I guess that's true. Are you from this area?" Bailey asked, eager to see how long she could keep TJ talking.

"I am. Born and raised right here in Crawfordville. I grew up with the Panacea Blue Crab Festival, the Sopchoppy Worm Gruntin' Festival, and the St. Marks Stone Crab Festival."

"That sounds exciting, especially the worm grunting," she replied, laughing.

"That's worm gruntin' and you've already missed it and the blue crabs, but if you're still around in December I'll take you to taste the stone crabs."

"I feel like I should ask about the worm gruntin' but worms are slithery like snakes so I'll skip over that. What's the difference between blue crabs and stone crabs?"

TJ laughed and reached out to grasp Bailey's hand. She moved Bailey's hand through the water and held it palm down on the surface. She continued to make the same movements with Bailey's hand as she went back to the conversation.

"Blue crabs are soft-shell crabs. You eat the whole body. Stone crabs are mostly harvested for their claws and then thrown back."

"That's so cruel," Bailey said, horrified.

"There's some that would agree with you. Their claws regenerate, though."

"Do you eat them?"

TJ shrugged. "If I can avoid thinking about it. I like crab, crawfish, and shrimp. And I eat meat, but sometimes I wish I didn't. As a society we aren't very civilized."

Bailey studied her face. TJ's lips were pursed in a grimace. She wasn't surprised to find that they agreed about the cruelty of the world. She jumped as she felt her hand being pushed.

"He touched me!" she exclaimed, laughing.

TJ laughed too. "I believe he is a she."

"Really? How do you know that?"

"I'm just making a guess based on the calf swimming beside her. By the way, do you plan on taking any pictures today?"

Bailey closed her eyes. For the first time in her life, her first thoughts weren't to capture what she was seeing. She was living in the moment and enjoying sharing it with TJ.

She picked up her camera and began snapping as the manatee used its large flexible lips to munch on the surface vegetation. Other than an occasional swing of a flipper or swat of a tail to control movement, the manatees floated along beside them. The calf remained underwater, staying close to the side of its mother.

"I wish I had an underwater camera," she said.

"Next time," TJ suggested.

Bailey smiled as she met TJ's eyes. Next time? That sounded good to her.

# CHAPTER THIRTEEN

Bailey climbed from the limousine and straightened to face the flood of flashing cameras. Attending a movie premiere always made her feel special and it brought a little extra attention. She waited for Mark to emerge from the car before starting the slow trek down the red carpet. Mona always had a way of surprising her when it came to events like this. Right down to the limo equipped with an escort already in it.

Mark Elbury seemed nice enough. An up-and-coming actor who had made several appearances on a popular sitcom, he was willing to do anything to keep his face in front of the cameras. He was also happy to play any part he was paid for. Bailey had made it clear to him on their ride to the theater that at the end of the night she would be going home alone. Mark didn't seem bothered by that news.

Breaking up the tour dates had been a great idea, along with leaving Chewie with Mr. Maxwell for the California portion. Besides, Chewie was probably being spoiled rotten and might not even miss her. She missed her fur-covered friend, even though this type of event was often fun and always entertaining.

The next segment of the tour would last for three weeks and she would bring Chewie for that. There were plenty of hotels that would allow her companion, and some would even offer doggie day care if there was a bookstore that didn't allow dogs. She would leave the details to Mona but made a mental note to stress the importance of Chewie's attendance as well as no male escort surprises.

She walked through the open doors into the theater and felt the cold gust of an overworked air conditioner. Thankful to be past the red-carpet portion of the entryway, she maneuvered around the photographers and other guests. She wasn't the famous actress that the hordes of press were waiting for, but some would still mention who she was. And as Mona said, if she played her part well those that didn't know who she was would want to.

She had arrived in California the day before. Tomorrow they would begin a grueling drive through four states, southeast to Arizona, north to Utah, and then across Nevada. Their final stop would be Sacramento. Two bookstores in each state. Mona had scheduled her in states that she had already completed books on. She had a copy of the itinerary, but she hadn't really studied it. Mona would direct every second, telling her where she needed to be and when, as well as when to eat and sleep.

She spotted Mona across the sea of people milling in the lobby and made her way to her.

"Honey, it's so good to see you," Mona said, kissing both of her cheeks and then pulling Mark close to kiss his cheek as well.

"You, too." She hoped she sounded more sincere than she felt. Not that it mattered. For the moment Mona was focused on Mark. She glanced around at the glamorous outfits and shiny made-for-television people. All of it seemed fake. Right down to the woman and man standing beside her. It wasn't that she didn't want to be here. Surprisingly, she found she was missing the laid-back, comfortable life in Florida.

Mona slid her arm through Bailey's and led her toward the auditorium. "You have to tell me what's been happening with you. Normally your first couple weeks are spent on the phone with me and I've barely spoken to you. What have you been doing? Oh, I loved those mountain lion pictures!"

"It was a panther."

"Well, it looked like a mountain lion. How close were you to it? It looked so close. Were you in any danger?"

Was she in any danger? Certainly not when she took the pictures. She still remembered how her heart had raced when TJ first told her that something was in the forest around them. But she wasn't scared. Was she? Okay, yeah, she might have been.

Mona turned away to greet someone and Bailey moved on to their seats. She wasn't eager to share her thoughts or feelings from the last couple weeks with Mona and she *really* didn't want to spend any time thinking about why she didn't. Mona had been the only constant in her life for over ten years, and she had always referred to her as a friend as well as her agent.

What would Mona think of Tim and Tubs? She would call them country folk, Bailey was sure. If she even noticed them. And yet Bailey liked them. And what would her publicist think of TJ? She might get a few moments of Mona's time due to her education, but it was the uniform and her good looks that Bailey knew would draw Mona in.

Mona didn't identify with any gender labels, but Bailey knew what she liked. A man or woman in uniform would make Mona's head turn every time. Bailey wouldn't call her shallow. She was only a love-'em-and-leave-'em type. She had heard Mona say more than once that relationships only slowed you down.

"Where did you run off to?" Mona said, sliding into the seat beside her.

"I didn't run off. I went to find our seats."

"You're okay then? Great! I'm going to get a drink."

Mona sprang from her seat and was racing back up the aisle before Bailey had a chance to answer. Had Mona always been so...so what? Energetic? No. Flighty. And why had she never noticed it before? Mona was at her best when they were at an event. She was a social butterfly. Maybe that's why they got along so well. Mona kept people engaged and allowed Bailey to be quiet and more like herself.

She thanked Mona for the glass of wine she handed her as she slid back into her seat as the lights dimmed. The opening credits flashed across the screen.

"What do you think of Mark?" Mona whispered in Bailey's ear.

Bailey shrugged.

Mona frowned. "I thought you'd be pleased. He's everything you normally ask for."

Bailey could hear Mona's pout even if she could not see it.

"Did something happen? He promised he would keep his distance," Mona continued.

"No," Bailey whispered. "Nothing happened. Can we talk about this later?"

"Of course, but I thought you'd be pleased," Mona said again.

"I appreciate your effort, but maybe next time I could make an appearance alone."

"I guess. Anything would be better than the alternative."

Bailey sighed. She knew the alternative Mona hinted at was having a woman as her escort. This wasn't the first time they'd had this conversation, and Mona had made clear her opinion. It was okay to have sex with a woman, but when it came to publicity only an escort of the opposite sex would do.

The superhero raced across the screen as the movie picked up where the last one had left the hero hanging. Not all heroes wore masks, but their outfits were always cool. And some were certainly in the sexy category. Captain Marvel, of course, and Black Widow.

And then there were women in uniform. She had gotten used to working with forest rangers and park service personnel. She had to admit, though, that TJ was different. She was something special. She had felt it before they had spent the morning on the river, but since then she hadn't been able to stop thinking about her.

Most of the time they had spent together in the canoe had been in silence. Bailey had found it comforting. She was used to sitting for hours watching and waiting for animals and apparently TJ was too. If TJ saw something she thought Bailey might not see she pointed it out, but she didn't feel the need to converse. Bailey had appreciated having a guide along. She had to admit that she would never have chosen to take a trip on the river by herself. And certainly not in an easy-to-flip canoe.

She thought about the first time they had met and then their meeting at the vet's office. She had felt an interest from TJ, but it was times like this when she replayed everything between them that she would start to doubt her intuition. She had asked TJ if she wanted to grab some lunch after their river trip and once again TJ had declined. Bailey had suggested picking up Chewie and going somewhere dog-friendly. She wasn't sure if she or Chewie had been the reason for TJ's lack of interest.

The lights came on around her and she realized the ending credits were scrolling up the screen. Like everyone around them, they remained in their seats, waiting to see what clip would play after the credits. Everyone clapped when it was over, and she wondered if she had missed a good movie. Hopefully, Mona would not want to recap it.

She knew she was off the hook when Mona linked her arm through Mark's on the way out. Feigning tiredness when they got outside, Bailey caught the first cab that approached. Mona would have all weekend to grill her about her time in Florida and right now she needed to be alone with her thoughts.

* * *

TJ slid into her truck and slammed the door. This was getting ridiculous. For the second time in two days, she had forgotten a meeting. It didn't matter that she had them on her calendar. She couldn't remember to check it. Her mind was preoccupied with hoping to run into Bailey.

She had driven by the Shell Point Reserve too many times to admit. She wasn't sure why she was playing this game. She was an adult and she hated drama games. She was going to walk right up and knock on Bailey's door and ask her to go to dinner. Worst-case scenario was that Bailey would say no, but TJ hoped she wouldn't.

She had gotten a vibe from Bailey. One that said she was interested. She had tried to ignore it; Bailey was only here temporarily. TJ wasn't much for one-night stands, but clearly she needed to do something to get Bailey out of her system before she was gone for good.

She turned left and followed the shoreline to Bailey's street. There were only a handful of cars in front of the condominium, and she didn't see Bailey's Jeep. Maybe she was out and this would be a wasted trip.

She knocked and stepped away from the door so she would be visible from the peephole. She waited. And waited. Should she knock again? Did she knock loud enough the first time? She approached the door and knocked again, this time a little harder.

She heard rustling at the condo door behind her and turned as it opened. An elderly gentleman stood in the crack of the open door.

"She's not home," he said a bit gruffly.

"Okay." Should she ask if he knew when she would be back? Before she could think it through a blond muzzle appeared at the man's knee.

"Chewie!" She knelt and reached out her hand to the dog.

The man hesitated at first but then opened the door enough for Chewie to reach out.

"What are you doing here, girl?" she asked as she ruffled Chewie's neck.

"She's staying with me while Ms. Everett is away," he said, opening the door up and joining them in the hallway. "I'm sorry if I was a little rude. I wasn't sure who you were until Chewie said you were okay."

"No problem. Do you know where Bailey is?" She would go find her Jeep and wait for her to return.

"She's off on her big book tour," he said proudly. "She's pretty famous, you know."

"Yeah. I know." So, Bailey had left for her book tour. She didn't know much about book tours or if Bailey's trip would span more than one state. Truth was she didn't know anything.

If Bailey's tour passed through every state, then she might be gone for a long time. She didn't believe she would leave Chewie for that long, though.

She gave Chewie another pat and took a few steps back.

"Thanks. I'll try to reach her when she returns."

She started to walk away and turned back. She pulled a card from her pocket and handed it to the gentleman.

"If you need any help with Chewie until she returns just give me a call. I'm happy to help."

He nodded and tucked her card in his shirt pocket.

She drove home, trying not to think about how disappointed she was. How long would Bailey be gone and why hadn't she asked when she was coming back? Thanks to Chewie, at least she knew Bailey *was* coming back.

Her grandmother was in the kitchen when she walked in, and she immediately put a pot of water on the stove.

"No, Grams, I don't want to talk. It's been a bad day and I'm going to bed."

"Teresa Jane, sit."

She groaned and then ducked as Katie swiped the dish towel at her.

"You have been moping around for days now. I've tried to ignore it, but it's time for you to come clean."

"It's nothing."

"Well, nothing is a lot like when you were gathering the courage to ask Laureen to the senior prom."

"Grams! It's nothing like that." She felt the blush covering her face and knew her grandmother would see right through her words.

"That's fine, Teresa Jane. Take your tea to your room, but remember when you're ready, I'll be waiting."

She couldn't remember her grandmother ever letting her off the hook when she knew something was bothering her, but she grabbed her tea and bolted for her bedroom before Grams could change her mind.

# CHAPTER FOURTEEN

TJ slammed on her brakes and hit reverse. Bailey's Jeep was sitting in the parking lot at the Shell Point Reserve. It felt like weeks since she had seen her instead of just the days it had been. She had run through so many conversations between them in her head. Would Bailey be happy to see her?

She parked beside Bailey's Jeep and turned the engine off. She could leave a note with her phone number on Bailey's windshield. Or she could wait for Bailey to return. Or she could muster up the courage to go and look for her.

She jumped out of the truck before she could change her mind. She followed the main path and took the split to the left when she reached the first intersection. How far would she walk before she gave up? Her shift had already ended, but she was still in uniform. She could pretend she was there working and not let Bailey know she had stopped because she saw her vehicle.

The forest was quiet around her with only an occasional chirp from a bird or croak from a frog. The canopy of trees covered the path in sporadic clusters. Hard sun-packed earth led to soggy paths as the trail moved up and down through the forest. She was in the forest so much for work that she couldn't remember the last time she had taken a walk on her own time.

She inhaled the musty damp smell around her as she entered another low spot. She felt the temperature drop as the sun's access was restricted. Dodging the muddy water pooled in the tire tracks, she looked ahead to a patch of wildflowers amidst tall pine trees. This section of the forest was due for a prescribed burn soon. The pine trees no longer showed crisp black bark at their bases and the vegetation was thick. There was also an abundance of dead trees, some still standing.

She had always enjoyed playing outside as a kid. Football games with pine tree defenders or pretending to be a police officer sneaking through a forest of robbers. As an only child, she counted on her imagination to conjure the best playmates.

She crested a small hill and spotted Bailey walking in front of her. She was wearing her standard multi-pocketed pants and a long-sleeved light-colored shirt. Today she had a wide-brimmed hat perched on top of her head. Her steps were slow and she was moving her head back and forth watching both sides of the trail. Chewie stopped and turned to face TJ immediately.

Now that she found them, she wasn't sure how to get her attention without frightening her. She squatted down to see if Chewie would approach. Her plan worked. As soon as Chewie began trotting toward her, Bailey turned.

"I can show you a great place to take photos," she called, hoping Bailey would welcome the intrusion.

* * *

Bailey jumped a little at the sound of TJ's voice, but it only took a second for her words to register. Did she want help from her? Of course she did.

"Okay."

TJ began walking, so she followed beside her. She couldn't help wondering if TJ's form of help meant walking without talking. She was determined not to break the silence, though.

She had walked a lot of forests over the years with only Chewie by her side. She didn't need company or conversation, but maybe TJ could show her another side of the shaded wonderland. With TJ around maybe she would feel closer to the nature that surrounded her rather than a photographer plucking out the pieces she preferred.

She often walked for hours appreciating the beauty and scents of a forest. Chronicling the life cycle of a dying tree that provided food and shelter to birds, insects, reptiles, and animals. These things she photographed and made money from, but oddly she never had felt like a part of it. She had known many nature enthusiasts and prying them out of the forest was never an easy task. She on the other hand had tried camping multiple times and had never made it through the night.

As they walked beyond the road that she knew led back to the parking lot and her car, she wondered how far TJ planned to walk. It didn't matter to her. She was determined to keep pace with the silent woman beside her, but she did worry about Chewie. She felt an occasional drop of saliva from Chewie's tongue on the back of her calf as the goldendoodle stayed right on her heels. She kept a close eye on her watch so she would know how long they had been walking. She and Chewie would need a water break soon.

She glanced at the woman beside her. There was a slight glisten of sweat at the edge of her hairline, but other than that she didn't appear to be exerting much of an effort. She had to imagine that TJ was used to walking quite a bit for her job. They were moving at a moderate pace. Not a saunter but not rushed either.

She stopped watching TJ and began appreciating the beauty of the forest around her. They stepped around a bend in the road, and beyond a row of pine trees she could see a small stretch of wildflowers. She couldn't call it a field because it was such a small area. Maybe ten or twenty yards in length and surrounded on three sides by dense undergrowth and tall pine trees. The flowers were mostly white with an occasional pink and purple thrown in. She immediately stopped and began snapping pictures.

TJ stood quietly nearby while Bailey moved up and down the road capturing the flowers from all sides. When she finished, she gave TJ a shy grin.

"Not always animals, huh?" TJ questioned.

"Not always," she answered snapping a few quick shots of TJ.

"Hey!"

"Sorry. I take a lot of pictures that I don't use. It helps me remember places and feelings when I'm laying out the book." That sounded like a good excuse, right? The truth was TJ looked amazing standing in the middle of the road. With the bend in the road, she looked like she was not on a path but surrounded on three sides by trees. She wore her standard gray shirt with sewn-on name tag. Her dark green pants hugged her waist and tapered down into her boots. She looked comfortable in her environment, and she blended into the surrounding brown and green background. She looked at ease and, best of all, Chewie was sitting at her feet. It was a picture she couldn't resist.

"Okay, but no more."

"But I could make you famous," she laughed, swishing her head as if to throw her hair over each shoulder.

TJ shook her head, but the edge of her mouth curled. "No thanks."

They began walking again and she immediately regretted not taking the time for a drink.

"How far are we going?" she finally asked.

"There's a trail around the next bend that leads back to the main road we started on. I thought you might like it because it passes a small body of water. There's normally a lot of animal activity there."

Her heart skipped a beat. She knew that water in Florida meant alligators and snakes. Did she need to remind TJ of her fears? No. Maybe they wouldn't see anything that slithered.

When they reached the bend in the road, TJ stopped.

"You should give your dog a drink so she's not tempted by the pond. You might also want to leash her."

"Okay." She took a bottle of water from her pack, pouring a small amount into Chewie's collapsible dish before taking a drink herself.

She looked to both sides of the road and couldn't see a road or a path.

"Where's the path?" she asked.

TJ pointed to a small break in the underbrush. "Right there."

"I don't see a path."

"Well, it's not really a path. It's more like a trail. Mostly it's used by deer and other animals to get to the pond."

She bent over to retrieve Chewie's dish, taking a moment for a few quick breaths. Her anxiety was starting to grow. Now she remembered why she didn't use anyone else to help her get her pictures. Before she realized it, she ended up getting stuck in a position that she couldn't get out of and still maintain her pride.

She tucked the empty bottle of water and Chewie's dish into her pack and took another deep breath. She could do this.

"Lead on," she said as she clipped Chewie's leash to her collar.

With every step that took them deeper and deeper into the forest, her thoughts ran through the gauntlet of animals they could face. Remembering the panther, she shuddered. Of course, there could be foxes, coyotes, bears, but the things that worried her most slithered on the ground. She was unable to enjoy the area they were passing through because her attention was focused on watching where she was stepping. Focused on avoiding thinking about the potential that a snake could be in a tree above or beside her.

She wondered if she would hyperventilate and pass out before they reached the location TJ was taking her to. Before she could give into her anxiety, TJ put out her hand to stop them. Pointing through the brush, TJ dropped to a knee. Bailey knelt beside her, pulling Chewie tight against her body. She slowly leaned closer to TJ until she could see what she was seeing.

A mother deer and a baby fawn stood at the edge of the pond. The mother had heard them and her head was up, but the baby was still drinking. She gradually lifted her camera and zoomed in on the deer. The baby still had spots and its small body barely reached the mother's underbelly.

TJ leaned close, whispering into her ear, "There's more on the right side."

The heat from TJ's breath swept down her body, and she fought the chills that followed. It was the most divine feeling she had ever felt. If only they weren't in a forest surrounded by wild animals and more than a mile from civilization.

Looking through the camera lens, she slowly moved her head to the right. Another mother and baby stood staring straight at her. She continually snapped pictures as she zoomed in and out, moving between the two families.

Most fawns were born in late spring or early summer, which was one of the reasons she had worked so hard to get the photos a few weeks ago. Seeing a fawn this late in the summer was a gift and now there were two more. One of these babies could possibly be the same one she had already photographed, but it didn't matter.

Being able to witness the simple beauty of a mother resting her head against her baby or a baby nuzzling against her mother's chest brought joy to her, and it would to the folks that bought her books too. The smallest fawn stepped to the water's edge and lowered its head. It hesitated a moment, staring into the water and Bailey held back a chuckle. There was no doubt it was seeing its own reflection.

When she finally lowered her camera, her eyes met TJ's. The pleased smile on TJ's face danced all the way to her eyes. TJ was clearly happy being able to show her the scene stretched out in front of them.

"Ready?" TJ asked, slowly standing.

She nodded. Standing, she placed a hand on Chewie's neck to remind her to stay close. It was an unnecessary action, but it also was a silent praise for the dog's good behavior. As they turned to continue down the trail, she noticed a slight frown on TJ's face before she turned away.

She tried to push away the disapproval she felt coming from her and remember only the happy look that preceded it. She wasn't sure why TJ didn't like Chewie, but when they got back on the main trail she was determined to find out. Chewie was the best dog in the world and didn't deserve TJ's attitude.

When they emerged from the trail, the heat from the sun found them immediately. TJ clapped her hands together above her head.

"Black fly," she said, wiping the smashed fly on her pants. "Sorry if I startled you. I couldn't take another minute of him buzzing by my head."

"That's okay. They're the worst. I had one get caught behind my sunglasses the other day. I would have killed him if I could have."

"The fat black ones are normally easy to kill. They're slow and don't scare easy. No-see-ums are worse though. Have you experienced them yet?"

"No-see-ums? I thought they were a myth."

"Unfortunately not. They usually hatch in the spring and the fall. Regular repellant doesn't work on them. I use Avon's Skin So Soft. It's the only thing that kind of works and doesn't leave you needing an immediate bath."

"I'm no—"

TJ threw out an arm to block Bailey's path and pushed her back a step. "Stop!"

"What?"

"The thing you've been hoping to avoid," TJ said in a whisper.

"What?" she repeated. She searched the path in front of them, starting to panic again.

"Right there." TJ pointed to the left side of the path where underbrush and an occasional small shrub covered the ground.

"I don't…Shit!"

Bailey jumped backward, pulling Chewie with her.

"That's a diamondback rattlesnake," TJ said as she maneuvered closer to get a better look. "If you stand right here you can get a perfect picture."

"How do you know that's what it is?"

"See the perfect diamond pattern across its back?"

"No, I can't." Standing her ground, she pulled the camera strap over her head and passed the camera to TJ. "I'll be staying right here anyway, though."

"Don't you want...?" TJ's voice trailed off as she finally looked over at Bailey. Her head tilted as she appraised her. She reached out slowly and took the camera from her.

After TJ had snapped a few pictures from all sides of the snake, they began walking again. TJ removed the camera strap from over her head and passed it back to Bailey.

"You weren't kidding about your dislike of them. Your face is white as a ghost," TJ acknowledged.

Bailey took a deep breath. It was time to confess. "I'm not good with any snake. They creep me out."

She was surprised when TJ laughed.

"It's not funny. I'm a nature photographer. I should be taking pictures of all creatures in nature."

"I can laugh because I don't like them either."

"But back there you acted all excited."

"It was only an act. I'm always cautious in case I run into one, but I certainly never seek them out."

A shiver rippled down Bailey's body. "I hate the way they sneak up on you."

TJ laughed again.

"And the way they slither. I can't believe how close you got to that one. Weren't you afraid it would strike?"

"I think it had eaten something, because it didn't seem eager to move. You'll be able to see the huge lump in its middle when you look at the pictures."

"*If* I look at the pictures," she said with a deep breath.

"Okay, how about something more gentle?" TJ said, pointing ahead of them in the road.

She froze. "Oh, please don't let it be another snake."

"It's a gopher turtle."

"Okay. Turtles are good."

They moved forward together. Unfazed by their approach, the turtle continued to make its way slowly across the road. She felt Chewie's head between her legs as she peered at the turtle.

"Check it out, girl," she encouraged Chewie.

Chewie slowly approached, moving behind the turtle. She lowered her head and sniffed its butt.

Bailey snapped a few pictures before the turtle disappeared into its hole.

"Did you know that over three hundred different species use gopher turtle holes as their home?" TJ informed her.

"Really? That's impressive."

"Even diamondback rattlesnakes like to hide in there."

"And the turtles don't mind?" Bailey asked in surprise.

"I guess it's hard for the snake to bite a turtle or maybe they just don't feel threatened."

"Yikes! Can you imagine trying to pierce or swallow a turtle shell?"

Bailey was surprised when the bend in the trail emerged into the parking lot. TJ went straight to her truck and opened the door. Bailey struggled to find the words to extend their time together.

"Hey," she called.

TJ turned halfway into the truck. "Yeah."

"Would you like to get some coffee?"

"Um, well," TJ stuttered.

Dang it. She had screwed up. How many times would TJ have to tell her she wasn't interested? She had thought when she saw TJ's truck parked beside her Jeep that TJ had come looking for her. That maybe their meeting today hadn't been accidental. Clearly, she had misunderstood and the best thing she could do now was offer TJ an out.

"That's okay. I should have realized you're working."

"No, I'm off now, but I really need a shower."

"Another time then?"

TJ nodded. "Yeah, sure."

"Tomorrow?" Bailey bit her tongue. Why couldn't she stop herself from talking?

"Okay. I can usually break away about ten. Can I text you?"

Bailey quickly pulled her phone from her pocket. "What's your number?"

TJ rattled off the numbers and immediately her cell chimed with an incoming text.

"Now you have my number, too," Bailey said. "Text when and where and I'll be there."

She quickly buckled Chewie into her seat belt without looking in TJ's direction. She didn't want to see any hesitancy or give TJ an avenue to back out now. She couldn't wait for tomorrow.

# CHAPTER FIFTEEN

TJ awoke with a killer headache. She had spent the previous evening waffling back and forth between where to take Bailey and how to cancel. Bailey had made the invitation. Why couldn't she embrace the opportunity to spend more time with her? It was what she wanted anyway.

The house was quiet as she made her way downstairs and grabbed an apple for breakfast. Since the evening she had bailed on Grams's invitation to talk there had been a bit of tension between them. She could tell Grams wanted to push her. To ask questions and delve into TJ's feelings, but she hadn't done that and it had created a barrier between them that TJ hated.

Grams's car was parked beside her truck and she felt guilty for leaving without saying anything to her. Of course, there was no expectation for her to do that, just a courtesy. She appreciated the parenting her grandmother had supplied as well as the roof over her head when she was younger. Their relationship had changed as TJ had gotten older, but there had always been a level of respect. TJ had never taken her anger at her parents out on her grandmother and she had always tried to be appreciative of her sacrifices.

Right now, though, thoughts of Bailey were drowning out everything in TJ's head. She didn't like it. Usually her thoughts were always on work. Where to go and what to do next. Bailey, however, had put a definite twist on that. And she still didn't have a decision on where to go on their date this morning.

*Date?* Was it a date? No. It wasn't.

She would suggest the diner. Since she didn't eat breakfast, she would be hungry by ten and Myra Jeans would offer food and coffee. She would text Bailey when she got to the office.

Joey was crossing the parking lot when she climbed from her truck.

"Mornin'," he called.

"Good morning, Joseph."

"Why do you do that?"

"What?"

"You know. Call me Joseph."

She gave him a good-natured bump with her shoulder. "That's your name, right?"

"Well, yeah, but—"

"You guys see this," Kurt interrupted Joey as they stepped through the glass doors into the Florida Fish and Wildlife office.

"What?" Joey asked, stepping forward eagerly.

Kurt tossed a magazine on the counter separating them from where he stood with Chandler and Neal. The magazine was open to a page with lots of small photographs.

"Wow!" Joey exclaimed, leaning in to get a better view.

"That's what I said too," Neal agreed as Kurt and Chandler laughed.

"I don't think that was the word you used," Kurt teased.

"Maybe not, but it meant the same thing," Neal answered.

TJ took a step forward and looked down at the magazine. On one side was a gossip column about the latest blockbuster superhero movie. Her eyes were immediately drawn to the other side of the page and a photo of Bailey in a low-cut sapphire blue dress with spaghetti straps.

"Do you watch that show?" she heard Joey ask.

The dress was molded to Bailey's body and flowed all the way to the red carpet she stood on.

"Do you, TJ?"

"What?" she asked, looking up to find all three men looking at her.

"That's Mark Elbury with her. Do you watch the show he's on?" Joey asked.

*With* her? TJ looked at the photo again. Standing beside Bailey, with his hand in the small of her back, stood a man in a tuxedo. He looked familiar, but TJ couldn't study him long enough to pinpoint from where. Her eyes could only see how he touched Bailey. Comfortable and possessive.

"Do you even know who he is, TJ?" Chandler prodded her.

"No. I mean yeah, he looks familiar." She turned and walked away before Joey or Chandler could question her further. She could hear them hypothesizing about the relationship between Bailey and her date.

She closed her door to block out their conversation. She felt like she had been kicked in the gut. Bailey had a boyfriend. Of course, she did. Why hadn't she asked her? That would have been a friendly question when they talked about all of Bailey's traveling.

Her phone dinged with a text message.

*Are we still on for coffee?*

It would have been an easy answer before she saw the picture, but now she needed time to process this new information. The thought of food made her queasy.

She quickly typed her reply before she changed her mind again. *No, caught up at work. Catch you another time.*

She wouldn't. She couldn't. Even though she had tried not to think about Bailey as someone she was interested in, she knew she was. She liked everything about her from the first moment they had met. The scared but strong woman on day one to yesterday's confident photographer. And yes, the woman in the sapphire blue dress.

She opened the cover on her laptop and dove into work. If she worked fast, she could get out of the office for the afternoon and away from any more conversation about Bailey and her boyfriend.

An hour or more had passed before she realized that Bailey hadn't responded to her text. She opened her phone and checked in case she had missed it. Or maybe in hopes she had missed one that explained the man in the tuxedo. Or why he had his hand on Bailey in such an intimate way.

She leaned back in her chair and closed her eyes. The vision she saw sent flutters through her midsection. She stood in a tuxedo with Bailey by her side. She could feel the silkiness of the dress as her hand rested in the small of Bailey's back. Cameras flashed around them and Bailey leaned toward her, whispering something in her ear and they both laughed.

Bailey's voice settled around TJ smoothly, so smoothly that it took her a moment to realize it was coming from the hallway. She opened her eyes to an amused expression on Randy's face.

"Me and the guys are going to Mo's for lunch at noon. You can go with us or take an early one now."

She nodded.

"So you're free now?" Bailey asked, stepping past Randy and into TJ's office.

"She's all yours," Randy said as he disappeared.

TJ hadn't missed Randy's innuendo. Apparently he was the only one of her coworkers who hadn't seen the picture of Bailey and her boyfriend.

"Shall we go?" Bailey asked, motioning toward the door.

"I saw the picture of you and your boyfriend." TJ heard the words coming out of her mouth and was surprised she had said them.

"As I told your coworkers, not my boyfriend."

TJ raised her eyebrows. "Oh yeah?"

"Yeah. He is an actor who was paid by my publicist. She seems to think I can't go anywhere alone."

"In that case, there is something you should know before you go out with me."

"Are we going out?"

"I...I mean go to lunch."

"Okay."

TJ walked around her desk and pushed her door closed, realizing too late that her action would make her coworkers gossip as much as her taking Bailey to lunch. Oh well, she had already started and now she needed to finish.

"Being seen with me will make the local rumor mill churn."

This time Bailey raised her eyebrows.

"I don't go out much so when I do it makes people talk," she continued.

"Talk about what?" Bailey asked.

"About me being out. With you."

"Ah, like a date?" Bailey grinned. "And that's something you do? Date women?"

"Yes. I mean no. I prefer women, but I don't date much. It's a small dating pool."

Bailey slipped her arm through TJ's, steering them toward the door.

"Then I'm happy to broaden the waters."

TJ's stomach shot into her throat and she swallowed hard. Did Bailey mean what she said or was she only playing with her? She wanted to ask, but instead she squeezed Bailey's hand between her arm and her side. She felt the chills go down her spine as Bailey tightened her grip on her bicep. With her head held high, she walked them through the lobby and held the front door open for Bailey.

* * *

Bailey slid into TJ's truck, pulling her seat belt on as TJ shut her door and walked around to the driver's seat. When TJ had texted to cancel their coffee date, she had tried to convince herself that work had gotten in the way. She knew it was brazen to come to her office anyway, but she wanted to see if TJ's initial hesitancy was lack of interest or something else.

Joey's harassment when she arrived at the Fish and Wildlife Office made her wonder if it was the something else. She was glad that she hadn't taken the cancellation at face value. She liked the way TJ smiled at her and couldn't be happier that they were going to lunch.

"Have you been to Myra Jeans?"

"I have not."

"It's comfort food, but they do have a few basic salads. Nothing fancy."

"Sounds perfect. I forgot to wear my fancy clothes today anyway."

TJ gave her a quick glance and Bailey felt her perusal.

"You look good anyway. Although it would be hard to top that blue dress."

"Liked that did you?" she teased, enjoying the quick flush that covered TJ's face.

"I was surprised at how well you clean up."

She laughed. "Nice comeback."

TJ shrugged as she turned the truck into an open parking lot in front of a white building with multiple signs announcing "ice cream." Bailey took advantage of TJ's distraction to study her as she parked the truck. Her hair was pulled back in a ponytail today and Bailey resisted the urge to run her fingers over the shaved section at the base of TJ's head. It was an interesting haircut, one that announced TJ's personality. Her hands held the steering wheel loosely as she backed into the parking spot.

"Butt first, huh." Bailey continued the teasing.

"Always. I don't like to be trapped."

"Oh, that's an avenue to be explored."

"Can it wait until we order? I'm starved."

Bailey nodded but knew she wouldn't bring it up again. It was an area she wasn't sure she wanted to delve into. The smell of burgers and fries helped distract her as did the small train that was running around a track along the top of the wall.

Bailey allowed TJ to steer the conversation back to the movie premiere but held firm in not releasing any information about the movie. TJ was clearly a fan too and they talked about the previous movies in the series while they waited for their food.

Before shoving the last bite of burger into her mouth, Bailey circled back to their previous conversation.

"Have you always dated women?"

"Pretty much from high school."

Bailey was surprised she had answered so easily so she pursued the subject.

"Anyone serious?"

TJ chuckled. "Like I said before. The dating pool here is pretty small. What about you?"

"I don't date."

"Anyone? Ever?"

"If you move around a lot, the dating pool gets even smaller."

TJ narrowed her eyes and leaned across the table toward her. "Are you telling me you have never gone out on a date?"

"I believe I'm out on one now."

"You're avoiding the question."

"Maybe, but how boring would I be if I answered honestly?"

"What are you doing tomorrow?" TJ asked.

"Probably working through all the pictures we took yesterday. Why?"

"There's somewhere I'd like to take you."

Bailey shrugged. "I'm game, I guess. Do you want to share where we're going?"

"Nope. And don't bring the dog."

# CHAPTER SIXTEEN

TJ had regretted her spontaneous decision to invite Bailey to Homosassa Springs almost from the moment she had made it. The joy she had seen on Bailey's face as she watched the manatees on their canoe trip was what had prompted her, but she hadn't thought through the whole process. With over three hours of driving facing them, the negatives were showing up in full force.

The streetlights were still on and the morning light was barely showing through the highest of tree limbs. Seven was her usual time to arrive at work so she was used to it. Bailey didn't appear to be a late sleeper, but they hadn't talked about it. The first manatee show would be at eleven and she wanted to catch it in case an afternoon thunderstorm ran them out of the park.

"I'm sorry it's so early," TJ said as Bailey climbed into her truck.

"I'm an early riser, so not a problem."

"And your dog?"

"She's with my neighbor."

Bailey turned to look out the window and TJ took that as a good sign. No small talk was going to be required.

She turned on to State Road 98 and headed south. It was a two-lane highway with a posted speed limit of sixty. The first forty miles or so the road was sandwiched between state and national forests with only an occasional house. She had seen lots of deer and wild pigs on this road as well as an occasional alligator. A silence had settled between them and TJ thought it was a comfortable one until Bailey finally spoke.

"She has a name, you know," Bailey said.

"What?"

"My dog. She has a name."

"Oh."

She could feel Bailey's eyes on her now and she felt like she had entered a conversation already in progress. She wondered what she had missed, but before she could ask Bailey spoke, a distinct edge in her voice.

"Really?"

Was Bailey upset that she told her she couldn't bring the dog today? Maybe she should have explained where they were going. "Dogs aren't allowed in the park where we're going and it's too hot to leave her in the truck."

Bailey shook her head. "I understand not bringing her. That's not a problem."

"Okay, then. What is the problem?"

She was starting to get frustrated. Should she turn around before they went any farther? They were barely into the first hour.

"Never mind," Bailey said, shifting in her seat to look out the window.

Yes, turning around seemed like the best option. She let the silence stretch as they entered the first town on their journey. Perry was known for its tree and lumber industry. With a little more than five thousand residents it was considered mostly rural. TJ knew it as the stinky town. Growing up, she hated traveling through Perry because of the smells from the papermill.

At the railroad tracks, she turned left onto a small, unmarked road and parked in front of the train depot.

"Are we taking a train?" Bailey asked curiously.

TJ chuckled. She was glad to have the tense silence between them broken. "No, it's a coffee shop. There aren't any passenger trains on this track anymore."

Bailey followed TJ up the stairs to a concrete sidewalk that stretched the length of the building. A pleasant tinkling of a wooden windchime sounded as soon as they passed through the open door. Built-in shelves lined the wall with items for sale— bags of coffee beans and locally made pottery.

TJ placed her order and took a seat at one of the small tables near the counter. Once they had both received their orders, TJ removed the lid from her coffee and took a small sip.

"I should have told you before we started how long of a drive this would be. We still have about two hours or so left, so now is the time to turn around, if you don't want to go."

"I do want to go," Bailey said. "I think. Of course, I don't even know where we're going."

TJ looked around until she spotted the rack of sightseeing pamphlets near the door. She walked over and grabbed the one for Homosassa Springs.

Bailey's eyes lit up as soon as she saw the manatee on the cover. "I want to go."

TJ stood, laughing. "Let's get back on the road then."

Outside of Perry, the speed limit increased again, and TJ set the cruise control. Bailey's head had been buried in the pamphlet since they left the coffee shop. Whatever her frustration with TJ had been seemed forgotten, at least for the moment, and TJ was relieved.

When they crossed the bridge into Fanning Springs, TJ turned into the state park entrance. "I'm ready for a bathroom break."

"Oh yeah. Me too."

TJ led the way through the tourist center to the bathrooms.

* * *

Bailey exited the bathroom and looked around the tourist center. TJ stood at the counter talking to a park service employee. When Bailey approached, TJ turned and met her.

"Need anything before we get back on the road?"

"Nope, I'm ready." She glanced around the center. "This artwork is amazing. It looks like Denise Dean's photographs."

"It is. She lives nearby."

"Wow. I didn't know she was from Florida."

TJ unlocked the truck with her key fob and waited for Bailey to climb in before continuing their conversation. "She grew up in Crawfordville and moved down here after she got married."

"I knew a lot of her photos had alligators in them, but I guess I thought maybe she was like me and moved around."

"Nope. Born and raised. The artwork she displays in the park's tourist center is for sale, but she donates the majority of the proceeds back to Florida State Parks."

When TJ didn't offer any additional information, Bailey opened the Homosassa Springs pamphlet again. TJ didn't seem eager for conversation, but she didn't seem against answering questions either. Bailey was impressed with her knowledge. "Do they really have a hippo at this park? That's not something you would expect to see in Florida."

"They do. Lu's story is long since he just turned sixty."

"I'm listening." Bailey shifted her focus away from the pamphlet.

"Lucifer was born in San Diego and sold to a writer and director of animal shows in the sixties. You remember *Flipper*, right?"

"Yes, the television show with the dolphin."

"Right. Ivan Tors was one of the producers on that show. If you back up to the early 1900s, Homosassa was a tourist attraction even then. The mullet train would stop to load fish, crabs, cedar, and spring water, and the passengers would enjoy the view of the spring with its many fresh and saltwater fish. When vehicles came along it became a roadside attraction. So, Ivan bought Lu and used him in a few movies. When he didn't need him, he would house him at Homosassa Springs along with other exotic animals, like Buck who was the stand-in for Gentle Ben. Remember that series?"

"I've never seen it, but I remember. Ben was a big black bear, right?"

"Yep. When the State of Florida purchased the park and made it into a state park, they sold off all the exotic animals and kept only the native ones. There was such a public outcry to keep Lu that he was declared an honorary citizen of Florida by the state legislature."

"I love that. It's hard to say where he might have ended up otherwise."

Finished with her story, TJ returned to her quiet contemplation, so Bailey buried her head back in the pamphlet. She kept coming back to the dog issue. It was clear TJ loved animals. Her telling of the story of Lu was passionate and engaging. She promised herself that she would make TJ talk about her issue with dogs before the day was over. For her, it felt like a barrier between them and she wanted it gone.

She looked up when TJ slowed the truck. A giant thirty-foot fiberglass manatee stood at the edge of the parking lot of the Homosassa Springs Wildlife Park. A mural of several manatees covered the wall of the brick building marked as the visitor center. TJ backed into a shaded spot, and they walked across the parking lot and entered through the glass doors, Bailey shivering when the air-conditioning washed over her. She shivered again when TJ's hands ran up and down her arms to warm her.

"We're only passing through so we'll be back outside in the warmth in a moment," TJ explained.

The room was filled with pictures, statues, and local artifacts. She followed TJ slowly, reading the plaques in front of each display. They stepped outside into a permanent roped-off area that herded pedestrians toward a small twenty-passenger barge. TJ took a seat in the front and Bailey slid onto the hard, plastic bench beside her.

"We're taking a boat to the park?" Bailey asked.

"Yep. You can drive to the main entrance or take a tram or boat."

She nodded as a few more people took seats around them. "I like this. It's like—"

"Foreplay," TJ said softly.

Bailey squeezed her eyes shut and then opened them again. TJ's body was shaking with laughter. She studied TJ's face as she turned to look at her. The stress lines that she thought were a permanent feature were gone and TJ's shoulders were relaxed as she leaned against the side of the boat.

Bailey shook her head. "I'd like to say that wasn't what I was thinking, but actually that is perfect."

"I know. Any time I go to an amusement park and they have entertainment to distract me while I stand in line, I can't help but think foreplay."

She settled into her seat, facing forward as a mustached man in a park shirt hopped aboard. He pulled in the lines and began to talk quickly.

"I'm Tom, your boat captain for today. I'm a volunteer, like most of the staff here at the visitor center. Our fifteen-minute ride will take us along Pepper Creek to the main entrance of the park. There are a few areas that are too narrow for two boats to pass so we might have to pull off for a few minutes while the return boat passes. I'll identify native wildlife and vegetation as we travel but feel free to ask any questions." He dropped the gear lever into reverse and began slowly backing away from the dock. "Please keep your arms and legs inside the boat at all times. Especially as we are leaving and entering the boat docks."

TJ sat quietly without providing any of her usual nature information. Bailey was sure it was because Tom talked nonstop. When the boat docked, she followed the flock of people through the metal winding bars and out into the sunshine.

"Do you plan on taking any pictures you might want to use professionally?" TJ asked, nodding at the camera dangling from Bailey's neck.

Bailey frowned. "I hadn't really thought about it. Why?"

"Professionals have to identify themselves at the park office and sign some paperwork."

"Oh. I don't mind doing that if it would make you feel better, but honestly my books are about catching the creatures in their natural habitats. Not pictures of animals in captivity."

TJ smiled. "I thought that would be the case. Let's head straight to the fishbowl. The manatee feeding will start in less than thirty minutes and that's the best time to see them."

"Lead the way."

# CHAPTER SEVENTEEN

They entered another air-conditioned visitor center with a café, gift shop, and information center. Bailey's stomach growled as she caught a whiff of the pizza being sold at the café counter. She must have slowed her steps because TJ bumped her gently.

"We'll come back as soon as we see the manatees. If we get the usual afternoon thunderstorms, they'll cancel the afternoon manatee show."

Bailey nodded, falling into step with TJ as they maneuvered around people moving in both directions. At the park entrance fee booth, TJ stopped and shoved a couple bills through the window. Bailey didn't want TJ to pay her way, but she wasn't going to argue with her in front of everyone.

Bailey followed TJ's example and held out her hand to receive the admission stamp on the back of it. She smiled at the purple outlined manatee now traveling with her. They exited the building and she followed TJ along a concrete path. At the fork was a manatee fountain. She snapped a quick photo before hurrying to catch up with TJ on the trail to the left. They followed along the river that began to veer around to the right. It seemed to dead-end at a round boat-looking building.

"Is this a freshwater spring?" Bailey asked as they descended the steps into the underwater viewing area.

"That's one of the best parts of this spring. Several vents combine to form the river headspring. Each vent has a different salt content and water quality, so the river is filled with a variety of saltwater and freshwater fish."

"You are completely correct, Officer Smith."

Bailey spun to see where the voice behind them had come from. A woman in a park service uniform stood at the base of the stairs. She had a broad smile that displayed her perfect teeth. Dark hair brushed the top of her shoulders as she walked toward them.

"I'm Officer Barry." She offered her hand to Bailey. "You can call me Heidi."

Bailey took her hand. "Hi, Heidi. I'm Bailey."

Heidi dropped her hand and pointed into the water outside the viewing glass. "Those are mullets. They're saltwater fish, but they like brackish water too. A little higher up near those rock enclosures are bream and that scary-looking fish with the long nose is a gar. They are both freshwater fish."

"The green one?"

"Colors under the water are deceiving. Gars are olive brown."

Heidi turned her back to the glass and met TJ's eyes. Bailey watched with curiosity as they each seemed to appraise each other before they started to laugh.

"Hey, loser," TJ teased as she embraced a chuckling Heidi.

"What are you doing in my neck of the woods?" Heidi asked.

"Are you feeding the manatees today?"

The clear deflection of TJ's answer seemed expected by Heidi and she rolled with the question.

"Yep. You should be able to see the first two on the other side."

"How many manatees do you have living here?" Bailey asked.

"There are five here right now. Three are permanent residents and two are being rehabilitated." Heidi walked to the other end of the viewing area. "Matilda, the one on the left, was injured by a boat propeller. It severely damaged her back and she can never be released. The other one, Stella, she was found with a fishing line wrapped around her flipper. Luckily, she was found before the damage was irreversible. With a little more rehabilitation she'll be released." Heidi glanced at her watch. "It's time. We feed them off the platform, if you want to watch."

Bailey nodded and, with a glance at TJ, followed Heidi up the stairs. Heidi moved to the end of the viewing platform where an assistant had rolled a wheelbarrow filled with green leafy vegetables. Bailey watched her maneuver around the audience that had gathered to see the manatee. It was like a silent dance as she positioned children and a woman in a wheelchair to the front of the group while casually chatting with everyone.

"Hi, everyone, my name is Officer Heidi Barry. I've been at Homosassa Springs for almost ten years and the majority of my time here has been working with the manatees. Today we're going to offer them a little snack to help bring them closer. Feel free to ask any questions."

An exuberant little boy about ten years old waved his hand in the air. When Heidi nodded at him, he asked, "How do you tell if they're boys or girls?"

Heidi laughed. "That's a good question. Male manatees have male body parts just like you."

"Wow," he concluded as he turned his head to the side. Bailey assumed he was trying to see under the manatee in front of them.

Heidi addressed the rest of the group. "Males and females have basically the same sex parts as humans. They can be identified by the opening's location to their anus."

"They poop?" the little boy asked with surprise as his father pulled him close and placed a hand over the little boy's mouth.

"What's your name?" Heidi took a knee in front of the boy.

Bailey liked the way she casually let the father know everything was okay and that she could handle his son's questions.

"I'm Riley."

"Hello, Riley. I'm so glad you could be here with us today. Are you having fun?"

"Yeah, it's awesome!"

"That's great." Heidi stood and addressed the group again. "To answer Riley's question, yes, manatees do poop and pee. Not that anyone swimming wants to think about that considering a manatee can consume sixty to two hundred pounds of vegetation a day."

Heidi paused while everyone chuckled and then she continued, "Our manatees are all West Indian Manatees. They can be found from the Gulf of Mexico all the way to South Carolina during the summer months, but when the ocean gets cold, they prefer the natural springs of Florida. This water is warmed by the earth and maintains a constant temperature of about seventy-two degrees."

While she talked she began throwing heads of lettuce into the water. Moving like bumper boats, the manatees leisurely swam toward the food.

"Manatees are very curious and like to touch things with their flippers and the stiff whiskers around their mouth. They can move each side of their lip pads independently and this allows them pull food into their mouth. A manatee can grow up to thirteen feet in length and weigh up to three thousand pounds."

"Do they breathe underwater?" a woman from the back of the group asked.

"No, they actually need air and you'll see them surface to breathe about every three to five minutes. If they're using a lot of energy, they may surface as often as every thirty seconds and if they're sleeping they can wait for twenty minutes or more."

Bailey watched the aquatic creatures as they swam around each other. Although you really couldn't call what they did swimming. It was more like they floated with an occasional swipe of a flipper or a flop of their flat paddle-shaped tail. She couldn't help smiling every time their little faces surfaced. When doing her research online, she had read that Christopher Columbus had entered a mermaid sighting in his logbook while in the Caribbean. He had written that the mermaids were not as beautiful as the sailors had been led to believe.

"What are you laughing at?" TJ whispered, bumping Bailey's shoulder.

Bailey turned and looked at her. TJ's face was inches from her own and her eyes strayed instantly to her lips. They looked soft and kissable. As her gaze lingered, she watched her pink lips grow into a smile. How long had she been staring? Too long, definitely. She met TJ's eyes and read the humor in them.

"I was thinking about how the manatees make beautiful mermaids."

TJ chuckled. "You're in a minority."

"Okay. Maybe not beautiful but certainly adorable."

A little face surfaced below them and then disappeared with the wave of a flipper, rolling deep into the water.

"I love their fingernails," Bailey added. "I didn't notice that when we saw them on the river."

"They're certainly unique creatures," TJ agreed.

Riley's high-pitched squeal to get Heidi's attention drew them back to the ranger and her crowd of observers.

"Where are the babies?" Riley called to Heidi.

"All of our manatees at Homosassa Springs are adults. Babies are normally born in the spring and early summer and they are about Riley's current size and weight when they are born."

This brought another round of laughter from the crowd.

"How often do they give birth?" someone from the group called.

"Every two to three years. A female doesn't normally give birth until they are between five and nine years old and the gestation period is thirteen months. Combine all that and it's a recipe for dwindling numbers. The manatee has no predators in nature. While human beings cause the majority of their deaths with watercraft, the most serious threat they face today is the loss of habitat. Are there any more questions?"

Bailey's stomach gave a rumble and she glanced at her watch, discovering to her surprise that an hour had passed since they arrived. They lingered behind the exiting crowd, watching as the manatees headed down the river. She enjoyed the occasional breeze from the nearby trees as well as the silence resulting from a departing Riley and family. She leaned on the railing as she watched the one remaining manatee and the colorful fish.

TJ had moved to chat with Heidi and her assistant, but Bailey had lingered behind. Curiosity about the relationship between TJ and Heidi wormed into her thoughts. She pushed it away. Jealousy was an uncomfortable feeling, one she wasn't ready to embrace. TJ was a friend and that was all. It was true that she enjoyed hanging out with her and wouldn't mind getting to know her better, but she had no claim to TJ.

"Ready to see the rest of the park?" TJ asked.

Bailey turned at the sound of her voice and nodded. They casually strolled across the platform that connected the underwater viewing area with the park and back under the trees, where the shade was welcome. Bailey could already feel her arms starting to burn.

"I either need to find some suntan lotion or I need to stay in the shade more," Bailey said, touching her forearms. "I can feel the burn already."

"There's a gift shop in the welcome center. It probably has lotion."

"Where the restaurant was?" Bailey asked eagerly.

TJ chuckled. "Ready for that pizza now?"

"I could eat some pizza," Heidi said as she joined them on the path.

Bailey felt a recurrence of the jealousy bug as Heidi stepped between them.

"Pizza it is then," TJ said.

"Really?" Heidi asked. "You don't mind if I join you and Bailey? I can share academy stories while we eat."

TJ shook her head. "Bailey doesn't care about your lame bragging."

"No lame bragging. Just a couple TJ fiasco stories."

"Now those I want to hear," Bailey interjected. Despite her initial jealous feelings toward Heidi, she did enjoy the banter between her and TJ. "You guys met at the academy?"

"Yep, she held the door open for me on the first day," Heidi explained. "I thought she was a typical northerner, but she turned out to be okay."

"Just because Crawfordville is north of here, it doesn't make me a northerner," TJ groused.

"What's wrong with being a northerner?" Bailey asked.

"See what you started, Smith. Always the troublemaker. You can explain to Ms. Bailey why you have issues with northerners."

"I'm pleading the fifth," TJ mumbled.

Heidi roared with laughter. "For the right slice of pizza, I can be bribed for information."

"Fantastic. You choose and I'll buy," Bailey encouraged. "TJ's silence makes me curious."

TJ held the door for them as they entered the welcome center. The air-conditioning was freezing on Bailey's sunburned arms and she couldn't stop the shiver. She looked into the gift shop as they passed and was glad to see a row of suntan lotion bottles near the cash register.

"Go grab some lotion," TJ suggested. "I'll get your pizza. What kind do you want?"

"That would be great. Pepperoni or plain cheese is fine. A water too, please."

"Got it."

Bailey watched TJ and Heidi standing in the pizza line while she purchased her lotion and several bite-sized pieces of candy. Heidi's smile was genuine as she gazed at TJ and then laughed at something she said. Bailey was annoyed that she was being so bothered by Heidi's clear knowledge and depth of friendship with TJ.

TJ was still a mystery to her, and of course there was the dog issue. She could never like someone that didn't like Chewie. Not that there was any chance of anything between her and TJ. They had fun together and that was the extent of their relationship. Maybe one day she would be able to consider TJ a friend.

Bailey slid onto the hard, plastic bench beside TJ. She had only hesitated a second when she saw TJ and Heidi had chosen a booth rather than a table with chairs. It was a chance to be close to TJ and she felt good about it. No pressure. No agonizing analysis.

"I didn't buy your pizza, but do I still get a story?" Bailey asked Heidi after she had curbed her hunger with a few bites of the warm, gooey pizza.

"I don't see why not. Smith, do you want to choose?"

Bailey laughed as TJ shook her head and focused on the table. The woman always in control was not even going to offer a suggestion. Bailey was pretty sure once Heidi started that TJ would have something to say. And it only took one line to prove her right.

"Why Officer Smith doesn't like northerners," Heidi started.

"Nope," TJ interrupted. "Choose something else."

"Okay, how about how Officer Smith was given the boot at the academy?"

"You were kicked out of the academy?" Bailey asked in surprise.

"Not the boot from the academy, the love boot from her girlfriend," Heidi explained. "Or rather the 'not so love' boot."

"Nope. Same story, Barry. Choose again."

"Okay, okay. I understand. You don't want to talk about past loves with your new love," Heidi teased.

"She's not—" TJ started.

"We're not," Bailey said at the same time. "I mean, we're friends."

"Really?" Heidi asked, leaning back in the booth. "You could have fooled me. And I've seen Smith work her moves on a lot of women. A lot of—"

"Barry! Enough," TJ interrupted. "Bailey and I are friends. She's from out of town and wanted to see the manatees. I thought this would be a good place to bring her."

* * *

TJ sighed. She knew she was in trouble when she saw Heidi. Their friendship had been during a tumultuous time in TJ's life. Her father had crawled back into her life after several years in jail and at the same time the woman she thought was the love of her life had dumped her. TJ's emotions had been frayed to the bone and she was doing everything possible to cover their exposure. Women were a distraction that she needed. Unfortunately, she was also trying to gain some respect at her job by scoring at the top of her academy graduation class.

"How about the morning of water rescue training?" TJ suggested. She knew it would display her lack of judgment as well as her destructive personal demeanor during that time in her life, but she hoped Bailey would recognize that she wasn't that person anymore.

"Oh, that's a good story," Heidi cooed as she settled into the bench.

TJ groaned. She hoped Heidi wouldn't embellish too much.

"So, we'd been at the academy about five months. We were almost ready to graduate and start two months of specialized training. Our instructors had weeded the class down to the best and most dedicated so they had started to loosen the restrictions. Smith and a few of her drinking buddies decided to go out and party one night. Thursday nights were 'drink and drowned' for college students and the academy is right down the road from Florida State University."

TJ watched a family in line order food while she listened to Heidi tell the story she hadn't thought about in a long time. Unfortunately, she remembered the night like it was yesterday and the entire story had never been shared with her classmates that didn't join them.

The five guys she had went with that night would never tell on her, if they even remembered what had happened in their drunken state. Heidi didn't know that it was the last time she had ever taken a drink of alcohol inside a college hangout. She would like to say she had learned her lesson, but honestly she had seen what her life was going to be if she didn't get a handle on it. She had dreams and goals and being in jail was not one of them.

She felt Bailey's leg touch hers and glanced up. Bailey's eyes convinced her that her reputation wasn't at risk. She gave Bailey a smile to let her know that she was okay with Heidi's betrayal of her younger self. Anyone who knew her currently would never imagine that she had done so many irresponsible things early in life.

Heidi continued excitedly as she got to the end of the story. "All six of them were given tickets for public intoxication, but Smith was taken to jail for urinating in public."

TJ smacked her head on the table before lifting it and giving Bailey a weak smile. "It was not my most shining moment. Sadly, we were all peeing, but I was the only one with my pants down when the cops arrived."

Bailey laughed. "It seems so unfair. And," she said, raising her eyebrows, "so unlike you."

"The instructors had a great time using her in place of the water rescue dummy the entire next day," Heidi added.

"My skin was shriveled like an old prune for weeks. On a happier side, the Tallahassee Police Department released me without putting an arrest on my record."

"And you graduated top in our class," Heidi reminded her.

TJ bobbed her head from side to side, taunting Heidi. "Yeah, there's that too."

Heidi slapped her hands on the table as she stood. "That's all the time I have for storytelling today, ladies." She gave a slight bow. "Just a reminder that gratuities are welcome. That's for you, Smith, since I'm sure you used your badge to get in free."

"Yeah, yeah, yeah," TJ said, catching the puzzled glance from Bailey. "I'll catch you next time."

Heidi moved toward the garbage can to dispose of her trash and Bailey stood to follow.

"I didn't see you pull out your badge when we entered."

"I didn't. I paid the park fee. It's a small way that I can support the company I work for essentially. Plus, it helps feed the animals."

She saw Bailey smile as she turned to follow Heidi. Hopefully she had reinstated her sterling character after that horrible story that Heidi had to tell.

They left the visitor center and she posed for Bailey in front of the stone manatee fountain. Then she guided Bailey to the right to explore the portion of the park they hadn't seen yet.

"That's Lu's enclosure." TJ directed Bailey's gaze toward the high fence to the left.

Bailey stopped and looked. The water swirled as Lu emerged within feet of the shore and slowly climbed the concrete bank to grab a snack from the pile of fruit left for him.

"Let's keep walking. The storm clouds are moving in."

TJ's steps faltered as Bailey slid her fingers down TJ's arm and clasped her hand. They walked together silently. TJ tried to be cool about holding Bailey's hand and at the same time gripping it hard enough not to let it slide away.

"Oh, I know that animal."

"That's Yuma. He only weighed a pound when he was found abandoned. He was the first Florida panther to come here. The other is Sakata. He was only a few months old when found. Both have imprinted on humans and can never be released into the wild."

"Oh," Bailey exclaimed as Yuma sprinted across the enclosure and pounced on a cantaloupe left for her by trainers. "I'm so glad I had the opportunity to get the pictures when the one you caught was released."

"I look forward to seeing those pictures," TJ said, remembering earlier that day when Bailey had shot a few pictures of her. She hadn't known Bailey at all then and she had felt shy around her. She snapped out of her reminiscing when she saw her favorite animals ahead.

"Look how beautiful the wolves are. So much like dogs, but so wild too."

"My dog has a name, you know?"

TJ turned in surprise at Bailey's words. "Why do you keep saying that?"

Bailey started walking toward the next enclosure where birds flapped in the flowing water. TJ hurried to catch up with her. She waited for Bailey to offer an explanation, and when she didn't, she prompted her again.

"Would you please explain why you keep saying that?"

Bailey stopped on the path, facing TJ. She watched her forehead wrinkle as she struggled with her words.

"I keep saying that in hopes you'll explain your obvious dislike for dogs."

"What are you talking about? I love dogs."

"That's not possible. You have avoided my dog like the plague."

"I slept with your dog!" TJ exclaimed. She shook her head as a nearby woman turned to look at her. She grasped Bailey by the elbow and escorted her off the path to an area free of people. "That didn't come out right, but you know what I mean."

"I do, but that was forced. You were mostly unconscious for the duration and every other opportunity you have avoided her."

Bailey took a deep breath and TJ could see how upset she was. She wanted to say she didn't know what Bailey was talking about, but the truth was that she had avoided Chewie in the beginning. There were some dogs you met that seemed more intelligent and they were easy to get attached to. She knew Bailey and Chewie wouldn't be staying around. The immense sense of loss she had felt when Breezie died was still an open wound; she had thought it would be easier to avoid Chewie and thereby avoid the loss she would feel when she was gone.

"I didn't mean to hurt you. I like Chewie."

"You do know her name."

"Of course, I do. I knew the moment I met you that she was a good dog."

"I couldn't understand why you would dislike dogs."

TJ sighed. If she wanted any kind of friendship with Bailey she needed to explain. "I love dogs. I had a dog. She was a golden retriever. It's only been a few months since she passed away."

"Oh, I'm so sorry."

"I'm getting used to living without her, but I'll always miss her. Breezie was a unique animal. She always knew exactly what I needed from her."

She took Bailey's hand. "Chewie seems like a great dog too. I guess subconsciously I might have been keeping her at a distance because she is so great and I knew you guys wouldn't be around long."

Bailey let out a huge breath. "I'm so relieved to hear you say that. I know it's crazy but she's so important to me that it's hard to like people that don't like her."

"I totally get that." TJ gave her a mischievous smile. "So, it's safe to say you like me?"

Bailey pulled her back onto the path. "As long as you don't pee in front of anyone here in the park."

"Seriously? I'm going to be hearing about this for a while now, aren't I?"

"At least for today."

TJ laughed as they started strolling along the path again.

"Let's go see Lu and then get on the road. I think I have an idea for dinner."

Bailey smiled and TJ was surprised when she didn't ask any questions.

# CHAPTER EIGHTEEN

Bailey glanced at the time on the truck panel. It had been three hours since they had pizza at the park and her stomach was starting to growl again. TJ had made a call as soon as they climbed in the truck. From what Bailey could hear of the conversation dinner reservations had been made but she had no idea where. Her eyes had drifted shut from the movement of the vehicle, but they had been on the road for over an hour.

"So, about these dinner plans you have," Bailey said, breaking the silence.

"We have about twenty minutes until we get there. I doubt that dinner will be served right away, though. It's not even four yet. Are you hungry?"

"I'm getting there."

"Sometimes they have a few appetizers. Let me call and see what's been prepared."

TJ quickly switched the Bluetooth from the car back to her phone before Bailey could even hear someone answer.

"Appetizers have been requested," TJ said without offering a greeting to whoever picked up the other end of the phone. "We could grab something along the way if it's a problem. It seems I'm traveling with a hungry bear."

Bailey took a swipe at her shoulder. She was getting more and more curious as to where TJ was taking her. Somewhere that TJ felt comfortable obviously, since she was joking with the host.

"Sounds good. See you soon." TJ ended the call and tossed her phone into her drink holder. "Dinner will be served about six, but they have miscellaneous cheeses and crackers to keep us going until then."

"Where are you taking me that you can call and talk to them like that? It's obviously not a restaurant. Are we going to someone's house? I'm really not dressed for a social call."

"You're dressed fine for this adventure, but if you must know, we're taking a boat cruise."

"Well, that sounds fun," Bailey said excitedly.

She glanced at TJ a few times to see if she was going to give any additional information, but apparently that was all she was telling. Bailey's mind considered many options, but Florida had so many rivers and boating adventure tours she knew she would never be able to guess.

She watched TJ turn the wheel with her right hand while her left rested casually on the windowsill, barely touching the steering wheel. She seemed comfortable and relaxed. The conversation they had earlier had cleared the air between them. Bailey was glad they had the opportunity to have it. She was also glad that TJ liked Chewie.

TJ turned at a park entrance sign and pulled to a stop beside the boat ramp. Bailey slid out of the truck and stretched. She hadn't meant to fall asleep, but the sun and their early start had conspired against her. She was wide awake now, though.

"Looks like our ride's here," TJ called across the hood of the truck.

Bailey looked toward the dock and spotted two people and a boat. It was white with a dark-blue stripe down the side and a Florida state flag flew from the top of the mast. A woman waved from the front.

"That woman looks like Denise Dean," Bailey said in surprise.

"Not just looks like. She is Denise Dean."

"Is that our ride? Are we getting on that boat with her?"

"Yep."

She felt TJ take her hand and tug her toward the boat. Her feet felt heavy and she willed them to move forward. Denise Dean was a world-famous photographer, and Bailey had once stood in line for over four hours to get her autograph. She wouldn't tell that story today. She was sure she already looked like a drooling fan.

She grasped TJ's hand tighter as they approached the boat. A thin, pale man with gray hair sprang onto the deck and offered his hand to assist them. TJ gave him a hug and then climbed into the boat, hugging Denise in turn. The grin on TJ's face was huge when she turned to help Bailey on board.

Bailey stepped close as she jumped onto the boat. "You could have given me a heads-up."

"And ruin the surprise? You should see the look on your face. We're ready to go," TJ said, turning to face their hosts.

The man untied the ropes on the dock, leaping back on board and taking the wheel. Bailey watched Denise assist him as he backed the boat away from the dock and then she stepped toward Bailey with her hand outstretched.

"That's my husband, Steven, and I'm—"

"Denise Dean," Bailey gushed. "It's a pleasure to meet you."

"Well, thank you. The pleasure is all mine." Denise patted the back of Bailey's hand while they shook. "Although the company you keep leaves something to be desired."

"Hey!" TJ stepped close, wrapping her arm around Denise's shoulders. "Why would you say something so mean?"

"Because it's been over a month since you visited and I didn't realize it was you at first," Denise teased. She pulled TJ into a tight hug and then pushed her away. "Are you going to introduce your guest?"

Bailey blushed. She was so elated to meet this woman that she had forgotten to introduce herself. She must look like an idiot. She jumped in before TJ could.

"I'm Bailey Everett. It's really nice to meet you."

Denise looked at the camera around Bailey's neck and then at TJ. "Did you bring me a photographer to play with?" she teased.

"She is. She also has several photography books published. That's why she's in Florida. She focuses on a different state in each book."

Denise raised her eyebrows. "You're *that* Bailey Everett. I've seen your work. Very nice." She pulled Bailey close as she turned them toward the front of the boat. "Let's talk shop."

Bailey's pulse raced. She was having a chat with Denise Dean. She was sure this ranked right up there with her best day ever. Especially given the smile that covered TJ's face. She smiled back at TJ as she leaned close to hear Denise's words over the sound of the boat.

* * *

TJ watched Bailey follow Denise to the cushioned seats at the front of the boat. The look on Bailey's face was priceless and she laughed again. Bringing her here had been a good idea.

"Didn't tell her who she would be riding with, did you?" Steven said with a chuckle.

"Never." TJ's voice was muffled against his chest as she hugged him again. "Where would be the fun in that? Did you see the look on her face?"

"She was surprised. What have you been up to?"

She had barely finished telling Steven about the capture of the panther when Denise came toward them with Bailey following.

"Did Denise fill you in on our history?" TJ asked Bailey as they approached.

"A little, but you're not off the hook," Bailey said as she helped Denise pour wine into glasses for her and Steven.

Denise produced a platter of cheese and crackers from the cooler under the front seats and handed Bailey two bottles of water. TJ took a seat beside her on the cushions lining the rear of the boat. Steven slowed the engine and turned in his chair to grab a few crackers and cheese squares from the platter as Bailey passed. Denise sat on the railing with her feet on the cushions.

TJ studied her friends. Denise was elegant and sophisticated with the appearance of a twelve-year-old on the playground. Peach tank top, cutoff blue jean shorts, and no shoes. Her hair was cut short around the base of her head and the top dangled across her eyes every time she turned her head. Steven was so pale that she often wondered how he managed to own two boats without a tan.

"So where are we?" Bailey asked, looking at the group.

"We are on the Silver River headed toward Silver Springs," TJ answered.

"Oh, let me," Steven called. "I'm TJ and I'll be your guide today," he said, in a high-pitched, squeaky voice.

"Stop teasing her, Steven," Denise chastised.

TJ shrugged at the look Bailey was giving her. "I used to insist on being the guide whenever I would travel with them."

"From about the time she was ten until she joined the FWC. Then she realized she didn't know everything." Steven chuckled.

"Steven!" Denise slid off the railing and pushed Steven's chair around to the front. "Let's you and me get us up the river and let TJ entertain her friend."

"Let's do that," Steven said, wrapping his arm around Denise and pulling her close. He looked over his shoulder at TJ. "Let me know if you need help with the entertainment."

TJ shook her head at him as she turned sideways in her seat. Bailey met her gaze for a moment and then went back to watching the water.

"I want to hear all about how you know Denise and Steven but not right now. Now I want to hear about the critters on the river."

"Okay, let's start right there." TJ pointed to a tree in the middle of the river. "That's an anhinga on that branch hanging over the river. The tan head means it's a female. The males are all black. They are sometimes called the snake bird because of their long necks. There are nearly five hundred different species of birds in Florida. It's kind of a bird-watching paradise, but there are plenty of other animals along a river too."

Four turtles lay on a log near the shoreline and slipped into the water as their boat drew close. "Those are river cooters. They like to sunbathe on the logs to dry the algae on their backs, but they're very skittish."

"Yeah, I bet. I can't believe how close that alligator is to them."

"Right, but they didn't run until we got close. They're not bothered by the alligator."

"Won't alligators eat them?"

TJ chuckled. "They will, but they don't seem to mind sunbathing near each other." She spotted a black bird in the sky about fifty feet above the river. "Oh, watch this."

"What kind of bird is that?"

"It's an osprey. They can spot fish in the water from over a hundred feet away. When they see their target, they bend their body, pointing their head down, and dive feet first toward the water."

"Wow. Do they go under?"

"Sometimes. They have the ability to close their nostrils."

The osprey disappeared underwater for a few seconds and then soared into the air with its catch.

"Did you see it shifting the fish in its talons when it came out of the water?" TJ asked. When Bailey nodded, she continued, "They turn the fish so it won't slow down their flight."

In the middle of the river on a small island, she spotted the white chest of another osprey high on a branch of a tree. On a nearby branch was an anhinga with its wings spread wide to each side. She pointed out the birds to Bailey.

"The osprey is a bird of prey. It has very dense plumage that is oily and helps prevent its feathers from getting waterlogged. The anhinga has to sit like that to dry their feathers."

"I always think of flamingos when I think of the birds of Florida."

"Most people do and few know that the mockingbird is actually the state bird. The few flamingos you might see in

Florida are mostly in the Everglades area, but there are some in captivity like we saw at Homosassa."

The boat's speed increased and TJ looked at Steven.

Denise was scrolling through images on her phone. "Someone just posted monkey pictures. If you guys can wait a little longer for dinner, we'll run up there and see if we can catch them."

"Yeah. They're worth seeing," TJ agreed, smiling when she saw the quizzical look on Bailey's face. "Yes, she said monkeys."

"Cool. I think I heard something about them once," Bailey said excitedly. "They were brought here in the 1930s for the Tarzan movies, right?"

TJ shifted back toward Bailey. "I've heard that story before, but it's not completely true. There were six Tarzan movies filmed here in the 1930s, but the monkeys were brought here for tourist revenue, not to be part of the movie. A local entrepreneur named Colonel Tooey ran jungle boat tours on the Silver River back then. He thought creating a monkey island would help his business, so he selected an island and then built a habitat. I've heard that he didn't know that rhesus macaque monkeys could swim, but others say he had actually ordered nonswimming squirrel monkeys and got these instead. Either way, his six rhesus monkeys were swimming off the island before he even made it back to his boat."

Bailey laughed. "I bet he was surprised."

Steven laughed with her. "Probably not as surprised as out-of-staters that run into monkeys while hiking nowadays in Ocala National Forest."

# CHAPTER NINETEEN

Bailey followed TJ and Denise to the front of the boat as they approached several brightly colored kayaks. Steven shut off the boat motor as they drifted toward the shoreline.

"There's one," he called, pointing into the trees.

Bailey looked in the direction he was pointing. There was a large dock on the left side of the river and she could see movement beyond it. She lifted her camera and used the zoom lens to bring the furry pink faces into view.

"I can see two and they're both headed toward us," she told the others.

"We often see them in this area," Denise said. "They like to sit on the dock railings."

As if they heard Denise's words and were willing to put on a show, one monkey after another came forward from the darkness of the trees and took a seat on the railing around the dock. Walking on all four feet, they traveled along the railing and then took a seat, lining up to face the river and their audience.

"I sure didn't expect to have monkey pictures from Florida," Bailey said as she snapped pictures. She glanced at TJ. "They're not in captivity now, right?"

"Correct. There are hundreds of them living near Silver Springs and in the Ocala National Forest."

"Oh, are we in the park now?"

"Technically yes," Steven answered. "All of Silver River is considered within the park, but we're about a mile or so away from where the glass bottom tour boats depart."

After about ten minutes or so, the monkeys began to leave the dock. They left in the order they arrived and continued walking on the railing until they were close enough to jump to a nearby tree.

"I guess the show is over," Bailey said, finally pulling the camera away from her face. "That was great. I'm glad we got to see them."

Steven started the boat engine again and pointed them down the river. TJ returned to the comfortable bench at the rear of the boat and Bailey followed her. There wasn't a lot of wind with the speed they were traveling, but there was a bit of shade in the rear of the boat.

Bailey nudged TJ. "So, tell me why you are making that face."

TJ grimaced. "Was I that obvious? I didn't want to ruin this for you."

"Only moderately obvious," Denise said.

"Extremely obvious," Steven added. "Go ahead and tell her the rest now that she's seen them."

"Tell me the rest of what?" Bailey asked.

TJ sighed and pulled her feet up on the bench, hugging her knees. "I've always loved the monkeys, especially as a kid. As a conservation officer I see the issues with nonnative animals and especially one without a natural predator."

"Alligators won't eat them?" Bailey asked.

"They can sometimes catch a naïve young one, but mostly no. So without a predator they reproduce at a rapid rate. In the early 1980s, my nature-loving employer began removing them in large numbers, so a couple hundred were trapped and sold to research labs or zoos or some had an unknown fate. The community erupted in opposition, and they were forced to stop. But in the last couple of years, I've heard rumors that they're concocting another plan and that this time they want to get rid of all of them."

"That's terrible," Bailey said sadly.

"Yes and no," Steven interjected. "They have a herpes virus that can be deadly to humans."

Bailey looked at Steven and then back at TJ.

"He's right," TJ said. "But there haven't been any confirmed cases of a monkey to human contraction. Scientists say it's spread through saliva and other bodily fluids and the monkeys have been known to bite and throw feces. Which doesn't help their cause much. No one cares much when the nonnative Burmese pythons are caught and killed, but the monkeys are cute. While a part of me understands the issues, the other part of me remembers how much I've enjoyed seeing them over the years."

Denise groaned. "We try not to dwell on what might happen and just enjoy them when we see them."

"That's a good way to look at it," Bailey said as she stood. "I'm going to give my dogsitter a call and check on Chewie."

She pulled her phone from her pocket and stepped away from TJ and Denise. She had noticed TJ watching her and that Denise had slid across the bench to sit beside her. She pulled up Mr. Maxwell's number and pressed dial. He answered on the first ring and seemed happy to hear from her. He began to rattle on and on about what he and Chewie had been doing all day. After his greeting, she had blocked him out, trying to hear the conversation going on behind her.

"She's pretty cool," Denise said.

"Yeah, we've had fun today."

She wasn't surprised that she agreed. She'd had a lot of fun today with TJ and meeting Denise Dean was certainly a bonus.

"We're glad you called us," Denise said. "It's nice to see you with someone you like."

"Oh, we're not together."

*Yikes.* TJ seemed pretty adamant about that. She was sure Denise was frowning by the tone of her voice.

"Well, I thought it was odd that your grandmother hadn't mentioned that you had a new love interest, but I have to say the way you guys interact it sure seems like you are together."

"Grams hasn't met her."

Denise laughed. "She's going to be sorry she stayed away so long, but I won't tell her if you don't want me to."

Mr. Maxwell pulled her back to the conversation, but she said her goodbyes as quickly as she could. TJ and Denise were talking about dinner and the mention of food made Bailey's stomach growl.

"It's all good," she said, returning to sit beside TJ. "Mr. Maxwell is spoiling her rotten."

"I declare that it is time to eat," Steven exclaimed. "TJ, take the wheel."

TJ slid behind the wheel as Steven followed Denise to the front of the boat.

Bailey moved to stand beside TJ and for the first time looked at the boat they were traveling in. Except for the exterior stripe everything inside and out was a pristine white. There were several electronic gadgets mounted around the wheel and an overhead cover that could be raised if needed.

"Are you scared?" TJ asked, bumping her.

"I don't think so. Should I be?" she teased.

"No, I'm a very good driver." TJ laughed maniacally as she slid her hands loosely back and forth across the steering wheel to imitate swerving.

Bailey shook her head. "Don't ruin our great day by wrecking this beautiful boat."

"Maybe you should drive then. Come here."

"No!" Bailey exclaimed.

"Really. Come here. I'll help you. There's nothing to it."

Bailey reluctantly slid between TJ and the wheel. TJ covered Bailey's hands with her own and placed them on the wheel.

"This is a twenty-one-foot Tahoe with a center console and an outboard motor."

Bailey closed her eyes, enjoying the vibration of TJ's voice and the warmth of her breath near her neck. *Crap!* Her eyes flew open as she searched the river in front of them for any obstructions. She took a deep breath, holding it for a second before releasing it.

"That's nice, but all I really care about is how do I know if the water is deep enough."

TJ laughed, pointing at one of the electrical gadgets. "That's a navigational system with a depth finder. You need at least three feet."

TJ shifted to Bailey's left, resting her hand on Bailey's hip and keeping her left hand within reach of the wheel. Bailey gripped the wheel, sliding her fingers into the molded spots along the sides of the wheel. It didn't feel much different from driving a car. She began to relax a little, except for the pressure of TJ's body against her back.

"On average the river flows at about three miles per hour, which is plenty fast enough. Steven dropped us into neutral, but if you feel like we're drifting too far to either side we can put it back into gear," TJ explained.

"I saw the No Wake sign earlier. How does that translate to speed?"

"It doesn't necessarily. A good driver could go as much as ten miles per hour and not produce a wake, but most stay under five. By law you're responsible for the wake you produce. You don't want to damage someone's dock or flip a kayaker. A wake can also do damage to the ecosystem on the riverbanks."

Bailey nodded as she noticed several kayaks coming into view ahead of them. "Things look crowded up ahead. You should take over."

TJ stepped behind her and wrapped her arms around her to grasp the steering wheel. Bailey stayed in the cocoon of her arms as a wave of warmth washed over her. She wanted to stay here forever. TJ's hands lingered on top of hers.

"I got it," TJ said, her voice a little deeper than Bailey had noticed before.

She leaned against her for a few minutes before forcing herself to duck out of TJ's embrace. She wasn't sure how they had reached this point. And she wasn't completely sure when she had started to feel differently toward TJ. She had thought TJ was attractive from the moment she met her, but now she was having feelings she wanted to explore. She wasn't sure TJ wanted to, though if you measured TJ's interest based on the feel of her embrace maybe there was more there than Bailey had thought.

Denise and Steven returned with a platter of sandwiches and a small dish of potato salad for each of them. Steven flipped a table into place beside them and set the platter on it. Bailey's mouth watered as she tried to wait the appropriate amount of time before grabbing a sandwich. They had been made on slider rolls and she could see how soft they were without even touching them.

"This half is turkey cold cuts and that half is veggie," Denise said, motioning to each side of the platter. "We weren't sure what you liked to eat, Bailey, so I wanted to have a meat-free option."

"I'll eat some meats, but I appreciate the veggie option."

"Me too!" TJ said, grabbing from both stacks of sandwiches.

Steven bumped TJ with his shoulder. "Like we didn't know that. Next time we'll do steaks."

"Oh yeah, next time we'll take the Thoroughbred," Denise added. "Then we can grill and have a real dinner."

"It's a houseboat," TJ explained to Bailey.

"Oh, cool. I've always thought it would be cool to live on one of those. You could change your front yard every day."

"I've spent plenty of nights on theirs," TJ said. "The rocking to sleep is not as soothing as people think."

"No," Steven said, laughing. "It took you plenty of nights before you didn't have motion sickness."

"I'm good now, but I prefer to have my feet on the shore before bed."

Bailey followed TJ's lead and grabbed a sandwich before digging into the potato salad. The roll was as soft as she had imagined. Everything tasted amazing and she was sure it wasn't only because she was starving.

Steven passed a can of soda to TJ and offered one to Bailey.

"She doesn't drink anything with carbonation," TJ explained.

"That's true," Bailey said, surprised that TJ knew that. "I'll stick with the water, but thanks for offering."

"I wish I didn't like soda," Denise added. "I could drink them all day and never touch water, but I know I would gain fifty pounds in a day."

"I've never cared for carbonation. Even as a kid I avoided it," Bailey explained.

"That's amazing. You must be the only kid in the world like that," Steven chimed in. "I like my carbonation mixed with alcohol."

Bailey laughed. "I'll drink a glass of wine, but I've never messed with the hard stuff."

"Well, I don't know if you can call it the hard stuff if you water it down with soda," Denise teased her husband.

"Hey, it's more alcohol than soda. I got this," he said, sliding into the driver's seat and pushing TJ off the other side.

"Damn, man!" TJ exclaimed as she regained her footing by holding on to his shirt.

He swatted playfully at her hand stretching the tail of his shirt.

"Children!" Denise interrupted TJ and Steven's banter. "So, Bailey, how long will you be staying in Florida?"

"A few more weeks at least," Bailey said, glancing at TJ. That was something TJ had not asked her. She only had the condo rented until the end of the month. The real estate agent had been bugging Mona about reserving it for another month. Mona knew she didn't stay places more than two months, but instead of saying no outright she had contacted Bailey to see.

For the first time, she was thinking about staying longer. She always enjoyed taking photographs and the thrill of returning to the same location to see what different animals might cross her path, but this time was different. She was preoccupied. Florida had more animals than she could cover with one book, so her lack of interest wasn't the photography side. She knew what it was. TJ was on her mind all the time now. Did she want to stay longer? She needed to make a decision. Did she want something more with TJ? She wasn't sure she was ready to think about that yet.

"So, have there been a lot of movies filmed on this river?" Bailey asked, deflecting her vague answer as to how long she would remain in Florida.

"Oh yeah," Steven chimed in. "In the 1930s it wasn't just Tarzan. There were several television episodes like *Sea Hunt* with Lloyd Bridges. You probably never heard of that one. There were scenes from James Dean's *Rebel Without a Cause* and the James Bond movie *Moonraker*. Silver Springs is probably the most famous for *Creature from the Black Lagoon*, though."

"Wakulla Springs, too," TJ added. "That's outside of Crawfordville. Have you been there yet?" she asked Bailey.

"No, but I've seen the signs. I feel like I've seen as much wildlife wandering around myself and with you than I would see at a park like that."

"That's probably true. Turtles, birds, gators, and an occasional manatee. Oh, and of course fish. Do you put fish in your books?" TJ asked.

"I haven't. I initially started out doing only mammals, but well, you know."

TJ laughed and looked at Steven and Denise. "There's no love lost on snakes."

"Right," Bailey agreed. "And when I went to Arizona it was hard to skip snakes—"

"And scorpions!" Denise added.

"That's really only the beginning for Arizona," Bailey continued. "They have a lot of venomous creatures like blister beetles, desert centipedes, and several varieties of spiders."

"And don't they have a dinosaur-like lizard?" TJ asked.

"Yep, that's the Gila monster. Sounds like a children's horror story and I didn't want to believe it when I first heard the name. It's true, though, and you can see them in my book. They are mostly nocturnal and usually only bite in self-defense, but they can grow up to almost two feet in length. Not something you want to encounter all alone, late at night."

"Did you use a guide to get your pictures?" TJ asked.

"I did. I prefer to work alone, but if I wanted to include those creatures then I had to go where they were." Bailey shivered involuntarily and TJ laughed.

"What did you envision when you started doing these books? Cute, little cuddly bears or creepy crawly creatures?" TJ teased.

Bailey laughed. "My agent asks me that all the time and I'm not sure. I just wanted to take pictures."

"Sunsets and mountains are nice," Denise laughed.

"Yes, I should have followed your example," Bailey agreed.

Much sooner than Bailey expected, they were returning to the dock where they had started their trip. Steven had turned on their running lights about ten minutes earlier, but full darkness was still thirty minutes or so away.

Bailey did what she could to help Steven prep the boat for travel as Denise brought the truck and trailer over to the ramp. Mostly she followed TJ around and helped or took over anything she thought she could handle. Securing anything that would blow out was the easiest once TJ showed her how the seats lifted for storage.

Within ten minutes the boat was loaded and they had said their goodbyes. Bailey was sad to see their time together end, and she hoped she would have a chance to visit with Denise again. She could remember the first Denise Dean picture she had ever seen. She had only been able to afford a small version of the print, but she still had it on the wall in her apartment in New York.

Bailey was surprised when Denise approached her with outstretched arms.

"You're a friend now, so hugs are required," Denise said with a smile.

Bailey embraced her and felt the warmth. She wasn't surprised that Denise was a hugger, but it made her think about how many people she had in her life that she hugged. She considered Mona a friend, but they didn't hug. Was it her? Or Mona? She enjoyed Denise's embrace and wondered if she had let it linger too long. She quickly stepped away to avoid any awkwardness.

She exchanged a quick hug with Steven and watched while he and Denise took turns squeezing TJ tight. She looked forward to hearing TJ's story of how they had all became friends. She hadn't asked Denise when they talked earlier. They had mostly talked about taking pictures and how she knew TJ.

# CHAPTER TWENTY

TJ waved to Denise and Steven and then walked around the truck. She had never been a door holder even when she was out on a date. It always felt weird to her. Maybe she dated taller women that didn't need a hand getting in her truck. Yeah, that must be it. Whatever it was, she pulled open Bailey's door and offered a hand to help her inside.

Bailey stepped forward but stopped when she was between TJ and the truck. She was inches from Bailey's body. So close she could touch her with only a small lean in her direction. She could feel Bailey's eyes on her. The day had faded to night and the streetlights that lined the dock were too far away from where TJ had parked to offer any light. The dome light in her truck didn't come on and she remembered turning it off the other night to better see a video clip Joey was showing her.

The world stood still. Should she kiss her? She wanted to kiss her.

She took a step closer, leaning into Bailey. She could feel Bailey's breath on her neck and she wished she could see her eyes. Did Bailey want her to kiss her? Bailey was the one that had stopped and turned toward her. Surely, that was a signal that contact was welcome.

She gripped the truck door with her right hand but gave her left permission to wander. She felt the goose bumps on Bailey's arm as her fingers lightly slid up under her shirt sleeve. She gripped her bicep and pulled their bodies together. The warmth was stunning. The flutter in her stomach took over and she bent her neck to close the distance between their lips.

She was going to kiss her. If Bailey didn't want this too, then she was going to have to tell her. Her night vision was starting to increase and at this distance she could almost see Bailey's eyes.

Kiss her now. What was she waiting for? She could feel Bailey's breath on her lips now and she knew the touch of them would be softer than a pillow.

"It's really dark out here," Bailey said softly.

"Uh...yeah." TJ cleared her throat. "I forgot I had turned off my dome light."

She felt Bailey nod and then she slid her hand into TJ's. She had watched Bailey stretch to get in the truck earlier and had thought about helping, but this time it felt natural. She grasped her hand and helped her slide onto the truck seat. She could have walked away at that point, but she didn't. She stood in the open door for a few more seconds before shutting the truck door.

She was going to be kicking herself for a long time for missing that moment. She should have kissed her.

She wasn't sure what to say when she climbed behind the steering wheel. Had she gone too far? Bailey had instigated the contact, but this wasn't familiar ground for TJ. The women she dated had been easy. She always knew where she stood with them. If they were on a date, then she knew the boundaries. This was different.

"We have about a three-hour drive ahead of us so I'm going to gas up before we get on the interstate," TJ said, pulling into a gas station.

"Great! I need some road snacks."

"Can you grab me a root beer, please?" TJ asked.

"Sure. Any snacks?"

"Chips and chocolate of any kind is fine."

TJ was still kicking herself when she pulled the truck closer to the store and watched Bailey wandering the store. It had been the perfect moment and she had missed it. What was she afraid of? She wasn't looking for a relationship and Bailey was perfect. She would be gone in a couple of weeks. She was still trying to decide if that was a good thing or a bad thing.

She jumped from the truck and went inside the store.

"I'm getting a drink with ice since we'll be on the road for a while. Would you like that too?" Bailey asked.

"Sure." TJ reached for the cup and filled it with ice and root beer before clipping on the lid. Bailey stood beside her, filling her cup with fruit punch. They fought about who would pay for the snacks at the counter and TJ finally let Bailey do it. Her argument that TJ had driven and filled the gas tank seemed worthy. She held the bag and drinks as Bailey settled into the seat, then passed them to her. Bailey set a bag of chips and M&M's on the console between them.

"Those are for you. I got popcorn if you want some."

TJ pulled onto the interstate and set the cruise control before she picked up the bag. It seemed like hours since they had eaten the sandwiches and she quickly consumed all the chips. It wasn't until the last one was in her mouth that she realized she hadn't offered Bailey even one.

"I'm sorry. I should have offered you a chip," TJ said with embarrassment. "I guess I was hungrier than I thought."

"Yeah, me too," Bailey said, tossing her empty popcorn bag into the trash bag.

"Should we stop and get some real food?" TJ asked.

"No, I'm better now. Let's get home. Eating might make me sleepy."

"You can sleep. I'm good for now and I'll wake you if that changes."

"I'll think about it, but right now I want to hear about how you met Denise and Steven."

"Oh that's a short story. Denise grew up beside my grams. Denise is about ten years younger than she is, but she followed Grams everywhere she went when they were growing up."

"How is it that you never mentioned you knew her?" Bailey prodded.

"Everyone that knows me knows that we're close so it's not something I think about. She's not really famous to me."

"Well, I think it is neat and I really appreciate you taking me there. I had a wonderful day and I got some great pictures."

"Will you use the monkeys in the book? They're not native to Florida."

"No, I won't, for that reason," Bailey said firmly. "But it was fun to see them."

TJ settled into the drive and easily answered all of Bailey's questions about the animals they had seen today. It wasn't long before they were merging onto Interstate 10 and heading west toward Tallahassee.

TJ reached for the M&M's and bumped Bailey's hand going for her drink. She quickly realized Bailey had picked up her root beer.

"That's the wrong cu—"

It was too late. Bailey already had a mouth full of carbonated soda. Her eyes grew huge and her arms flailed. TJ took less than a second to think before pulling Bailey's mouth to hers and accepting the root beer and then turning her eyes back to the road.

She had taken gum and even candy from other women's mouths, but never anything like this. It was disgusting and gross, and yet she was a little bit thrilled. She swallowed warm root beer, which tasted horrible, but she had also felt Bailey's lips. And she had been right—they were really, really soft.

She sat in the awkward silence, waiting to see how Bailey was going to react.

When Bailey finally spoke her voice was soft. "I can't believe you did that."

"I can't believe *you* did that," TJ responded, breaking into laughter. "I thought you were going to spit it in my truck."

"I didn't know what to do. I was shocked by the taste."

"And yet you willingly spit it into my mouth."

"You offered!" Bailey exclaimed. "I don't know what I would have done, but it wouldn't have been that."

Bailey went silent and TJ kept glancing at her. It appeared Bailey was still in shock.

"That was really so gross, you know," Bailey finally said. "We can never tell anyone."

TJ chuckled. "You're right." She held up her right hand. "Pinky swear."

Bailey hooked her pinky around TJ's, still shaking her head. "I swear never to tell a soul what happened here tonight."

TJ's chuckle turned to a full laugh. "I still can't believe you did that."

"I can't believe it either, but I can't believe you offered that as an option. I could have spit it back in your cup."

"Yeah, because that's less disgusting."

"Well, you wouldn't have to drink it!"

TJ gave her a big grin. "Does that count as our first kiss?"

"No! Absolutely not."

"Why not?"

"Because we are never speaking of it again. I'm erasing it from my memory."

TJ laughed. "Yeah, I know you're right. No one would ever understand if we told."

Bailey punched her arm. "You pinky swore that you wouldn't tell. You better not."

"I won't. I've wiped it from my mind too." But she knew it wouldn't be easy to forget the softness of Bailey's lips. "So, how did you become a photographer?"

"I—"

"Wait. I don't even know where you're from? New York, right?"

Bailey was silent for a few seconds and TJ glanced over at her.

"Was that too personal?"

"No. I was just thinking about how I wanted to answer. If you read my bio, it'll say New York, but I was born and raised in a suburb of Massachusetts. I barely made it to graduation and I haven't been back. Now I consider New York my home, I guess."

TJ could hear what wasn't spoken and she knew enough lesbians who left less-than-hospitable homes as soon as they were old enough. She wanted to ask why Bailey had left but it didn't seem important.

"And how did you decide to be a photographer?"

"When I moved to New York, I found a little one-room apartment over a camera shop. It wasn't completely a coincidence. I was visiting the shop when I saw their apartment for rent sign. When the man who owned the store found out I was interested in photography, he gave me a job and began teaching me."

"So, on-the-job training?"

"Mostly. Mr. Anderson let me borrow his camera and I would travel to every park in the city. There are over fifteen hundred in New York City."

"No way. Fifteen hundred?"

"Yep. I'd come back with tons of photos. Birds, squirrels, and occasionally a non-city animal in one of the more rural parks. Mr. Anderson would give me pointers on what would make the photo better and I'd go back out again. The Internet had information but it wasn't what it is today so I'd play around and experiment with the settings on the camera."

"Mr. Anderson helped you get started then."

"He did. He didn't know a lot about taking photos, but he had an eye for composition and how to frame a subject. And he was a master at developing them."

"Do you still develop your own shots? Not many places do that kind of developing anymore."

"You're right. Everything is digital now. I don't have a darkroom, but I've always wanted to. I really like waiting for the picture to appear and feeling like I had a hand in its creation."

"Why don't you?"

"There is no space in my apartment and Mr. Anderson passed away about six years ago." Her brow wrinkled in thought.

"Honestly, until this very moment I had forgotten how much I enjoyed it. After my first book, my life was taken over by doing another one. Having an agent means never straying from what brings in the money. Mona keeps me on track."

TJ didn't ask any more questions. She could hear something in Bailey's voice. Maybe remorse or regret at something she had lost.

Several hours later TJ pulled to a stop bedside Bailey's Jeep and slid the gear shifter to park. She couldn't believe the day was over. This morning she couldn't wait for the day to be over and now she didn't want it to end.

"Do you want to come over for dinner tomorrow?" she asked, surprising herself and apparently Bailey, judging by the look on her face.

"I would. Can I—"

"Yes, bring Chewie."

Bailey smiled. "I was going to ask if I could bring anything, but bringing Chewie is the best." Bailey opened the door and slid to the ground. "She probably won't be happy that I've been gone all day."

"Okay. We'll make it up to her tomorrow. She can run all she wants."

# CHAPTER TWENTY-ONE

TJ crested the small hill at the end of her driveway and was surprised to see light pouring from the living room window. She circled to the side of the house and parked beside her grandmother's Volkswagen bug. It was a medium blue that the dealership called ocean blue, but TJ called it Smurf blue.

"Grams," TJ called as she opened the back door.

"In here," Katie answered.

Her grandmother stood at the kitchen counter peeling apples. It was almost ten and her grams looked like she was only starting her day. TJ crossed the room and kissed her on the cheek.

"What are you doing up?"

"Getting a start on tomorrow's baking."

"Oh, yum, are you making apple pie?"

"I am. Did you have a good day?"

TJ dropped into a chair at the kitchen table. "I did."

"You sound surprised."

"I am."

"Why's that? She sounds lovely."

TJ laughed. "Denise called you, didn't she?"

"She might have."

Grams placed a bowl of apples in front of TJ. "Help me and we'll have fresh applesauce for dinner tomorrow, too."

TJ slid the knife around the apple, separating the peel from the meat of the apple, and then sliced the apple. Should she suffer the inevitable teasing from her grandmother about inviting Bailey to dinner or wait and call Bailey to cancel. There wasn't a place she could take Bailey that wouldn't cause talk and Grams was putting too much work in for TJ to cancel on her.

"Spill it," Katie said, sitting down beside her.

"What?"

"Whatever it is that you aren't telling me."

"I invited her over for dinner tomorrow."

"Well, that's great! I can't wait to meet her."

"Yeah, that's what I'm afraid of." TJ laughed as she ducked the fresh-cut apple peel her grandmother threw at her.

* * *

Bailey buckled Chewie's seat belt and slid behind the wheel of her Jeep. She wasn't nervous about going to TJ's house for dinner. Okay, maybe a little. She was definitely nervous about the connection she had felt between them yesterday. TJ's hot and cold interest in her was confusing at the least. Maybe tonight she would be able to get TJ to talk about herself more. Being in TJ's space would be enlightening and for that she was excited.

It was a short drive down Highway 98 to the dirt driveway that led to TJ's farm. She wasn't sure it would be considered a farm by most people's standard since there weren't any animals. Having lived in the city most of her life, though, she considered anything over two acres a farm.

The driveway was a mixture of sand, dirt, and crushed oyster shells, which made for an easy-to-follow white trail. The trees and brush on the sides were cleared back, leaving several feet of green grass on each side. Lots of mature trees, mostly pine and water oak, offered shading until she came within sight of the house.

She didn't remember much about the house or property from when she dropped TJ off after she had been sick. She had been distracted by the situation. Today she had the time to appreciate the charm of the wraparound porch that hugged the one-story farmhouse.

TJ's personal and work trucks peeked out from behind the house, but she wasn't sure she was supposed to knock on the back door. She split the difference and parked on the side of the house closer to the front door.

As she helped Chewie out of the Jeep, she noticed another vehicle beside TJ's truck. A little Volkswagen hatchback was nestled closest to the rear door of the house. Did TJ have company? Or maybe that was her grandmother's car.

She clipped on Chewie's leash and started toward the front of the house. The squeak of the screen door on the back porch stopped her. A woman with a petite frame and short gray hair stood at the top of the porch stairs. She gave a little wave, motioning Bailey toward the rear of the house. Chewie eagerly changed direction and Bailey followed.

The woman held the door open with her backside as she bent to greet Chewie.

"Easy," Bailey reminded the dog as they approached.

The woman didn't appear frail—in fact she was quite the opposite—but Chewie could get a little overeager when meeting someone new. Based on her greeting of the dog, the woman was an animal lover.

"Hi," Bailey said tentatively, wishing she could remember TJ's grandmother's name. "I believe TJ is expec—"

"Hey," TJ said enthusiastically as she emerged from the house barefoot. The cuff of her denim jeans drug on the floor and the T-shirt was stenciled with FWC across the front. "Come on in, Bailey. This is my grandmother, Katie. Grams, this is Bailey Everett and her dog, Chewie."

"Hi, it's so nice to meet you, Bailey. Come in. Come in." Katie patted Bailey's shoulder as she passed in front of her. "Your dog is beautiful."

"Thank you. She loves meeting new people and seems to have a fondness for you already," Bailey said as Chewie took a seat at Katie's feet, her head held high as she stretched for pets from the dangling hand.

"TJ and I are definitely dog lovers, as I'm sure TJ has mentioned."

"Well—" Bailey said hesitantly, meeting TJ's eyes.

TJ held up her hand to stop Bailey from saying anything else. "We had some confusion about my level of dog love, Grams, but I think we have it worked out now. Right, Bailey?"

Bailey nodded as she watched Chewie move from Katie's feet to TJ's. It was like the dog had always known them. She resisted the urge to give the leash a tug to bring Chewie back to her side.

Bailey followed them through the door, appraising the cute design as well as the wonderful smells. She hadn't seen the kitchen when she had dropped TJ off and she appreciated that it wasn't too small or too large. Tucked into the left corner in front of a large single pane window was a restaurant-style seating booth. A long countertop stretched the length on two sides and a small island with barstools was adjacent to the sink.

"Wow, that's a great smell," Bailey exclaimed.

"Grams decided to make a ham so Chewie would have a bone. If that's okay with you, of course," TJ said, quickly adding the last.

"I don't normally give her human food, but I guess it's okay this time."

"Most of the meat has cooked off of it, but we won't force the issue. You can decide when you see it." Katie moved into the kitchen and began to gather dishes.

"I know it's only four, but Grams and I like to eat early so we can have dessert before bed."

"I won't argue with that. Can I help with anything?"

"Nope, have a seat and watch us work. Turn that dog loose. She can't hurt anything in here," Katie told her.

Bailey looked at TJ and she nodded. "The doggie door in the hallway goes into a small, fenced section, so she's safe."

Bailey unclipped Chewie and settled onto the cushioned bench seat at the table.

"Breezie, that was my dog," TJ continued, "always stayed close to the house, but I put in the fence to keep her safe at night."

"You never know what might be lurking around outside after dark," Katie added. "TJ brought a camera home from work when my flower bed was being torn up every night. I was pretty sure it was an armadillo, but it was fun to watch it on the video anyway."

"I love them," Bailey added. "The way they scurry around is so cute."

"They are cute but can be very destructive. Just ask my flowers. You'd think living with a conservation officer that I could have more wildlife control."

TJ shrugged at her grandmother's joking. "What can I say? Armadillos love mulch."

Bailey was enjoying watching TJ and her grandmother maneuver around each other and the kitchen. It was a dance they had clearly been doing for a while. She reached out and took the plates from TJ as she approached the table.

"I guess the mulch hides many insects beneath its surface," Bailey added.

"That it does."

TJ set a dish of homemade scalloped potatoes and one of mixed vegetables on the table. She turned in time to take the plate of ham from her grandmother.

Katie pulled a fist-sized ham bone from the freezer and held it out for Bailey to see.

"It should be cooled enough by now. I can give it to her or we can skip it."

They all looked at Chewie, who licked her lips and laid her head on the floor, looking up at them.

Bailey blew out a breath. "How can I say no to that face?"

"Great," Katie said as she disappeared into the hallway.

Bailey heard the door open and TJ's grandmother cooing to Chewie as she led her into the fenced yard.

"She may not go home with me after this treatment," Bailey joked.

TJ slid across from her and began filling her plate, passing each dish to Bailey as she finished.

"Grams and I wouldn't complain."

"Why don't you get another dog?" Bailey asked as the door closed in the hallway and Katie returned to the kitchen.

TJ shrugged. "We aren't ready yet."

"You aren't ready yet, my dear." Katie held up her hand. "And that's okay. You take your time healing. I can wait. I've missed the unwavering love that only a dog can offer, though."

"I'm sure Chewie would be happy to be your surrogate until you get a new dog."

"Chewie is welcome to stay with us any time."

TJ nodded her agreement.

"Mr. Maxwell has been great about keeping her when I go anywhere I can't take her."

"Karl?" Katie asked as she exchanged a look with TJ.

"What?" Bailey asked with concern.

"Nothing," TJ said, gently digging an elbow into her grandmother's side. "Mr. Maxwell is a nice man."

"I didn't say he wasn't," Katie said quickly.

"What?" Bailey asked again when Katie laughed.

"Stop it, Grams. He was good to Breezie even if he was using her to get close to you."

"Oh," Bailey said and then laughed with them. "I could see that. He's pretty flirty even with me."

Bailey waited patiently for Katie to fill her plate before she took her first bite. The potatoes were cheesy and perfect with the steamed vegetables and salty ham. She couldn't remember the last time she had a home-cooked meal. She wasn't sure what she had expected coming to dinner at TJ's house, but this wasn't it. She had to attribute much of the comfortable feeling to Katie's hospitality. Everything about the woman and the kitchen exuded warmth and contentment.

She tried to eat slowly, but the food was so good her plate was empty before she realized it. She glanced up casually to make sure TJ and her grandmother weren't watching her stuff food into her mouth. TJ met her eyes and dropped her fork loudly on her empty plate.

"That was so good, Grams. I'd eat another plateful, but I know there's an apple pie cooling on the counter."

"And I'm about to cut it. Who's in?"

"Oh, I don't—" Bailey started.

"We both are!" TJ cut her off. "Make it small if you must, but don't miss out completely."

Bailey smiled. Her stomach was full, but she had been considering adding more potatoes to her plate anyway. "Okay, yes. I'm in."

Her eyes met TJ's and her smile widened. A lot like the TJ she had enjoyed yesterday with Denise and Steven, the woman across from her was relaxed and jovial. She tried to match her image of TJ that first time they met in the forest to this woman. She had seen the serious, professional side of TJ in other work situations but without a doubt this was her favorite version.

"And is there vanilla ice cream?" Bailey asked. "Or is that sacrilege, based on the homemade deliciousness of the pie?"

TJ jumped up from the table and pulled open the freezer door. "Nothing wrong with decorating the pie," she said, dropping a half gallon of vanilla-bean ice cream on the table. She added a scoop of ice cream to the top of each slice of pie and it immediately began to melt. The bowls were emptied as quickly as they had been filled.

"I may never walk again," Bailey groaned.

"Let's test that theory," TJ said, standing. "I could use a walk. Grams?"

"I'll sit on the porch, but that's as far as I plan to walk tonight."

Bailey laughed and followed TJ out the back door. Chewie followed them, but she seemed reluctant to leave Katie's side. Or maybe it was the hope of another bone.

"You can stay, girl," Bailey encouraged her.

Chewie threw herself on the floor at Katie's feet and Bailey shook her head.

"I guess she's made her decision."

"Since Chewie isn't coming with us, do you want to ride or walk?" TJ asked.

"Hmmm, that sounds exciting. What would we be riding?"

"A dirt bike or a four-wheeler. Come look and then you can decide."

Bailey followed TJ to a three-stall garage across the yard from the house. TJ unlocked the walk-in door on the side and hit the button to lift the middle overhead door. The light coming in showed a dirt bike and four-wheeler sitting side by side. Shadowed in the far stall was a large tractor and near where they stood was a mowing tractor and miscellaneous lawncare items.

TJ sat on the dirt bike as Bailey wandered around looking at the bins filled with nuts, bolts, and screws.

"My father collected stuff like that. He always thought it would come in handy. I guess it does. Whenever we need something around the house, Grams or I will wander out here and then return with it or at least something that works."

"Your dad's not around anymore?"

TJ looked around the garage before answering Bailey's question. "He died right before my twenty-first birthday."

"I'm sorry. I guess."

"I guess?"

"Well, instinct told me to say I was sorry. I mean it's sad to lose a father, but then I'm reminded that having him stay might have been worse."

"I see. No, he wasn't a bad man. He was in and out of jail all through my teenage years. Mostly petty crimes. He liked to steal cars and smoke dope. I was happiest when it was just Grams and me." TJ rubbed the dust from the mirror of the bike she sat on. "It's been ten years, but not long enough for the remorse to go away."

"Remorse?"

"Yes, remorse for not taking advantage of the time I had with him. I blamed him for Mom leaving when I was five. Even though I came back to Crawfordville several years before he passed away, I didn't really clear the air with him."

"I'm sure he knew you loved him, but why did you come back?"

TJ smiled. "You don't love my little red town?"

Bailey chuckled. "It doesn't seem like the place a young lesbian would enjoy."

"It certainly wasn't that. I guess I could say I came back for Grams, but truth is I missed being here."

"Where were you?"

"Citrus County. In the area around Homosassa Springs. That's where Denise and Steven lived. I moved in with them after graduating from the academy."

"So, you've worked in Wakulla County for ten years?"

"Yep. Combined with growing up here, you could say I know this area like the back of my hand. What about you?"

"This area is certainly pretty."

"True. How did you manage to avoid a New England or New York accent?"

Bailey shrugged. "I move around a lot. So, what about that ride?"

TJ tilted her head, but she didn't push for more answers. "What's your poison?"

"I find the dirt bike alluring, but I guess my conservative side says four-wheeler."

TJ handed her a helmet and leaned over to switch on the key before pushing the start button. "The accelerator is a thumb lever, right here. Brake is—"

"Aren't you driving?" Bailey asked in surprise.

"I can if you want me to."

"I do. I've never driven anything like this."

TJ buckled her helmet and swung her leg over the gas tank between Bailey and the handlebars. She revved the engine a few times and then popped it into gear.

"Ready?" she asked.

"What should I hold on to?"

"Me," TJ said over her shoulder. She waited until she felt Bailey's fingers wrap around her belt loops. "This time we'll play it safe for your conservative side, but next time we'll go faster."

"Next time?"

\* \* \*

Bailey squealed again as TJ accelerated hard on the little hills. Her arms were wrapped tight around TJ's middle. She couldn't tell if TJ accidentally pressed the accelerator hard or if she had intended to surprise her, but her goal seemed to be to keep Bailey's arms where they were.

She braced herself against TJ's back as they circled the trail and headed back across the stretch of little hills. She wasn't sure what passenger rules were, but clinging tightly to TJ felt so good.

She was surprised at the way she felt around TJ. Truth was she had felt it the first moment she had met her in the forest. She had ignored it because that was what she did. She had stopped putting herself out there for others to hurt. It wasn't that she didn't care about others. She did, but she also had the ability to turn off her feelings.

She had always felt like there was something wrong with her. When her friends and coworkers were delving into others' lives, asking about their wants and desires, she noticed that she had to remind herself to ask as well. Common questions like "How was your weekend?" or "How is your family?" didn't come naturally to her. Maybe it didn't come naturally to anyone and she was making more out of it than was necessary. Still, she had always felt like something was missing.

The passionate "I can't live without you" love that she saw on television or read about in books seemed unobtainable. She couldn't imagine feeling that way about someone. She had had a few girlfriends and had enjoyed those first few weeks of lovesick headiness, following each other everywhere and talking or texting continually, but it always dissipated quickly. When she met people like Denise and Steven who had been together for so long, she always watched them, wondering if they were pretending. When she saw a couple that seemed sincere, it made her feel all the more that something was wrong with her.

"Have you had enough?" TJ asked over her shoulder. "It's going to be too dark to see shortly."

"Yes, let's head back."

TJ punched the accelerator and then let off, forcing a surprised Bailey backward and then slamming her into TJ's back.

Bailey punched her arm. "Stop it," she said, laughing.

TJ pressed the accelerator twice more in rapid succession.

Bailey squeezed her arms as tight as she could around TJ's stomach.

"Stop, stop. I give. You win," TJ gasped.

Bailey was laughing so hard she didn't release her immediately.

"Seriously, you're squishing my apple pie."

"Not sorry," Bailey said, sliding her hands back to TJ's belt loops. "Stop driving crazy or you might see my apple pie again."

"Puking is not allowed. And Grams will make you stay at the house with her and Chewie next time."

"Oh, the threats."

Bailey slid off as soon as TJ stopped the four-wheeler. In the final minutes of the ride, her laughter had drifted away, leaving an emptiness. She hadn't realized until then how much fun she was having, and the realization that the evening was coming to end brought unexpected sadness.

TJ locked the garage and they walked side by side across the yard. Darkness was starting to settle over the pasture and the trees were like giant hovering beasts.

"Want to stay for popcorn?" TJ asked softly.

"Hmmm."

"Or not."

"Do you think there is any apple pie left?"

TJ laughed. "Absolutely."

"I wonder where those two are," Bailey said as they stepped onto the empty porch.

"I bet I know. Follow me."

TJ opened the kitchen door and slid off her shoes. Bailey did the same. Walking quietly, they stopped at the entrance to the living room. Grams sat in her recliner with her head resting against the back and Chewie lay on the couch beside her. Neither of them opened their eyes at the intrusion.

TJ stepped back into the kitchen and pulled two bowls from the cabinet. Bailey grabbed the ice cream from the freezer and two spoons from the dish strainer. Catching the microwave before the time ran out to avoid the beep, they quietly added ice cream to the top of their warm apple pie.

TJ led the way onto the back porch and Bailey happily followed. She slid a bite into her mouth before her butt even touched the chair.

"This is possibly the best pie I've ever had."

"My grams is certainly the best cook in town."

"Truth is that I don't even like apple pie or cherry or peach. Berries are okay, but really pie should be coconut or chocolate cream."

"That's good to know. Any other secrets you want to share?"

Bailey looked at TJ. Her silhouette was all she could see even with the light coming through from the kitchen.

"I don't stay long enough in any one spot to make real friends."

"Is that a threat or a warning?"

"Funny." Bailey took another bite of the pie. What was she trying to say? That she was surprised at how much she enjoyed TJ's company? Or that she liked having someone to joke around with?

"Sorry. I wasn't trying to be insensitive," TJ said.

"I know. You deflect emotions with humor."

"Wow. That's insightful and very accurate. But enough about me. Let's talk about your inability to make friends."

Bailey chuckled. Coming from anyone else she might have been offended. She had been trying to be honest. The night was still and quiet and seemed to call for honesty.

"It's not an inability really. More of a lack of desire," Bailey explained.

"Oh, so this is a warning."

"Would you call us friends?" Bailey asked.

"I certainly think we're getting there. Don't you?"

"Yeah, I guess so."

"That's a lot of enthusiasm. I won't force you to keep my company or to stay in touch once you leave."

She wasn't sure if TJ was joking, but she didn't want her to think she didn't care. She did. She cared what TJ thought. Maybe she *was* capable of feeling something. What would TJ think about being her experiment? Probably not the best way to move forward.

"I've had a really good time with you."

"So have I. Let's just agree to enjoy whatever moments we have until you leave," TJ suggested.

"Agreed."

Was it that easy? She didn't have to worry about hurting TJ if she left and never looked back. That seemed unlikely, but she'd take TJ at her word for now. That niggling part in the back of her mind still wanted to analyze the what-ifs. What if she didn't want to leave TJ without looking back? What if she wanted to remain friends? What if she wanted to explore being more than friends?

"Your ice cream is melting," TJ said softly.

Bailey mixed the melting cream with pie crust and took a bite.

"Stop making things difficult," TJ demanded.

Bailey looked at her and frowned even though she was pretty sure she couldn't be seen in the darkness. She liked the way TJ had pulled one foot up on the chair and leaned on her knee.

"You're frowning at me, aren't you?"

Bailey released a sigh. "I don't know how to keep things simple."

"Just enjoy the moment. Whatever happens will happen."

"And you won't be upset if I walk away?"

"I didn't say that. I've kind of gotten used to having you around and I've really enjoyed the last two days."

"See? It's not simple."

"I would be hurt, maybe even crushed." TJ chuckled. "But life goes on. I wouldn't stop living without you."

TJ stood and pulled Bailey to her feet.

"If everyone spent weeks analyzing how to move forward there would be no kissing. What would a world be like if there was no kissing?"

Bailey held her breath. TJ's face was inches from her own, and even without contact she could taste the ice cream and pie on TJ's tongue. She wanted to move toward her. To encourage her. *Oh, please kiss me.* She felt and heard TJ take a deep breath. In the dark, she couldn't tell if it was a resigned sigh or if TJ was gathering the strength to do what they both wanted.

Bailey couldn't wait any longer. Her fear that TJ would walk away from this moment without kissing her was larger than her fear of acting on an impulse. Tentatively she stretched her neck forward, barely allowing her lips to make contact with TJ's. She pulled back for a moment and then pushed forward again. TJ met her eagerly.

How had she been so wrong about this woman? TJ wasn't the cold, hard person she had thought she was when they met. She was soft in all the right places and her touch was warm. *Oh, when did her hand get under my shirt?* This wasn't happening. They were making out on TJ's grandmother's porch. *Oh, yes they were! And it was incredible.*

Bailey broke the kiss and sucked in a breath of air. Had she forgotten how to kiss? TJ must think she was an idiot. In the darkness beside her, she heard TJ inhale deeply.

"Grams!" TJ exclaimed, dropping her arms and turning toward the kitchen door.

Katie and Chewie stood looking out through the open door.

"Sorry," Katie said, laughing. "I didn't know you were out here in the dark. I was listening for the motorcycle."

Bailey took a step away from TJ and reached out to run her fingers through Chewie's fur as she sat at her side. "I should get home."

"Oh, don't let me rush you off," Katie said. "I'm getting some pie and going back to my chair."

Bailey waited to see what TJ would do when her grandmother left. Would they kiss again? She wasn't in any hurry to leave if that was the option for staying.

"Sorry about that," TJ said softly.

"It's okay. I should get home." She pushed open the screen door and Chewie ran ahead of her to the car.

"I hope we can do this again soon."

"Yeah." She opened the car door and Chewie climbed across her seat. "Me too."

*Soon. Soon.*

She buckled hers and Chewie's seat belts and dropped the car into gear. In the rearview mirror, she could see TJ standing on the porch watching her leave.

Maybe leaving without looking back wasn't one of the options.

# CHAPTER TWENTY-TWO

TJ spent days thinking about Bailey and resisting the urge to visit her. So, they had kissed. Did that mean she was supposed to call her or that she could call her? She had never had a problem making decisions, but lately she was second-guessing herself at every turn. Even her work was suffering.

As if to prove a point, she realized the sounds of a nearby bird was not normal chirping. It was the frantic cry of something in trouble. She began to jog toward the sound. This area of the forest was dry, but the direction she was moving was not. She really hoped she would reach the source of the sound before she reached the water.

She pushed through the bramble of bushes and briars. She could hear the change in the sounds around her and knew she was close to the swamp. She chose each step carefully, watching the ground for anything that slithered. She spied the mother bird before she saw the nest floating on the water below the limb where she sat.

TJ didn't hesitate, wading quickly into the water and praying that it wouldn't be too deep when she reached the nest. It was less than three feet from the edge of the water so she felt fairly confident she could make it. Belatedly remembering the rules of personal safety, she called Joey to back her up. She wasn't going to wait for him, but at least he would be headed her direction if things went wrong.

She stepped back out of the water and pulled a rescue rope from her pocket. A knife and a rope were two of the most important things she carried with her. She tossed the rope over a nearby branch, making a knot, and then tied the other end around her stomach.

She waded into the water again. Stagnant water in Florida was seldom cold even in the fall, but it was still shocking as it seeped into her boots. The mud on the bottom was squishy but not suctioning so much that she couldn't lift her feet.

The mother bird had stopped squawking and that was good news. Her noise could bring predators. It also gave TJ the feeling that she wasn't going to dive bomb her head when she approached her babies. She unbuttoned her FWC shirt and wrapped it around her arms before scooping up the nest, babies and all.

She safely returned to the bank and looked around. Now she had to decide where to put the nest. The water wasn't moving, so the nest had probably dropped directly under where it had been positioned. There was a fork in the tree near where the mother bird sat.

She heard Joey coming through the thicket and called him to her location. She was happy to see he had brought a scoop net, which she quickly set the nest in. She climbed the tree and Joey handed the handle of the scoop net up to her. She pulled it up until she could reach the nest, sliding it into the crook of the tree. She tossed the net back to Joey and scurried down the tree.

They moved a distance away, waited silently until the mother returned to the nest, then walked silently away. When they were back on the main path, she felt free to talk again.

"Thanks for coming so quickly."

"No problem. I was in the area." He looked her up and down. "You're a mess."

She looked down at her wet pants. They were soaked but salvageable. She twisted the shirt in her hands, wringing the water from it before sliding it back over her tank top.

"Nice," Joey said, laughing. "Good as new."

She gave him a wave as she headed back to her truck, grateful that the rescue had taken up some of her day and taken her mind away from Bailey.

She pulled a tarp from behind the seat of her truck and covered the driver's area. This wasn't the first time she had wet clothes and with her job it wouldn't be the last. She returned to the office and closed out her day before heading home, anxious to get home and out of her wet clothes.

* * *

Bailey looked up as TJ stepped onto the porch. She almost laughed at the puzzled tilt of TJ's head and the way she hesitated to come closer.

"Welcome home," Bailey said.

"Uh, thanks."

TJ stepped out of the shade and Bailey was able to see her wet clothes.

"Oh wow. Hard day at work?" she asked.

"You could say that."

"Another wildlife rescue adventure I see," Katie said as she opened the back door. "Go ahead and strip right there because you are not stepping a foot in my house."

Bailey watched the blush wash across TJ's face and again she held back a laugh.

"I should be going," Bailey said as she stood.

"Oh no, Bailey. I promised you dinner," Grams said, looking back and forth between Bailey and TJ. "Come help me in the kitchen and we'll give TJ room to get over her shyness."

Finally giving in to her laughter, Bailey followed TJ's grandmother into the house. She stood at the table grating carrots for a salad and trying not to look through the window on the back door. TJ paced back and forth for a few minutes and then slowly began to remove her boots. She turned her back to Bailey as her pants and shirt came off. Dressed in nothing but a black tank top and thigh-length boxers, she pulled open the kitchen door and walked through. Bailey didn't meet her eyes, not that TJ was looking at her either, but she did watch her backside until it disappeared.

She had expected TJ to have a fit body because of her job and that had been mostly confirmed when TJ was sick. The wet undergarments hugging TJ's body today left a lot less to Bailey's imagination. The width of her shoulders narrowed into the curve of her waist and the tight muscles of her buttocks. Bailey swallowed hard and focused on the carrots in front of her, afraid to look around for fear that TJ's grandmother was watching her.

Quickly finishing with the carrots, she added them to the bowl of shredded lettuce, following with a handful of sliced radishes. Finally glancing up, she realized that Katie had everything else on the table and was adding plates and silverware. She hurried to help her.

"What do you think of Florida?" Katie asked.

"I like it. Even though it's hot."

"True. How do we compare with the other states you've been in?"

"I was surprised at how green it is. When you think of Florida, you think of palm trees and beaches."

"We have a little of that here, but being so far north we do have the green too. Some folks say we are actually part of South Georgia rather than Florida."

"I can see that."

Chewie leapt through the doggie door, her head held high. "You look proud of yourself. Did you clear the yard of geckos?" she asked the dog.

Chewie's tongue emerged and she gave a few happy pants. Bailey took that to mean yes. She called her back onto the porch and gave her some water and a bowl of kibble.

"She probably wouldn't bother us, but I'll leave her on the porch while we eat," Bailey told Katie when she came back in.

"Sounds good. Or you can put her in the front like we did last night. Let's sit down. TJ should be back in a minute. She's fast at showering."

Bailey took a seat across from TJ's grandmother, leaving the head of the small table for TJ. Bailey gave a contented sigh. Gathering the meal with Katie and greeting TJ when she returned from work were daily rituals that she could get used to. She felt at peace here. At home even. More than she had ever felt at her apartment in New York. Being with TJ and her grandmother was what she had always thought being with family should feel like.

TJ slid into her chair and looked at them quizzically. "What are you waiting for?"

"We were waiting for you," Katie said, giving TJ's arm a slap. "Don't act like we have no manners."

TJ laughed. "We have manners, but I can't wait. Everything smells so good."

"I agree," Bailey added, following TJ's lead and spooning rice onto her plate before passing the dish to Katie.

"Where's Chewie?" TJ asked, adding a large scoop of green, leafy mash to her plate before passing the dish to Bailey.

"She's having her dinner on the back porch," Bailey explained, putting a tiny dab of the greens on her plate. She had always stayed away from any cooked greens. Spinach, kale, or collards, it didn't matter, she couldn't tell them apart anyway. Once cooked they became a mushy mess. Today, though, she would try them.

"You don't have to eat them," TJ said, interrupting Bailey's fork halfway to her mouth.

"Well, they smell good," Bailey said, putting a smile on her face.

"Grams adds bacon so they have a good taste too, but some people don't like the texture. I thought you might be one of those people, based on the look on your face."

"I won't be offended if you don't like them, Bailey. You might have to develop a taste for them. Hang around here long enough though and we'll get you all hooked up."

Bailey moved the fork to her mouth and slowly chewed the greens. They were a bit stringy but warm and they did taste of bacon. Not as bad as she had expected. She would eat the rest on her plate, but then she'd stick with the chicken and rice.

She looked up to see Grams and TJ watching her. "Not bad."

Katie nodded. "I'll take that."

Bailey listened while TJ recounted her day and the baby bird rescue. Then Katie told them about her trip to Ohio to visit her friend. Bailey nodded a lot and made appreciative noises while she ate, but mostly she enjoyed the family camaraderie.

After the table was cleared and dishes washed, Bailey followed TJ to the porch swing. The daily thundershowers had passed while they ate and the frogs were now enjoying the aftermath. Their energetic chirping filled the air.

"If you were wondering how I came to be crashing your dinner, I ran into your grandmother at the grocery store. Apparently she didn't approve of the canned soup I was buying," Bailey explained.

"That sounds like Grams."

The squeak of the swing threatened to cover the chirp of the frogs, and Bailey put her toe out to stop it. TJ was quiet and Bailey strained to read her face. Was TJ upset that she was there? There was no reason not to ask.

"Are you upset that I'm here?"

"Oh no. I'm happy to see you."

"And yet you're being extra quiet tonight."

"It's been a long day."

Chewie came through the doggie door and rested her head on Bailey's knee.

"I guess it's time for us to go."

"I'm sure Grams has something planned for dessert."

"Tempting, for sure. What do you think, Chewie?"

Chewie was focused on the wall above Bailey's head and didn't even acknowledge Bailey's mention of her name.

"What is it, girl?" Bailey asked, turning in her seat to see behind her.

"It's a green tree frog," TJ said, pointing to a small lump near the windowsill.

Bailey jumped to her feet and was through the screen door before TJ could question her destination.

She returned a few seconds later with her camera.

"Oh, picture time," TJ said.

Bailey shrugged. "Sorry, I can't help myself. He's really cute and so green."

"Then you'll like the anoles. Let me see if I can find one."

"What's an anole?" Bailey asked.

"It's a lizard. A lot of people call them geckos."

"Oh, I know what those are. I've never heard anole, though."

TJ stepped outside. "Yeah, here. You have to see him before I mess with him."

Bailey frowned. "What happens when you mess with him?"

"He morphs into a snake."

"What!" Bailey froze in midstep.

"I'm kidding. He changes color."

"Really." Bailey came toward her and snapped a couple pictures of the lime-green lizard lying on the rock ridge that lined the flower bed.

TJ stepped forward and squatted beside it. When it took a hop, she shifted with it. Bailey moved with them, snapping pictures. TJ finally coaxed it into her left hand, slapping the right one over it to hold it in.

"Do they bite?" Bailey asked.

"They can, but I'm not squeezing him so hopefully he won't. There are over four thousand species of lizards in the world and about seventy of them live in Florida. The majority aren't native, but this little guy is, though. He's a green anole."

TJ placed him on the side of the house and stepped away so Bailey could see.

"Oh, he turned brown."

"Yes, most people think they change to match their surroundings, but the truth is green is their happy color. Brown or black means they feel threatened or uncomfortable. They'll also turn white for a really short time when they're shedding their skin."

"He's already turning green again," Bailey said as she followed him up the wall with her camera. "Oh, what's he doing now? Are those pushups?"

"Yep, that's his mating ritual. I think he likes you. Watch for the red flap of skin under his chin." TJ paused as the anole flared his dewlap.

"I'm impressed. Do you think it's for me or Chewie?"

Chewie jumped at the lizard, trying to get close enough to sniff him.

"I'm sorry to say probably neither." She pointed at a smaller lizard farther up the wall.

Bailey took a few more pictures and then turned the camera on TJ.

"Hey, stop that!"

"Come on. Pose for a shot or two. You know you want to," Bailey teased as the camera continued to whirl.

TJ grabbed a stick Chewie had been carrying around earlier and gave it a toss.

"Perfect. Action shots."

TJ tried to ignore Bailey and the camera as she chased Chewie around the yard. After a few minutes, she collapsed on the porch, Chewie at her side.

Bailey walked around the yard snapping pictures of the house and farm before joining TJ with a shrug. "Pictures help me remember the feelings of the moment after I'm gone."

"You could stay."

"What happened to 'distance makes the heart grow fonder'?"

Registering Bailey's dismissal of her comment, TJ didn't push.

* * *

Bailey inserted the camera card into her computer and began to browse the pictures she had taken throughout the day. When she got to the lizard shots, she slowed. The first pictures of TJ bounding around the yard were blurry.

She contemplated TJ's words. "You could stay." *Right.* She wasn't sure if TJ meant for the night, which would have been awkward with Katie in the house, or permanently. She wasn't sure she was ready to think about the possibility of that.

She moved to the final pictures on the memory card, which showed TJ sitting on the porch with Chewie. They were clear and solid. It seemed natural and perfect. Yes, perfect. Was her life finally coming into focus?

# CHAPTER TWENTY-THREE

"Go visit her."

"What?" TJ pulled the earbuds from her ears and dropped them on the coffee table in front of her.

"Just go visit her already," Grams repeated.

"Go visit who?"

"Teresa Jane, do not play dumb with me. I'm not going to watch you bumble around this house again tonight. If you refuse to visit Bailey, then please go to work."

TJ chuckled. "I've been at work all day and if Bailey wanted to see me then she would call."

"When have you ever been the one waiting on a phone call? Get off your butt and go see her. Take her for dinner or better yet a picnic. Then you can take Chewie too."

"Seriously, Grams. You have this all planned out. Why don't you call her?"

Grams squeezed TJ's cheek and cooed at her. "I can do it for you if you're too scared."

TJ shook her cheek loose. "I'm not scared. I just don't want to bother her."

Grams shook her head. "I'm going to bingo with Nellie. Don't let me see you sitting here with those dang things in your ears when I get back."

The kitchen door slammed, and TJ sank back on the couch.

"They're called earbuds. And I like music." She resisted the urge to add, "So there." It was her evening to spend any way she wanted. She didn't have to see Bailey if she didn't want to. But that was the problem, wasn't it? She wanted to.

She had been checking her phone repeatedly for the last two days in hopes Bailey would call or text. Nothing. Instead of doing something about that she was sitting at home. Why? Grams was right. She had never before waited on anyone.

Her truck tires threw gravel as she pulled out of the driveway. Now that she was in motion, she was in a hurry to get to where she was going. Which was where? Was she going to show up at Bailey's door without calling? No. She couldn't do that.

She would drive through Shell Point and maybe she'd run into her. Yeah. That was a good idea. She just happened to be in the area. Was there any chance Bailey would buy that? She didn't and it was her idea.

She stopped at the store on the corner as she turned off of Highway 98. Procrastinating was not her thing either, but she really was thirsty, right? And she had left the house without eating dinner. She walked up and down every aisle in the little store. The hot dogs under the heat lamp were almost dehydrated and the pizza slices were so shiny with grease her stomach clenched at the sight. She grabbed a pack of peanut butter crackers and a soda.

In the car, she tucked the crackers into her center console. Peanut butter would make her breath stink. She knew being worried about that was ridiculous, but she still couldn't bring herself to eat one. Even when her stomach growled. She was committed to making one swipe through Shell Point and then she was going to Mack's and having a cheeseburger and fries. Comfort food always made her feel better. At least while she was eating it.

She lowered her window as she reached Pelican Bay Road and then sat a little longer than necessary at the stop sign. The blue waters of the Gulf of Mexico stretched in front of her as far as she could see. There was a hint of salt in the air and she felt the stresses she had been carrying blow away with the breeze.

As she drove the half-mile strip to Bailey's condo, she changed her mind about the peanut butter crackers. Pulling into the public parking area in front of the beach pavilion, she climbed out of the truck with the crackers and her soda. She sat on the picnic table and rested her feet on the bench. Opening the pack of crackers, she shoved an entire one in her mouth.

"TJ?"

Her head jerked in the direction of Bailey's voice. The cracker grew dry in her mouth as the peanut butter acted like glue between her tongue and the roof of her mouth.

*Crap! I have peanut butter breath.*

"What are you doing here?" Bailey asked, stepping on the bench to sit beside her on the table.

"I...uh...was in the area."

Bailey laughed.

"What? I was."

"I don't doubt that, but why were you in the area?"

"I was...I mean...I...uh."

Bailey laughed harder. "Why can't you admit that you came here to see me?"

"Maybe I was here to see Chewie."

They both looked up as Chewie splashed through the water in front of them.

"She's happy to see you too," Bailey said.

"I can see that," TJ said, standing. She took a step and tossed the remaining crackers into a nearby trash can. She wasn't sure what she had expected, but she was certain things weren't going as she thought. She had come here because she couldn't stop thinking about Bailey, but now she felt awkward and was unsure of what to say. "I should go."

"Wait," Bailey said, reaching out her hand. Her fingers stretched toward TJ like the arms of a starfish desperate to catch the retreating tide of the Gulf waters.

TJ stared at Bailey's hand. Without taking a step, she could easily grasp it. Her mind raced with images of what could happen if she did. Without conscious thought, she raised her arm and entwined her fingers with Bailey's. The warmth of the connection raced up TJ's arm, streaming into every part of her body.

TJ followed the pull of Bailey's arm until she stood between Bailey's legs. She locked her eyes on Bailey's, trying to convey all the things she felt. The desire and the fear of wanting something more than she ever had in her life. She placed her palms on Bailey's thighs and froze as Bailey's fingers danced up her arms and into her hair.

* * *

The softness on her fingers of the bristles of the shaved hair on TJ's neck sent a shiver of desire through Bailey's body. She let all thoughts fade as she stared into TJ's smoldering brown eyes. Her wants and desires seemed to be written in the swirling chocolate there, and Bailey felt it all. All the what-ifs flashed through her mind again. What if the geographical distance between them didn't matter and things could work out? What if she kissed TJ? What if she gave in to having what she wanted without fear of the consequences?

The smell of saltwater and decaying vegetation reached Bailey's senses, reminding her where they were. She slid her feet to the ground and stood, causing TJ to take a step backward. She felt Chewie come to a screeching halt at her side and glanced down to see her tail whipping back and forth as she pushed her nose into TJ's hand.

Bailey knew in the pit of her stomach that if they walked away from this moment it would be lost forever. She couldn't let it pass. She didn't want to leave Florida and wonder if she might have had a chance at something she had given up on. Something that could awaken that part of her she thought she had forgotten.

"Right. I'm going now," TJ said as she bent and scratched Chewie's head.

"Wait. Do you want a drink?"

"I...uh."

"No pressure. I just opened a bottle of merlot, though, if you're interested."

They both looked down at Chewie as her nose pushed into TJ's hand again. It wasn't a reminder that she was there to be petted but more of a prod to answer the question. Bailey smiled. Her dog was working on her behalf. Together she and Chewie would open TJ's heart to what they had to offer.

"I'd like that," TJ finally answered.

Bailey clipped the leash to Chewie's collar and the three of them crossed the road together. She wanted to take TJ's hand but hesitated. TJ had pulled away from her each time they took a step closer to each other. If she touched her now, would TJ climb in her truck and leave before they even reached her apartment? She needed to keep things light and trust that they were following a path that had already been marked for them.

"Did you work today?" she asked.

"Yes."

She glanced at TJ and saw a small smile starting to spread across her face. She felt TJ's fingers slide around her hand, their fingers entwining easily. She relaxed and leaned into TJ's strong grip, knowing a decision had been made and, in that moment, it did not matter what she did or said. Even if she was leaving for her tour in a few days, their path would not change.

Bailey had felt this almost from the moment they had met, but she had resisted, afraid of obtaining something she had wanted for so long and the loss that inevitably would follow. Now it felt good not to care. TJ fit easily into her life. When she had been sick and staying with her, Bailey had never felt uncomfortable or a sense of urgency to get TJ out of her space. What if she moved here and TJ was always beside her?

Chewie led the way up the stairs and Bailey followed. Her fingers returned TJ's tight grip as she clung to that what-if. She unlocked the door and pushed it open, allowing TJ to enter first. Unclipped, Chewie settled onto her bed with a big sigh. Bailey almost laughed. Chewie's matter-of-fact indication that she knew she would not be a part of what came next was humorous. Until she met TJ's eyes.

The emotions swirling in them—fear, desire, resolve, were mesmerizing, and Bailey couldn't look away. She was on the verge of having everything she ever wanted. She knew TJ was seeing those same emotions in her eyes and more. Attraction, arousal, and love. *Wait...love? Where did that come from?*

As the words sank into her soul, she watched fear win the battle and register in TJ's eyes. Bailey knew in a second TJ would be gone and she would be left cold and alone in an empty room. She couldn't let that happen.

She dropped Chewie's leash and her keys and, taking a step forward, pushed TJ backward, feeling the gasp she made when her back hit the wall. She pressed her lips to TJ's lightly, giving TJ a chance to respond or reject. Bailey was already gone. She needed TJ as much as she needed her next breath.

Bailey eagerly deepened the kiss when TJ wrapped her arms around her, pulling their bodies tight. She spread her fingers across Bailey's back and pressed into her flesh, clinging to her like you would to a life preserver in a tumultuous ocean. The taste of TJ's mouth was sweet and earthy with a tinge of salt. *Yum. Peanut butter.*

TJ's tongue danced across Bailey's lips, enticing Bailey's tongue to follow each stroke. It was a dance to a song that only they could hear. Bailey pulled away and took several quick gasps. Her head was fuzzy, and flashes of light careened in the darkness behind her eyelids. She did not open her eyes, though. She only needed to feel TJ's body to know this was right.

* * *

TJ felt the tickle of Bailey's hair across the backs of her hands and lifted her fingers, letting the strands fall between them. Cradling the back of her head, she devoured her mouth. She rocked her lower body against Bailey's hips and thighs, searching for the pressure it craved. The contact was hard and then light as they each moved to stoke the fire that was raging inside them.

TJ felt her legs grow weak. She was not going to be able to stand much longer. She pushed Bailey toward the couch. Taking advantage of the small gap between their bodies, she ran her palms across Bailey's chest, feeling the swell of her breasts and letting her fingers play across each nipple. She lifted Bailey's shirt over her head and unhooked her bra, dropping them to the floor before allowing her tongue to follow the path her hands had taken.

"Oh...wait...TJ...stop."

"Stop?"

"No, don't stop."

TJ greedily covered Bailey's mouth with her own and then pulled away again.

"Stop. Don't stop. I'm so confused," she teased.

"Do not stop." Bailey pulled TJ down the hallway. "Bed. Now."

# CHAPTER TWENTY-FOUR

TJ bent her toes before moving each foot into a stretch. She did not have to open her eyes to remember where she was. She was lying on her side and Bailey's soft breathing was caressing her ear. Bailey's body was like fire against her back and warm pillows were cradled in front of her. She was a toasty little sandwich and she felt happier than she could ever remember.

TJ had no plans to ever move again. Being in bed with Bailey was the best thing ever and she refused to let herself think of the day she would leave. Whether that would be soon or was weeks away, this moment was worth all the future turmoil her mind was telling her to brace for.

The pillow in front of her moved and she opened her eyes. Chewie stretched all four legs and rolled onto her back, looking TJ in the eyes.

She rubbed Chewie's belly and chuckled softly. She didn't remember the dog climbing onto the bed, but apparently she had waited for the activities to stop and then joined them. Her belly was pink and her fur short and soft. TJ absently petted her while her mind sifted through the events of the previous night.

Bailey had been an attentive lover. Not that TJ was surprised. She had thought Bailey would be perfect and now she knew that was true. She pushed away again thoughts of when Bailey would leave and instead focused on how she might convince Bailey to spend the day with her. She had an urge to go to the beach. It might not be warm enough to swim, but the sun was already high in the sky. They could hold hands and walk in the sand, the two things TJ loved most about going to the beach.

"Are you awake?" Bailey asked.

"Yes."

"I thought I felt your hand moving."

"Chewie needed some morning love," TJ said, rolling over to face Bailey.

"I'm so sorry."

TJ frowned. "Why are you sorry?"

"My dog is in bed with us."

"I'm okay with that. Aren't you?"

Bailey sighed. "Yes, I am, but I wasn't sure that's what you imagined waking up to."

TJ kissed Bailey and then sent a kiss with her hand to Chewie's head. "I'll take Chewie every morning if it means I can spend the night with you."

"Oh."

"Oh?"

"I have to leave—"

TJ placed her finger against Bailey's lips. "Don't say it. Not yet. Can I have today before we think about that? Let's go to the beach."

"Really? I'd like that."

TJ jumped to her feet and began pulling on her clothes. "I need to run home and shower. Maybe pack a few things," she said. Her voice was muffled as she pulled her shirt over her head.

"Okay. Should I meet you somewhere? I'm not sure...well, I mean...I'm not ready to face your grandmother yet."

TJ laughed, motioning back and forth between them. "Because of this?"

"Well, yeah. I took advantage of her granddaughter."

TJ flopped onto the bed beside Bailey and kissed her again. "I like the sound of that. You don't need to worry about Grams. Who do you think prodded me to come over here last night?"

"You had to be prodded?"

"Not prodded exactly. Just encouraged."

"Encouraged? You didn't want to come see me?"

TJ shook her head. "This isn't coming out right. I was moping around the house because I wanted to see you and Grams helped me work up the courage."

"I see. You aren't as cocky as I thought then?"

"Cocky? Absolutely not. I'm confident and brave." TJ rolled to her feet. "And maybe a little cocky."

TJ darted out the door to avoid the pillow Bailey threw. "I'll be back to get you in an hour."

"I'll be ready," Bailey called.

TJ's phone dinged with a text message as she slid into her truck.

*Can we take Chewie?*

She sent Bailey a quick *yes* back before getting on the road, her mind running through all the beaches in the area and trying to decide which one would be the best for the three of them. Mashes Sands was closest, but there wasn't a lot of sand for walking and it was small so it could be crowded. Alligator Point was the best idea. It was a twenty-minute drive, but there would be plenty of space to get away from other people.

The house was quiet even though Grams seldom slept past seven in the morning. TJ took a two-minute shower and threw on jeans and a long-sleeved T-shirt. There was always a breeze coming off the Gulf so she was not worried about being too hot. She could always roll up her pant legs if she wanted to wade in the water.

She put a large blanket and her beach canopy for a little shade in the truck. She pulled a small blue cooler off the shelf in the pantry. The strap caught on a couple cans of soup, and they went flying with a clatter.

"Who's making all the ruckus?" Grams asked, swinging open the pantry door.

"Sorry," TJ said, brushing past her to the freezer. "I needed the cooler."

"Headed to the beach, huh? Looks like you had a good night."

"Um...yeah. Sorry, I didn't call."

"Teresa Jane, I stopped waiting for you to call twenty years ago. You did miss a wonderful dinner last night, though."

Her stomach gave a rumble in response and they both laughed.

"Want me to pack a lunch for you?" Grams asked.

"No, we'll grab something at Angelo's."

"Okay."

TJ threw a few bottles of water and two ice packs in the cooler. Grams followed her to the door.

"I'll be home all day if you want to drop Chewie off."

"We're taking her with us, but I might take you up on that if Bailey agrees to go to dinner with me tonight."

"Sounds good. Have fun."

* * *

TJ held the door open as Bailey followed Chewie into the truck.

"This was a great idea," Bailey said as she slid a steamed shrimp into her mouth.

"I was starving, and I thought you might be too."

"I was and I appreciate that too, but I meant it was a great idea to peel all the shrimp before we left the restaurant."

"It's not my first beach trip, lady," TJ teased. "And I didn't forget Chewie." She pulled an edible bone from the compartment in her door and passed it to Chewie.

Bailey smiled. "I can't believe I thought you didn't like dogs. You are so sweet."

"I am sweet. Aren't I?"

"And cocky."

"Ah shucks," TJ said, laughing. She turned left, following the two-lane road toward the beach. She rolled the windows down and Bailey slid against her to give Chewie access to the window.

"I should have rolled them down sooner," TJ said, patting Bailey's leg.

"Chewie loves the salty, dead sea animal smell."

"Don't we all."

TJ stopped at the red light and waited until the signal cleared the one-lane road ahead. Then she pulled in the small oyster-shell-covered parking lot. She jumped out and ran around the truck to hold Bailey's door. Bailey gave TJ's hand a squeeze as she stepped around her and clipped the leash to Chewie's collar.

TJ swung the cooler bag over her shoulder and turned, holding Bailey's bag out to her. "Do you need your purse?"

"First, it's not a purse. It's a backpack. And yes, I need it. My camera is in it."

"Okay, then," TJ said. "Here is your backpack purse."

Bailey swatted TJ's arm as she pulled her camera from the pack. She held it up with one hand and snapped a couple pictures of TJ.

"Stop that," TJ said, covering her face.

Bailey hung the camera around her neck and shivered. "That breeze is a little chilly."

"I think I have..." TJ mumbled as her head disappeared inside the truck. "Yep, I have a denim jacket."

Bailey pulled on the jacket and laced her arms through the straps of her backpack. "Much better. Thank you."

TJ led the way to the wooden sidewalk, and they followed it to the white sandy beach. There were a few figures in the distance but no one in their immediate area.

"You can turn Chewie loose if you want," TJ suggested.

"I'm going to walk her to the water first."

"Give me your camera and I'll put our stuff over there away from the water."

TJ opened the sun canopy and put sand in the pockets to keep it from blowing away. When she finished, Bailey was at the water's edge with her arm resting around Chewie's neck. It was a picture of serenity and beauty and TJ grabbed Bailey's camera.

She snapped several shots before tucking the camera back under the canopy.

Bailey stood and slid her hand into TJ's when she stopped beside her. Free from her leash, Chewie began to run through the surf, chasing the waves and the little birds looking for their lunch.

"Are you seeing anyone?" TJ blurted and then ducked her head. "I guess I should have asked that before last night."

Bailey squeezed her hand. "I'm not seeing anyone. I don't even date much."

"When was your last relationship?"

"Okay, so I don't date at all."

"It's been a while, huh?"

"I've never had a relationship. Not because there wasn't opportunity but more because I didn't want someone in my space." Bailey sighed. "Once I left home, I wanted to be alone. I wasn't strong enough to resist someone who would try to control me so I stayed away from everyone. I focused on learning photography and trying to make enough money to live."

"You were eager to leave home?"

"Yeah, but my parents were even more eager for me to go."

"That sucks, but sometimes getting away is the best thing."

"It was. I learned to develop pictures and fell in love with photography. Mr. Anderson, the camera shop owner, was the first person to think I was worth something."

TJ began walking again. She wanted to hear more about Bailey's early photography days, but she could see that Bailey was deep in thought. Besides she was happy just to walk beside her and watch Chewie race about.

After a short stroll, they returned to the blanket and lay side by side, staring up at the light-blue sky filled with clouds. Even Chewie was content to take a nap beside them.

"I love the way the clouds seem to glide across the sky," Bailey said dreamily.

"Yeah, me too. This was one of my favorite things to do as a kid."

"Watch the clouds drift by?"

"That and trying to identify all the animals hidden in them."
Bailey laughed. "I can see little TJ doing that."

"There always seemed to be a lot of bear-shaped ones.
Although, the long ones could be—"

"Don't say it. I don't want to think about things that slither
right now."

"I was going to say alligators, just for the record."

\* \* \*

Bailey pushed the door closed and leaned against it. TJ's kiss
made her ache for more. It was the first time in her life she
wanted more of someone, she realized. Did she mean something
permanent? She could see a life with TJ, but could TJ see a life
with her? They had talked a lot on the beach today, but they did
not talk about what was happening between them and what it
might mean for the future.

She could work anywhere once her photos were taken. Was
she willing to sell her apartment in New York and move to
Florida? Yes, she was. She couldn't believe she was saying that,
but it was true. She liked her apartment in the city, but she liked
the way TJ made her feel more.

TJ was everything she had ever dared to dream about. Long
ago she had given up the hope of meeting someone she truly
wanted to spend time around. Someone who was strong and
kind and TJ was all of those things.

She loved how close TJ was to her grandmother; she really
liked Katie, too. She felt comfortable when she was in their
home. She knew she didn't need to feel embarrassed about
spending the night with TJ when she went to their house again.
TJ had convinced her that Katie was truly happy about what
was happening between them. Even more than happy, she was
encouraging it.

She put some kibble in Chewie's bowl and prepared for bed.
As she crawled under the covers, Chewie rested her head on the
bed beside her.

"Come on, girl," Bailey said, patting the spot beside her.

Chewie made two circles and then curled against Bailey's stomach.

"What a great day. You like her, don't you?"

Chewie's tail thumped a few times and Bailey patted her head.

"I like her too."

# CHAPTER TWENTY-FIVE

TJ hit the brakes. What in the hell was she doing? She turned at the marina entrance and quickly left Shell Point. If Bailey wanted to see her, she would call. Bailey's words had been echoing in her head for the last few days.

*I've never had a relationship. Not because there wasn't opportunity but more because I didn't want someone in my space.*

Bailey's words had made her feel unsure about what she thought was happening between them. That had made her short-tempered and her coworkers were paying the price.

Bailey had been clear about her expectations and TJ should have paid attention to her warning. She could beat herself up, but it wasn't like she had gotten attached on purpose. She had been sure that she had everything under control and that she was keeping her feelings for Bailey in check. Then she had given in to the moment and everything changed.

She pulled into the office. She wasn't surprised that this was where she ended up. It was her day off, but if she continued to wander, she would find herself on Bailey's doorstep again.

A knock on her window made her jump. Allison, a casual friend from another law enforcement agency, stood outside the window, waving energetically. Allison had hit on all of the single FWC officers at one time or another, including TJ. She had never considered one of Allison's offers and certainly wasn't in the mood for it today, but she hit the button to lower the window anyway.

"TJ! Aren't you off today? What are you doing here?"

"I had…I needed…I mean. Well, shit. I don't know why I'm here. I was out driving and my truck brought me here."

Allison slapped the top of her door. "You're so funny."

TJ pushed the door open, forcing Allison out of her way.

"Right. I'm a comedian."

"You are. I always say that. TJ is so funny. Do you want to go out on Friday night?"

"Oh, I think I'm busy with, ah, Grams. Yeah, Grams and I have dinner plans."

"I thought your grandmother was out of town."

TJ took a few steps away from Allison. "Yeah, right. She's back now."

"Okay. Maybe another time then."

"Right, another time."

TJ waved and jogged toward the entrance. She didn't mind Allison as a friend, but she hated how forward she could be. Plus she never seemed to get the hint that TJ wasn't interested in her. Even after years of making excuses.

She pulled open the door and Joey fell through it. Kurt stood against the other door with his face pressed against the glass.

"Is she gone?" Joey asked.

"Are you two hiding from Allison?" TJ asked with irritation.

"No, of course not," Kurt said.

"No way," Joey added. "We wanted to see you dodge her."

"Funny. You guys need to knock it off. She's nice and I like spending time with her."

They fell into each other, laughing. "Every time we see you guys you're running away from her."

"That's not true. I like her just fine. She's a little forward sometimes, but she's nice."

"Keep telling yourself that and maybe one day you'll tolerate her embrace instead of running from it. We're headed for burgers. Want to go with us?"

"Nope. I'm not spending my time off hanging with you guys."

"Your loss."

She turned away from their laughter and was surprised to see Bailey standing right in front of her. After driving to Shell Point to see if she could accidentally run into her, she had convinced herself that Bailey didn't want to see her again. And here she was, but she wasn't smiling.

"Hey, I was looking for you."

"You were looking for me?" Bailey tilted her head. "At the place where you work?"

"Okay, well, I was looking for you earlier, but then I came here."

"Now you found me."

Bailey stared at her for a few seconds and TJ's mind raced as she thought about what to say. She couldn't say the things she felt. She would sound crazy.

Bailey waved her hand. "I need to go."

TJ followed her out the door. "Wait. I really was looking for you. I wanted—"

"I need to go. Chewie is home alone."

"I wanted to tell you that I had a great time the other day." Oh, she really was an idiot. Couldn't she think of anything else to say?

Bailey took a deep breath. "I did as well. That's why I came by to see you."

"Oh, cool."

"Really? I could have sworn I just heard you say you were merely tolerating me."

"You? No."

"Whatever." Bailey turned away and unlocked her car. "It doesn't matter."

"Wait. What doesn't matter?"

"Just let it go, TJ."

"Let what go? What's going on here?"

"Nothing apparently, so I'm leaving."

* * *

The words Bailey had overheard had cut deeply. She couldn't believe that TJ was treating their connection so lightly. She would cut her a small break since it was her coworkers she had been talking to and TJ probably wouldn't tell them the truth. But to hear her say she tolerated Bailey was more than disrespectful. It hurt. If TJ was sick of her or only tolerating her, then the least she could do was tell her the truth. She shook her head. She knew better than to trust anyone. Being burned hurt worse than she had imagined it would.

"You're so afraid of believing in someone you would walk away without even explaining?"

Bailey shrugged. What could she say? TJ was right. She could feel the tears threatening to fall. There wasn't anything she could say. She needed to get to Chewie now more than ever.

"You see the world through damaged lenses and you've already decided what I'm going to say and do," TJ said with finality.

Bailey slid into her car and closed the door. Leaving was the only option at this point. And leaving quickly. Before she started to cry. She couldn't look at TJ. She couldn't bear to see the pain and disappointment in her eyes.

She was pulling into the covered parking at the condo before she even realized that she had driven so far. She wasn't sure if her heart or her head hurt the most. She had believed that something was happening between her and TJ. Something that was good. Something that would last.

Chewie eagerly met her at the door and she clipped on her leash. She didn't rush Chewie, but she didn't linger outside with her either. Her phone beeped with a text message as they were walking into the condo.

Mona was checking to see if she was packed. Of course, she was. She texted her back a thumbs-up emoji in hopes of avoiding a chat. Why was she waiting until the end of the week? She had everything prepped to leave. She had decided to hold on to her condo so she could come back, but now she wasn't sure she wanted to.

She could spend the next few days packing and leave for good. That wasn't what she wanted, though. A part of her was still holding on to the image of her and TJ together. In the past, she would come in and out of a state while she was working, but her feelings for TJ had made this time feel different. Right now, she needed to run. To get away from the pain ripping through her chest.

She moved around her condo packing last-minute items. Even though she knew she wouldn't get a good night sleep, she decided to wait a day anyway. Starting out in the morning was the best idea. Taking her glass of wine to bed, she turned on the television, leaned her head against the headboard, and closed her eyes. She felt some relief with her decision to leave early. Or maybe it was regaining control of her life that felt better than waiting around and wishing things were different.

# CHAPTER TWENTY-SIX

TJ left the house early. Grams wouldn't tolerate her hanging around again. She was still reeling from her conversation with Bailey the previous day. What had Bailey meant about tolerating her?

Realization slapped TJ in the face. Bailey had overheard the conversation about Allison and she thought TJ had been talking about her. Why? Why would she have thought that? It didn't matter. All that mattered was that there had been a huge misunderstanding and she needed to set it straight.

She made a U-turn and headed toward Shell Point. At the corner of Highway 98 and Shell Point Road she swerved into the convenience store. She couldn't go empty-handed. She needed gifts. She grabbed a pack of peanut M&M's and a miniature box of Milk-Bones for Chewie. On the checkout counter were individually wrapped plastic roses. It was a commercial convenience-store red rose, but it would work for today though. She could make it up to Bailey with something better later.

She carried her hodge-podge of gifts up the stairs to Bailey's second-story condominium. She knocked on the door and waited. There was a doorbell, so she rang that too after a few minutes. Still no answer. Okay, so sometimes spontaneous wasn't the best idea. She should have texted or slowed down long enough to look in the parking lot for Bailey's Jeep.

She knocked again and heard the door across the hall open behind her. She turned to see Mr. Maxwell peeking through his door.

"Hello, Mr. Maxwell."

She pushed her gifts behind her back as his gaze crossed over them.

"Are you looking for Ms. Everett?" he asked.

TJ resisted rolling her eyes. What else would she be doing standing outside Bailey's door, knocking? "I am, but I don't believe she's home."

"That's true. She left for her book tour this morning."

"Oh."

She hadn't thought about the book tour in days. What had Bailey said about it? It would last several weeks.

"Okay. I'll send her a text. Thanks."

She left quickly before he could ask any questions. She should have called before she ran over here like an idiot. The stupid convenience-store rose felt even more ridiculous now; she dropped it in a trash can as she left the building.

She climbed into her truck and tore open the M&M's, throwing several into her mouth. She pulled out her phone to send Bailey a text, but it rang before she could do it.

"Hey, Grams."

"Honey, are you at the office? Have you seen the news?"

"No, what's going on?"

"The hurricane in the Gulf has changed direction and is headed our way. Landfall is expected tomorrow."

"I thought it was headed for Texas."

"I guess it changed its mind."

"I'll go by the office and then I'll be home to tie everything down," TJ said hastily.

"Okay, see you soon."

The last time she had seen anything about the storm was that it was projected to be a Category Three when it made landfall in Texas. She hadn't thought to ask Grams how large it was now expected to be.

The office was a flurry of activity when she arrived. The officers on duty were prepping equipment and pulling traps. If an animal was caught in a trap during a hurricane it could be days before they could get out to check on them. All traps needed to be brought in.

"Hey, Smith, glad you're here. We need to get rolling with our emergency plans," Randy said as she stepped through the door.

"When is the projected landfall?"

"About ten in the morning, but we'll start feeling the effects in a few hours."

"I need to run home and then I'll come back."

"Okay. We're calling everyone in for today and then we'll keep a minimal shift here overnight. Everyone will be on call tomorrow."

"Sounds good. I'll be back as soon as I can."

She swung by the grocery store and grabbed a few cases of water. They kept the pantry fully stocked during hurricane season so they didn't need any additional food.

Grams was waiting on the porch when she flew in the driveway. She unloaded the water and began moving all the patio furniture against the house. After everything on the porch was tied down she walked the yard. Grams followed her.

"How strong is it supposed to be when it hits?" TJ asked.

"It's almost a Four, but they don't think it will grow much more. The outer bands will start hitting soon."

"It must be moving fast so that's good."

"Absolutely," Grams agreed. If the hurricane slowed down over the warm water, it would grow in strength.

"I need to go back to the office for a few hours, but I'll be back before it's too late. You'll be okay, right?"

"Of course. Hurry back, though."

"I'll bring pizza and we'll have a hurricane party."

"Sounds good. You should call Bailey and ask her and Chewie to come here," Grams suggested.

"That's where I was when you called. She's already left for her book tour."

"Oh."

TJ could hear the disappointment in Grams's voice. "At least she'll be far enough north to be out of the storm."

"Yes, that's true."

\* \* \*

TJ slammed the truck door and squeezed the water from her hair. The rain had started about twenty minutes earlier and had caught her almost a mile from her truck. Thankfully, this was the last trap she needed to gather before returning to the station. She radioed Joey to make sure he was finished too. She was glad to hear all of his traps were empty and he was headed back to the station.

She gathered with all of her coworkers in the lobby and they listened to Captain Westmore's briefing. She wasn't at all panicked about the upcoming hurricane. It certainly wasn't her first one. Two of them, in fact, had been Category Five hurricanes. She had been a kid when Hurricane Andrew devastated Homestead and the southern tip of Florida, but she remembered clearly Michael a few years ago. Between those two there had been three others a bit smaller that had come close but gone west instead.

She had learned early on not to panic when a hurricane entered the Gulf of Mexico. It had so many choices at that point. It could head straight for Texas as a few had or into the coast between Texas and Florida like Katrina had in 2005. Or it could ping-pong around and bounce back into the Tampa area.

Meteorologists tried to get it right and sometimes they did, but mostly she kept prepared during the season and then sat back and watched. She had a generator that would kick on automatically if they lost power. It would run the refrigerator and air-conditioning if they needed it.

"Okay, head home and take care of your families. Stay close to your radios in case you're needed," Captain Westmore said as he dismissed them.

TJ ordered a pizza from the app on her phone and then picked it up after waiting in line to fill her gas tank.

A few hours later, she lay on her bed listening to the rain hammering the window. She and Grams had eaten pizza and watched a movie when she got home, and this was the first moment she had to herself since she had left Bailey's condo that morning.

She wanted to send Bailey a text, but it was a few minutes after midnight. Clearing up the misunderstanding between them had seemed urgent earlier but now it wasn't as pressing. Maybe Bailey was rubbing off on her. Their paths had crossed but that didn't mean they would stay in touch, right?

Dang, she did sound like Bailey. She typed out a message, deleted it, and then typed it again. She didn't mention the hurricane. Only a short explanation of the assumed misunderstanding. Bailey had returned to her world, and for all TJ knew she wasn't even thinking about her or the state of Florida. She had to believe if Bailey knew about the incoming hurricane she would have texted her already.

# CHAPTER TWENTY-SEVEN

Bailey pushed open the door as the chime sounded to alert Danny that someone had entered his shop.

"Bailey!" Danny exclaimed. "It's so good to see you."

"Hey, Danny. How's things going?"

"Good. Real good. I haven't seen you in five or six years—"

"Since your dad—"

"Yeah, since Dad passed away. How have you been?"

"Good." She glanced around the shop. Her books still held a spot of honor on the shelf behind a row of cameras protected by a glass case.

Danny came to stand beside her, his arm resting lightly on her shoulders.

"He was really proud of you. Told everyone that came into the shop about your books."

Bailey smiled at him. "Thanks. He was really proud of you too. I don't think I ever saw him as happy as he was when you agreed to take over the store."

"It was a win-win for me, that's for sure." He motioned around the store. "It keeps me going and Dad close. Things are still mostly the same in the back. You're welcome to look around."

Bailey nodded. "I'd like that."

"Take all the time you want. I'll be cutting photos."

Bailey opened the solid door separating the commercial part of the store from the work area. The smell of vinegar still lingered in the air, but she could see Danny was making the transition to a more eco-friendly and less-toxic process.

*"You're doing a great job, Bailey. You're a natural."*

Mr. Anderson's words played through her mind. She had forgotten how much she enjoyed developing film herself. Pictures became even more of a work of art to her then than they were to her now. Mr. Anderson had never minded if she developed her photos. In fact often he would help her play with using longer or shorter exposures to change the pictures.

She could do this. She could make her own darkroom and learn to experiment again. And she could do it anywhere. Even in Florida. To be closer to TJ but also to have a more permanent home and a yard for Chewie.

With newfound enthusiasm she said goodbye to Danny and rode the subway back to her apartment. Chewie was spending some time with her previous owners so she jumped online and began looking at property in Wakulla County.

* * *

"TJ, wake up!"

She sat straight up in bed, trying to get her bearings. "What is it?"

"The storm turned east," Grams said as she pushed open TJ's bedroom door.

She grabbed the remote and turned the volume up on the television. She had fallen asleep to the flickering glow the previous night.

"People from Cedar Key to Homosassa are preparing for a direct hit from this Category Four storm," the announcer said enthusiastically.

TJ jumped out of bed. "There's a lot of wildlife management land there. They'll need help rounding up animals caught in the storm. You'll be okay if I go, right?"

"Of course. Stay safe and keep in touch."

She grabbed an overnight bag and threw in some clothes. The call from Captain Westmore came as she was pulling out of her driveway. He was sending as many volunteers as wanted to go. It would take a few hours to load the vehicles so they would be about an hour behind the eye of the storm. He said calls were already coming from the Tampa office requesting assistance.

She loaded all the traps she had unloaded the previous day along with carrying kennels and as many towels as would fit behind the seat of her truck. The gas cans in the storage area were kept filled and she loaded several into the back of her truck. Her final items were cleanup equipment and a few chainsaws and tree trimmers, as well as a leaf blower and several pairs of gloves.

TJ brought up the rear of the convoy. With five FWC trucks in front of her, she settled back to organize her thoughts. What they did in the next several days would be critical to rescuing any lost or injured animals, especially babies.

* * *

Bailey walked Chewie around the small area of grass again.

"Please, Chewie, go potty. I won't be able to take you out for the next couple hours."

Finally finding the perfect spot, Chewie completed the requested task and followed Bailey into the bookstore. In the time she had had Chewie with her, she had only had one store that didn't allow Chewie to accompany her. Once they saw how well she behaved, they seldom said no. Chewie would find a spot under the table at Bailey's feet and sleep for the few hours they were there. No one would even notice her.

"It's about time you got here," Mona exclaimed.

"I've been in the parking lot for ten minutes trying to get Chewie to go to the bathroom."

"You should have called and told me. I could have stayed with her. The manager was starting to stare daggers into me. He was sure you weren't going to show given the hurricane that's hitting Florida."

"What?"

"He was sure you weren't going to show."

"I heard that. Did you say there is a hurricane hitting Florida?"

"Yeah, I thought you knew. It was headed straight for the area you had been staying but veered off early this morning. Now it's hitting farther south. Homosassa, I think."

Bailey sank into the chair at the table behind a pile of her latest book. "I didn't know. Poor Lu."

"Who's Lu? I thought that ranger dudette was named JT or something."

"Lu is the rhino at Homosassa Springs. And the conservation officer's name is TJ." Bailey pulled her cell phone from her pocket. "I should try to reach her and make sure they're okay."

"The hurricane didn't hit where she lives. I'm sure she's fine. Here comes the manager. You need to make nice since you're so late."

"I'm not late," she mumbled for only Mona to hear before sticking out her hand to greet the manager.

"Ms. Everett, we are so glad to see you. Is everything positioned okay for you? There are several bottles of wat— Yikes! What is that?"

Bailey quickly stepped between him and Chewie.

"I'm so sorry to startle you. That's my dog. Chewie. I believe my agent cleared that with you."

"Oh yes. Whatever you want is fine. I was just surprised."

He made no effort to pet Chewie, so she laid back down under the table and returned to her nap.

"Anyway, if you need more water just let us know. I'll be in the front of the store directing people to this area, but Henry will be right here with you."

He motioned for a young man to join him and made introductions before hurrying toward the front of the store.

She was glad the manager moved away as his nervous energy was starting to flow toward her. Henry was more laid-back. She took her seat as she studied him. She guessed his age as about twenty-five. Out of college but maybe not on a career path yet. He didn't seem interested in chatting but positioned himself at the end of the table to control the flow of patrons. Clearly this wasn't his first book signing.

Her mind returned to the hurricane hitting Florida. She wished she could discreetly look at the news on her phone. That wasn't going to be possible for a while, but she sent a quick text to TJ asking for an update on her and Katie's safety. She didn't mention her stupidity at misconstruing the situation at TJ's office or how glad she had been to receive TJ's explanation. They could discuss that later. Right now, she needed to know TJ and Katie were okay. She slid her phone under her leg so she would feel it vibrate when TJ answered and focused on the first woman approaching her table.

"Thank you for coming," Bailey said with a huge plastered-on smile. "What's your name?"

"I'm Sandy and thank you for all the pictures. My four-year-old grandson and I flip through the New York City one every night before bed."

"That's so sweet. What's your grandson's name?" Bailey asked.

"Ethan. His name is Ethan and he loves squirrels."

Bailey quickly added a personalized note to Ethan before handing the book to Sandy.

"I buy all the new ones too," Sandy said, blushing, as she handed two more books to Bailey to sign. "I wasn't able to get in to see you the last time you were here. The line was really long."

"I'm so sorry for that, Sandy." Bailey looked up at the woman and saw Henry pressing in on them. She gave him a nod and quickly signed the rest of Sandy's books before handing them back to her with a sincere smile. "Thank you for making another attempt. I really appreciate your support."

"I've been waiting a few hours, but I'm so glad I did. You are the nicest woman and your pictures transport me to so many new locations. Please keep producing new books."

Bailey smiled at her again as Henry ushered Sandy away from the table. She took the book from the next person in line.

Two hours later she wiggled her fingers from the cramp of holding a pen. She didn't mind signing books, but two hours was her limit. She stood and stretched as Henry escorted the stragglers toward the exit. She quickly pulled her phone from the pocket where she had stuffed it an hour ago when her hope for a response had dwindled. There was still no text from TJ. Nothing but silence.

# CHAPTER TWENTY-EIGHT

TJ jumped from the back of the truck and joined the group of people standing nearby. The devastation around them was catastrophic, trees bent like matchsticks and debris blown all around. This was their third stop of the day.

Gathering a handful of multicolored flags, she logged into the Forest Service GPS tracking device and began walking the area assigned to her. She walked slowly and listened hard for any sound of babies inside of trees or under rocks and debris. She had found one nest of raccoon babies inside the base of a stump earlier. After placing a flag beside it, she logged it into the GPS system. The local workers would monitor it and make sure the mother returned. They wouldn't move a nest unless it was in danger from rising water. The babies didn't seem in distress from hunger or injury so leaving them in place was the best call.

She heard rustling to her right and froze. A squirrel scampered up and into a hole in a nearby tree. TJ began walking again. The squirrel was old enough to take care of itself and if there were babies nearby they would be taken care of too.

Hurricane recovery was different from recovery after a fire. They didn't need to help the animals find food. Most vegetation eaters wouldn't have to go high for food since many trees were on the forest floor now. Worm and insect eaters would find the damp ground a smorgasbord.

Yesterday when they arrived at the Homosassa ranger station they didn't have enough hours of daylight to do much more than unload equipment. Then she had received an offer to follow a few zealous rangers on a mission to look for nocturnal critters. She was happy to say they hadn't located any animals in distress. She had managed to drop her cell phone into a pool of brackish water, though. Sadly, she had not secured the seal on the waterproof bag the last time she had looked at her phone. With help from one of the other rangers she had waded in and retrieved it, but it was dead. Not a big deal since phone lines were down from the storm anyway. She sent a message through a coworker to Grams so she would know she was operating off the grid. She gave her the local office number in the event she needed anything. First stop on her way home would be to purchase a new phone, but for now there were more important things to worry about.

* * *

Bailey sent another text to TJ. She had vowed last night after she had received no response that she wasn't going to text again, but this morning she had conveniently forgotten that promise. She wasn't worried so much since the hurricane had not hit TJ's area, but she would feel better if she made contact with her.

"Doesn't she live with her grandmother? Call her," Mona insisted.

"That would be weird, and I don't have her number anyway."

Mona wrinkled her nose. "What's with you? Why wouldn't it be okay for you to check on them concerning the hurricane?"

"It would be weird. That's all." What would she say to Katie? "TJ won't answer my calls so I'm calling you." Yep, it would be weird.

"Okay, then let's talk work. You're finished in Florida, right? Where are you going to next? And when?"

"I'm mostly finished, I guess. I thought maybe I'd go to Idaho." *Idaho?* Where did that come from? She wasn't sure where she would go next. She wasn't even sure when. Or if she was ready to leave TJ and Florida behind. But she did know she wasn't ready to have a conversation with Mona about her plans for establishing a more permanent residence.

# CHAPTER TWENTY-NINE

TJ settled into the padded chair and sipped her beer. She hadn't stopped for more than two minutes in the last four days. When her team had headed back to Crawfordville the day before, she had veered off and gone to see Denise. She was glad that she had. A good meal and ten hours of sleep had her feeling like herself again. She still needed to pick up a new cell phone, but for the moment she was enjoying the peace and quiet.

"How's that girl of yours?" Steven asked as he sank into the chair on the other side of the small white metal table.

"Not my girl."

"Okay, how's that girl you were traveling with?" he said laughing.

"She's on a book tour so I'm not sure."

"When does she come back?"

"When does who come back?" Denise asked as she pulled another chair to join them at the table.

"Bailey," Steven said with raised eyebrows.

"How is Bailey? I really liked her."

"She's on a book tour," TJ said, hiding her disappointment with a shrug. Bailey had not told her she was leaving. Hell, she didn't even know if Bailey was coming back, and without her phone she didn't even know if Bailey had responded to her text.

"Steven, can you refill my drink?" Denise asked.

Denise's eyes were locked on TJ as she passed her glass to her husband and TJ knew she was about to be peppered with questions.

"When did she leave?" Denise asked before Steven was even out of the room.

"Before the hurricane."

"And when is she coming back?"

TJ shrugged again.

"Use words, Teresa Jane."

"Don't call me that!"

"It's your name and the only thing appropriate when you're acting like this. What did you do to her?"

"Why do you think I did something?"

"Because you always act defensive when you feel guilty."

TJ sighed. "I think she overheard a conversation I was having with the guys at work. It gave her the wrong impression."

"Did you talk to her and explain?"

"I tried, but it wasn't until she left that I realized why she was upset."

"So, fix it now."

"I sent her a text," TJ said, taking a drink and looking away from Denise.

"Really? A text. That's a weak effort. You don't want to fix it? You're happy that she's gone?" Denise asked.

"No to both of those. I just don't know what to say. She made it clear she wasn't a relationship kind of person."

"And now you're afraid to put yourself out there for her. Well, I have news for you, if you don't ever put yourself out there you won't ever have the joy of complete love. To receive, you have to give and sometimes that means being the one who takes the risk."

"I hear you, but I think Bailey made it clear where she stands. She was in it for the fun, not for long term. I would be a fool to ask her for more."

"Sometimes being a fool is worth it."

Denise's words played through TJ's mind as she began her drive back to Crawfordville. Being around Bailey made her happier than she could ever remember. Bailey was different. She felt complete when they were together.

She took the exit ramp Denise had told her had an AT&T store. After purchasing a new phone, she waited, not very patiently, for her contacts to download and then sat in her truck staring at it. She knew what she wanted to say but not how to say it. Would Bailey think she was an idiot for even attempting to pursue her?

After giving a lot of thought to the words she wanted to say, she typed a text to Bailey. Maybe Denise was right about putting yourself out there. She already felt better. If Bailey wanted to give them a chance, then she was ready. And if Bailey didn't... Well, she'd worry about that when the time came.

\* \* \*

"I don't understand why you have to cancel the rest of your tour. The hurricane didn't—"

"It's not about the hurricane. I need to see TJ."

"But I don't understand," Mona whined.

"You wouldn't," Bailey said, turning to leave.

"Bailey, wait. That's not fair. Tell me what's going on."

"I'm in love with her and I need to tell her in person."

Bailey closed her eyes and leaned against the wall. She had finally said it aloud. She was in love with TJ and for the first time in her life it mattered what someone else thought. She had misunderstood what she had overheard and then she had overreacted and now she had to fix it. In person, not over the phone. She had to look TJ in the eye and tell her that she didn't want to live without her.

"Oh," Mona said softly.

"If you're not okay with it, I can find a new agent."

"Of course, I'm okay with it. I'm just surprised is all."

"I'm surprised too but probably not the same as you. TJ has changed my life for the better and I don't want to live without her."

"I'm surprised to hear you talking like this, but I have to say that I've seen the change in you. When we met in California you seemed happier."

"I am. Now, can you reschedule the rest of the tour?"

"I'll get on it right now. Call me when you get back to Florida."

"I will." *After I talk to TJ.*

# CHAPTER THIRTY

Bailey took another sip of cold coffee. It had been almost five hours since she had stopped the last time and she was relieved to arrive at TJ's place. Or she would be. Her need for a bathroom, already conspicuous, became fairly urgent when she stepped out of the Jeep. As Chewie jumped out and immediately took advantage of the grassy yard, she tried not to watch.

Bailey looked up as Katie pushed open the screened porch door.

"Bailey!" Katie exclaimed. "When did you get back?"

"We just arrived. Is TJ at work? I didn't see her truck."

"She's at work today, but not at the office. She's leading a volunteer crew to clean up the migratory bird nests around Gander River."

"Oh," Bailey said, trying to hide her disappointment.

Katie looked at her watch. "If you hurry, you can probably still catch them at the entrance to the Preserve. Do you know where that is?"

"I do, but I don't want to bother her."

"I'm sure she would love to see you. Besides, I would appreciate Chewie's company."

"Really? I left sort of suddenly, and I wasn't sure she would want to see me."

Katie sat and pointed to the chair opposite her. "Sit. Teresa Jane doesn't express her feelings very well, but I can read her like a book. Being around you has brought joy into her life again."

"Thank you for saying that. She makes me happy too."

"Well, I'm sure glad to hear you say that. The last thing I wanted was to encourage her and have you break her heart."

"I would never do that. At least not on purpose."

"Communication is the key to happiness. You'll have your work cut out for you. That's for sure," Katie laughed. "But you can come to me anytime and I might have a few secrets on how to get her to talk."

"Oh yes! I would love to hear them."

"Always start with a cup of tea. I have her preprogrammed. Now, quit dancing around. Go find her."

"Thanks," Bailey called as she gave Chewie a pat. She ran out the door. And then ran back in and asked to use the restroom.

\* \* \*

TJ jumped into the bed of her truck and addressed the crowd.

"We'll divide up into the trucks for the ride out. Make sure you have everything you need for the next four to six hours—water, sunscreen, and mosquito repellent being the most important items. Most of you have participated in this kind of cleanup before, but I'll have more instructions when we see what needs to be accomplished. Now let's go have fun. Any questions?"

No one seemed to have any, so she jumped down and headed for the driver's seat. As she watched the volunteers head for their rides, her eyes caught Bailey's. She froze. It had been almost two weeks since TJ had seen her and seeing her here felt like a dream. She looked fantastic. Her hair was pulled back in a ponytail and a camera hung around her neck. She was dressed in shorts and athletic shoes rather than her normal hiking boots.

She heard truck engines starting around her and shrugged at Bailey.

"I need to go. Can I call you when I finish today?"

"Of course."

She watched Bailey in her side mirror and was surprised to see her joining the other volunteers climbing in the bed of her truck.

The drive to Gander River would take about twenty minutes with the volunteers, double the time it would take without people in the bed of her truck. She was disappointed she could only see the back of Bailey's head in her mirror. She wanted to know why Bailey was here. She hadn't bothered to answer TJ's apologetic text and that had made her think Bailey wasn't coming back.

Her phone vibrated and she swiped to answer the call from Grams.

"Hey," she said. "We're headed out to the river. What's up?"

She knew Grams would understand by her wording that she wasn't alone.

"So you've already left the parking lot?"

"Yes, why?"

"I wasn't going to call but then I thought I should. I really don't want to get involved in your personal life, but you should know Bailey came back this morning. She was here looking for you and I told her where you were."

"I know. She's in the back of my truck."

"Oh good. You talked then."

"No, we haven't. Do you know why she's here?"

"Just talk to her, Teresa Jane, and don't be afraid to lead with your heart."

"I hear you, Grams. I'll talk to you tonight."

She disconnected the call and dropped her phone back into the waterproof bag that held her wallet. Grams's message was loud and clear. Bailey had returned to see her. Maybe for work too, but her first stop had been to look for TJ. That had to mean something. She took a deep breath and let it out slowly. Maybe Bailey was willing to give this thing between them a chance.

Lost in her own thoughts, TJ barely heard the rambling of the volunteer seated beside her. She muttered an occasional yes and gave a head nod to keep the one-sided flow of conversation going. But as soon as she pulled to a stop, she raced around to help Bailey and the other volunteers out of the truck.

"We need to talk," she said to Bailey as she took her hand to help her out of the truck.

"We do," Bailey agreed.

The next volunteer was reaching for assistance, and the buzz of activity was increasing around them.

"And I'll be around so we can do that," Bailey continued. "But not here."

TJ nodded as a volunteer looped his arm through Bailey's. "Let's get you decked out in some work gear," he said as he pulled her away from TJ.

TJ spent the next few hours trying hard to avoid looking in Bailey's direction. She knew if she did she would lose focus on what they needed to accomplish today. This was a national wildlife refuge area so ultimately it was the responsibility of the US Fish and Wildlife Service, but they were happy to help out.

Migrating birds would begin coming through this area over the next couple of months and the habitats needed to be checked for deterioration and stability. She and her coworkers would help document which, if any, of the highest platforms used by great blue herons and osprey needed bracing supports. Both types of birds were known to return to the same nests year after year. The volunteers would handle the lower nests. Though she was anxious to talk to Bailey, tending to these tasks made the hours pass a little more quickly.

TJ made a note on her clipboard and then her gaze drifted as it had numerous times to Bailey's group, which was working further down the shoreline. Bailey was standing in the water, too, with her arms over her head, supporting the man-made predator obstacles against the pole while another volunteer attached them. Knee-high rubber boots that had clearly been borrowed from one of the other volunteers now covered her feet, but there was still a bit of lovely skin showing between the top of them and the hem of her shorts.

A ripple in the water behind Bailey interrupted TJ's admiration of the scene. *Shit, shit, shit!* A foot-long snake was gliding straight for the back of her leg! TJ shuddered. She hated snakes, but based on their run-in with the diamondback rattler, Bailey didn't only dislike them, she was terrified of them. The snake was likely nonvenomous, but she knew Bailey would never step foot in Florida again if a snake swam into her boot. Pushing through the water as fast as she could, TJ steeled herself, grabbed the snake by its tail, and flung it out toward the bay and far away from Bailey.

"Hey, was that a snake?" a nearby voice called to TJ.

Excited voices began to shout around her.

"Snake!"

"Snake?"

"Where's a snake?"

Bailey spun quickly and nearly collided with TJ.

"Is there a snake?" Bailey asked, her eyes wide with panic.

"It's fine," TJ assured her.

Bailey's head whipped from side to side. "Really? There was a snake? Where…?" Her voice rose.

"There was, but it was tiny really. I shooed it away."

"It was huge," a male voice injected, "and she grabbed it by the tail and tossed it halfway to Tampa. It was awesome!"

TJ grasped Bailey's upper arm and guided her out of the water. "Can we talk?"

"You grabbed a snake?" Bailey asked.

"I might have."

"Why in the world would you do that? Are you trying to scare me to death?"

TJ pulled her to the other side of the truck away from curious eyes and ears. She couldn't believe Bailey would really think she was trying to scare her with a snake—on purpose.

\* \* \*

"Stop pulling me around!" Bailey exclaimed. "I need to leave. I don't want to see a snake."

She couldn't believe TJ would intentionally bring a snake to scare her, especially when she had been honest with her about how she felt about them. She would have left when she saw the body of water they would be working in, but the volunteers convinced her that the ruckus made by all of them would scare any critters away. Besides, she had ridden in with everyone else in the back of the FWC trucks, so she was trapped.

"Bailey, stop. Please," TJ begged. "I need to talk to you."

She looked at TJ, reading only sincerity in her flushed face and red-rimmed eyes and then she remembered their shared dislike for snakes. If TJ touched a snake willingly, then someone was in danger and that someone was her.

"I can't even...Not until I know what went on with the snake."

"It was swimming toward you and I got rid of it. It was really small."

"How small?" Bailey asked, certain by now that TJ was going to understate what she'd done.

TJ held up her hands to show the distance. Bailey mentally doubled its size and shuddered.

"Was it venomous?"

"I don't think so."

"You didn't know? And you grabbed it anyway? Why? Why would you do that?"

"It was going for your boot," TJ said softly. "I didn't want to risk it."

Bailey was silent for a few seconds, studying TJ's face, which contained equal measures of embarrassment and...fear?

"You touched a snake to protect me?"

TJ chuckled uneasily. "Yeah. I guess I did."

No one had ever risked their own safety for her. TJ sacrificed her own safety and she could have been bitten? Maybe she was. "Are you hurt?"

"No."

"I'm sorry I didn't ask that first. I was scared."

"Yeah, me too. And not just of the snake. I was afraid if it swam into your boot, you might leave Florida and never come back."

Bailey took a step away from TJ and looked at her. "Who said that wasn't my plan already?"

TJ gave her a half-grin. "Grams."

"She told me she wouldn't tell you about our conversation."

"She didn't, but she did suggest that I follow my heart."

"And are you going to do that?"

TJ pulled her close, pressing her lips against Bailey's. Deepening the kiss, they ignored the catcalls from TJ's nearby coworkers.

Bailey could finally see her future. Her life was in focus.

Bella Books, Inc.

*Women. Books. Even Better Together.*

P.O. Box 10543
Tallahassee, FL 32302
Phone: (800) 729-4992
**www.BellaBooks.com**

## *More Titles from Bella Books*

**Mabel and Everything After – Hannah Safren**
978-1-64247-390-2 | 274 pgs | paperback: $17.95 | eBook: $9.99
A law student and a wannabe brewery owner find that the path to a
fairy tale happily-ever-after is often the long and scenic route.

**To Be With You – TJ O'Shea**
978-1-64247-419-0 | 348 pgs | paperback: $19.95 | eBook: $9.99
Sometimes the choice is between loving safely or loving bravely.

**I Dare You to Love Me – Lori G. Matthews**
978-1-64247-389-6 | 292 pgs | paperback: $18.95 | eBook: $9.99
An enemy-to-lovers romance about daring to follow your heart, even
when it's the hardest thing to do.

**The Lady Adventurers Club - Karen Frost**
978-1-64247-414-5 | 300 pgs | paperback: $18.95 | eBook: $9.99
Four women. One undiscovered Egyptian tomb. One (maybe) angry
Egyptian goddess. What could possibly go wrong?

**Golden Hour - Kat Jackson**
978-1-64247-397-1 | 250 pgs | paperback: $17.95 | eBook: $9.99
Life would be so much easier if Lina were afraid of something
basic—like spiders—instead of something significant. Something like
real, true, healthy love.

**Schuss – E. J. Noyes**
978-1-64247-430-5 | 276 pgs | paperback: $17.95 | eBook: $9.99
They're best friends who both want something more, but what if
admitting it ruins the best friendship either of them have had?